Praise for **Andrew Vachss**

"Hard-boiled fiction at its best."
—*Chicago Tribune*

"Many writers try to cover the same ground as Vachss. A handful are as good. **None are better."** —*People*

"Some of the **cleanest, meanest, stripped-down-and-sparkling prose ever penned."**
—*Austin Chronicle*

"Vachss is red-hot and as serious as a punctured lung." —*Playboy*

"Gritty, frightening, **compelling and ultimately satisfying."** —*The Plain Dealer*

"Vachss's writing is like **a dark roller-coaster ride of fear, love and hate."** —*The Times-Picayune*

"The Burke books **make the noir-film genre look practically pastel."** —*The Philadelphia Inquirer*

"One of **the most hard-boiled and important crime series ever published."**
—*The Huntsville Times*

ANDREW VACHSS

MASK MARKET

Andrew Vachss has been a federal investigator of sexually transmitted diseases, a social services caseworker, and a labor organizer, and has directed a maximum-security prison for "aggressive-violent" youth. Now a lawyer in private practice, he represents children and youths exclusively. A native New Yorker, he now divides his time between the city of his birth and the Pacific Northwest.

The dedicated Web site for Vachss and his work is www.vachss.com.

ALSO BY ANDREW VACHSS

MASK MARKET

ANDREW VACHSS

MASK MARKET

A BURKE NOVEL

Vintage Crime/Black Lizard
Vintage Books
A Division of Random House, Inc.
New York

FIRST VINTAGE CRIME/BLACK LIZARD EDITION, AUGUST 2007

The Library of Congress has cataloged the Pantheon edition as follows:
Vachss, Andrew H.
Mask market / Andrew Vachss.
p. cm.
1. Burke (Fictitious character)—Fiction.
2. Private investigators—New York (State)—
New York—Fiction. 3. New York, (N.Y.)—Fiction.
4. Missing persons—Fiction. I. Title.
PS3572.A33M37 2006
813'.54—dc22 20048285

Vintage ISBN: 978-0-307-27830-2

Book design by Virginia Tan

www.vintagebooks.com

Printed in the United States of America
10 9 8 7 6 5 4 3 2 1

for . . .

Eddie Adams, who risked his life to show us the truth;
Joe LaMonte, who finally found his way to the door;
Eddie Little, who fell off the Horse no man can ride
    forever;
Rex Miller, who told it big;
Son Seals, who left to work a better room;

and for . . .

Steve: childhood pal, crime partner, lover of science,
    doomed boy.

MASK MARKET

I'm not the client," the ferret seated across from me said. He was as thin as a garrote, with a library-paste complexion, the skin surrounding his veined-quartz eyes as papery as dried flowers. He was always room temperature. "You know me, Burke. I only work the middle."

"I don't know you," I lied. "You knew—you *say* you knew—my brother. But if you did—"

"Yeah, I know he's gone," the ferret said, meeting my eyes, the way you do when you've got nothing to hide. With him, it was an invitation to search an empty room. "But you've got the same name, right? He never had any first name that I knew; so what would I call you, I meet you for the first time?"

It's impossible to actually look into my eyes, because you have to do it one at a time. One eye is a lot lighter than the other, and they don't track together anymore.

A few years ago, I was tricked into an ambush. The crossfire cost me my looks, and my partner her life. I mourn her every day—the hollow blue heart tattooed between the last two knuckles of my right hand is Pansy's tombstone—but I don't miss my old face. True, it was a lot more anonymous than the one I've got now. Back then, I was a walking John Doe: average height, average weight . . . generic lineup filler. But a lot of different people had seen that face in a lot of different places. And the State had a lot of photographs of it, too—they don't throw out old mug shots.

I'd come into the ER without a trace of ID, dropped at the door by the Prof and Clarence—they knew I was way past risking the do-it-yourself kit we kept around for gunshot wounds.

Since the government doesn't pay the freight for cosmetic surgery on derelicts, the hospital went into financial triage, no extras. So the neat, round keloid scar on my right cheek is still there, and the top of my left ear is still as flat as if it had been snipped off. And when the student surgeons repaired the cheekbone on the right side of my face, they pulled the skin so tight that it looked like one of the bullets I took had been laced with Botox. My once-black hair is steel-gray now—it turned that shade while I was in a coma from the slugs, and never went back.

The night man sitting across from me calls himself Charlie Jones—the kind of motel-register name you hear a lot down where I live. A long time ago, I'd done a few jobs he'd brought to me. The way Charlie works it, he makes his living from finder's fees. Kind of a felonious matchmaker—you tell him the problem you need solved, he finds you a pro who specializes in it.

Charlie pointedly looked down at my hands. I kept them flat on the chipped blue Formica tabletop, palms down. He placed his own hands in the same position, showing me his ID.

The backs of his frail-looking hands were incongruously cabled with thick veins. The skin around his fingernails was beta-carotene orange. The tip of the little finger on his right hand was missing. I nodded my confirmation. Yeah, he was the man I remembered.

Charlie looked at my own hands for a minute, then up at me. The Burke he knew never had a tattoo, but he nodded, just as I had. Charlie was a tightrope dancer—perfect balance was his survival tool. His nod told me not to worry about whether he believed the story that I was Burke's brother. By him, it was true enough. Where we live, that's the same as *good* enough.

"It's a nice story," I said, watching as he lit his third cigarette of the meet. Burke was a heavy smoker. Me, I don't smoke . . . except when I need to convince someone out of my past that I'm still me.

"It's not *my* story," Charlie reminded me. "Your brother, he was an ace at finding people. Best tracker in the city. I figure he must have taught you some things."

Charlie never invested himself emotionally in any matches he made. He was way past indifferent, as colorless as the ice storm that grayed the window of the no-name diner where we were meeting. But Charlie had something besides balance going for him. He was a pure specialist, a middleman who never got middled. What that means is, Charlie wouldn't do anything *except* make his matches.

Everyone in our world knows this. And for extra insurance, Charlie made sure he never knew the whole story. So, if he got swept up in a net, he wouldn't have anything to trade, even if he wanted to make a deal. Sure, he could say a man told him about a problem.

And he might have given the man a number to call. He had liked the guy, even if he'd only met him that one time. Felt sorry for him. In Charlie's vast experience, drunks who babbled about hiring a hit man were just blowing off steam. You give them a number to call— *any* number at all, even one you remembered from a bathroom wall—it helps them play out the fantasy, that's all. *"What!? You mean, his wife's really* dead? *Damn! I guess you just never know, huh, officer?"*

"This guy, he must not be in a hurry," I said.

"I wouldn't know," Charlie replied. His mantra.

"It's been three weeks since you reached out."

"Yeah, it took you a long time to get back to me. I figured, with the phone number being the same and all . . ."

"Most of those calls are people looking for my brother. I can't do a lot of the things he used to do."

"Yeah," he said, an unspoken *I don't want to know* woven through his voice like the anchor thread in a tapestry.

"But, still, three weeks," I reminded him. "I mean, how do you know the guy still wants . . . whatever he wants?"

Charlie shrugged.

"You get paid whether I ever call him or not?"

Charlie lit another cigarette. "He knows these things take time. You don't call, someone else will."

I waited a few seconds. Then said, "You want to write down his number for me?"

"I'll say the number," the ferret told me. "You want it on paper, you do the writing."

*C*ity people call winter the Hawk. Not because of the way it swoops down, but because it hunts. Gets cold enough in this town, people die. Some freeze to death waiting for the landlord to get heat back into their building. Some use their ovens for warmth, and wake up in flames. Some don't have buildings to die in.

I pulled out a prepaid cell phone, bought in a South Bronx bodega from a guy who had a dozen of them in a gym bag, and punched in the number Charlie had given me. A 718 area code—could be anywhere in the city except Manhattan, but a landline, for sure.

"Hello?" White male, somewhere in his forties.

"You were expecting my call," I said.

"Who are—? Oh, okay, yeah."

"I might be able to help you. But I can't know unless we talk."

"Just tell me—"

"You know the city?"

"If you mean Manhattan, sure."

"You got transportation?"

"A car?"

"That'll do," I said. I gave him the information I wanted him to have, walked to the end of the alley I'd been using as an office, and put the cell phone on top of a garbage can. Whoever found it would see there were plenty of minutes left. Probably use it to call his parole officer.

I pulled the glove off my left hand, fished a Metrocard out of my side pocket, and dropped below the sidewalk.

Charlie," said the little black man with the age-less, aristocratic face. "That boy's one diesel of a weasel. He might slouch, but he'd never vouch."

"I know, Prof. But no matter who this guys turns out to be, there's no way that it's me he's looking for. If anyone asked Charlie to put him in touch with a *specific* guy, it would have spooked him right out of the play."

The only father I'd ever known closed his eyes, looking into the past. The ambush that had almost taken me off the count years ago had been set up by a middle-man, too. Only, that time, I was told the client wanted me for the job. Me and only me.

"How much green just to make the scene?" he asked.

"Two to meet. For me to listen. That's as far as it's gone."

"It's a good number," the little man mused. "That's serious money, not crazy money."

"The job is finding someone, Prof."

"Charlie don't find people," the little man said. "He finds even one, he's all done."

"I did meet him, though."

"Charlie?"

"Yeah. And I called the spot."

"So, if he was fingering you . . ."

"Right. That diner, it's down by the waterfront. All kinds of bums hanging around. And, in this weather, you could put a dozen men on the street in body armor, and nobody'd even look twice."

"There's something else about Charlie," the Prof said, nodding to himself.

"What?"

"Maybe he's going along with you being your own brother, maybe he's not." The little man's voice dropped and hardened at the same time. "But he knows what number he called to get you to show up. You be Burke, you be his brother, don't make no difference. Because Charlie, he knows you not by yourself. You got family. He can't snap no trap on *all* of us. He double-crosses you, he's out of the middle. For as long as he lives. No way our boy bets *that* number."

Icicles fringed the bottom of the venom-yellow streetlight reflected in my rearview mirror, turning it into one of those old-fashioned parlor lamps, the kind with tassels hanging off the bottom of the shade.

I felt right at home. Waiting.

I'd set the meet for one in the morning, at a West Side bar in a building slated for demolition. New York is a big piece of machinery; it needs its gears greased to keep running. So the whole neighborhood was getting plowed over, like a field being readied for a different crop. That's Manhattan today—all the money goes up top, while the infrastructure wastes away from neglect. The famous skyline is a cheap trick now, a sleight-of-hand to draw your eye from the truth, as illusory as a bodybuilder with osteoporosis.

In the neighborhood I'd picked, strip joints where "upscale" meant five bucks for a bottle of Bud Light were driving out residential buildings. Only the rumors that our sports-whore mayor was going to find a way to green-light massive razing so he could build a gigantic football stadium near the Javits Center kept the whole area from being leveled. Building owners were laying in the cut, waiting to see the City's hole card.

My '69 Plymouth was huddled against the alley wall, its black-and-primer body mottled into an urban camouflage pattern. Anonymous, near-invisible. Like me, to most.

A cinnamon Audi sedan—a big one, probably an A8—circled the block for the third time, cruising for a place to park. I figured it for the guy I had been waiting for. There was an open space in front of a fire hydrant just across from me, but parking tickets can cost you more than money—ask David Berkowitz.

My watch read six minutes short of the meet time when a man came up the sidewalk toward the bar. He was bareheaded, hunched over against the razoring wind, wearing a camel's-hair topcoat with a white scarf. The kind of guy who would drive a hundred-grand car, and be used to parking it indoors.

I let him get inside before I made my move. I hadn't seen enough of his face to pick him out of a crowd, but I wasn't worried—it wasn't the kind of joint where you checked your coat.

He was standing at the bar, facing the doorway, the camel's-hair coat opened to reveal a charcoal-gray suit, white shirt, and geometric-pattern tie that flashed green-gold in the dim light. He had a shot glass in his right hand, a pair of butter-colored gloves in his left.

I walked toward him. He saw a man in a well-traveled army jacket, winter jeans, and work boots. If anyone asked him later, he would say the man's hair was covered with a watch cap that came down over the top of his ears, and his eyes were unreadable behind the heavy lenses of horn-rimmed glasses. My face was temporarily unscarred, thanks to Michelle's deft touch with the tube of Covermark she always carries.

The man coming toward him had a pair of gloves, too . . . on his hands.

I nodded my head to my left. He stepped away from the bar and walked in the direction I had indicated. I slipped past him and took a seat in an empty wood booth, facing the door. He sat down across from me.

Up close, he was older than his voice, but a guy who took care of himself, or had people do it for him: hundred-dollar haircuts, facials, manicures. I was guessing a heavy pill regimen, regular workouts, maybe even a little nip-and-tuck, too.

"Are you—?"

I held up two fingers.

He nodded, reached into the inside pocket of his coat, and brought out a plain white envelope. He put it on the table between us. I picked it up, slipped it into a side pocket.

"You're not going to count it?"

"You want something done, what's in it for you to stiff me on the front end?" I told him.

"That's right," he said, nodding vigorously.

I waited.

"Uh, is this a good place to talk?" he said, looking over his right shoulder.

"Depends on what you're going to say."

"I wouldn't want the waiter to—"

"They don't have any here," I told him. "Go to the bar, get a refill on whatever you're drinking, a whiskey double for me, and bring them back. Nobody'll bother us."

It was warm in the bar, but, even all wrapped up, I wasn't uncomfortable. When I was a young man, I had done some time in Africa. I was on the ground as the Nigerian military slaughtered a million people, made the whole "independent" country that tried to call itself Biafra disappear. The UN, that useless herd of toothless tigers, wouldn't call it genocide—that would mean they might have to send in troops. Didn't call what went down in Rwanda by its right name, either. Same for the Sudan. But they drew the line in Kosovo. Ethnic cleansing? Go ahead; just remember to keep it dark.

I got out of Biafra just before it fell, and I took home malaria as a permanent souvenir. Ever since, I can wear a leather jacket in July and not break a sweat. But the Hawk can find my bone marrow under the heaviest cover.

The man came back, sat down, put my whiskey in front of me, held up his own drink. "To a successful partnership," he said.

I didn't raise my glass, or my eyes.

He put down his drink without taking a sip. "I was told you specialize in finding people."

"Okay."

"Yes. Well . . . I, I need someone found."

If life was a movie, I would have asked him why he wanted the person found. He would have told me a long story. Being hard-bitten and cynical, I wouldn't have believed him. But, being down on my luck, I would have taken the case anyway. Unless he'd been a gorgeous girl—then I would have taken it for nothing, of course.

I shrugged my shoulders.

"Can you tell me how much it would cost to do that? Find . . . the person, I mean."

"No," I said. "I can't tell you that. Here's how it works: You pay me by the day. I keep looking until I find whoever you're looking for, or until you tell me to quit trying."

"Well, how much is it a day, then?"

"Same as you just paid me. I cover all expenses out of that. And there's a twenty-G bonus if I turn up what you want."

"Ten thousand a week," he said, the slightest trace of a question mark at the end of the sentence.

"We don't take weekends off," I told him. "One week, that's fourteen. Payable in advance."

"That could run into a lot of money."

"Uh-huh."

"I'll have to think that one over."

"You know where to find me," I said.

"Well, actually, I don't. I mean, the man who I . . . spoke to, he just took my number, and you called me, remember?"

"Yes, I remember."

"So how do I . . . ? Oh. You mean, now or never, right?"

"Right."

He took a hit off his drink. "I don't walk around with that kind of cash," he said. "Who does?"

"Best of luck with your search," I said, moving my untouched glass to the side as I started to stand up.

"Wait," he said. "I've got it."

I settled back into my seat. If we were still in that movie, I would have told him that lying was a bad way to start a relationship. If we were going to work together, I would need the truth, all the way. Down here, we play it different: "true" means you can spend it.

"Not on me," he said. "But close by. In my car. I keep an emergency stash. You never know. . . ."

I let my mouth twitch. Let him guess what that meant.

"Hold on to this," he said, handing me a black CD in a pale-pink plastic jewel case, as if it sealed a bargain between us. "I'll be back in a few minutes, and we'll go over everything."

I pocketed the CD. Folded my gloved hands like a kid waiting for the teacher to come back.

He got up and left. I counted to thirty; then I got up, too, heading for the restrooms. I walked past the twin doors until I found myself in the open space behind the bar. I crossed the space, moving like the Prof had taught me a million years ago. I can't phantom through a room without displacing the air like he does, but I can move smooth enough not to disrupt the visuals unless someone's staring directly at me.

The back door had a heavy alarm box next to it, but I could see it was unplugged. I opened the door just wide enough to slide through, clicked it *soft* behind me, and made my way down a short flight of metal steps to the alley.

I didn't want my car. I knew what direction he'd come from; if I cut the alley right, I'd come out close enough to see that camel's-hair coat.

Nothing.

Quick choice: was he still behind me, or ahead? I felt the Hawk's bite, remembered how the guy was dressed, and figured he'd be moving as quick as he could. I took off the glasses, switched my black watch cap for a red one, hunched my shoulders against the wind, and started covering ground.

I saw him cross ahead of me, moving toward the river. I gambled on another alley, and drew the right card. I marked the direction he was going in, and moved out ahead.

The big Audi was parked mid-block, a purebred among mutts. I floated into a doorway, wrapping the shadows around my shoulders. If he just took off, instead of getting something from inside his ride and walking back to the bar, I'd figure he was busy on a cell phone, and company was coming—I wouldn't be there when it arrived. But if he really kept that kind of cash in his car, I wanted that license number.

He walked past me on the opposite side of the street. I stayed motionless, but he never glanced my way.

Two men came toward him from the far end of the block, walking with too much space between them to be having a conversation. The guy in the camel's-hair coat was almost to his car before he saw them. He put his hands up and started backing away, making a warding-off motion with his palms.

A car door opened. A man in a black-and-gold warm-up suit stepped onto the sidewalk behind the man in the camel's-hair coat. He brought his two hands together and spread his feet in one flowing motion. The man in the camel's-hair coat went down. The shooter waved the other two back with his free hand, then walked over to the man lying on the sidewalk, an extended-barrel pistol held in profile. The whole thing was over in seconds, as choreographed as an MTV video, on mute.

A vapor-colored sedan pulled out of its parking spot. The shooter got into the back seat, and it drove off. The two men who had blocked the target were gone.

The street stayed quiet.

I took a long deep breath through my nose, filling my stomach. I let it out slowly, expanding my chest as I did.

Then I got gone.

My Plymouth looks like a candidate for the junkyard. But it's a Rolex under all the rust, including an independent rear suspension transplanted from a wrecked Viper some rich guy had thought made him immune to physics, and a hogged-out Mopar big-block with enough torque to compete in a tractor pull. So I feathered the throttle, even though I wasn't worried about snow on the streets.

The same year my car had been born, the mayor had been a guy named Lindsay. He was the ideal politician, a tall, good-looking, Yale-graduate, war-veteran, "fusion" Republican who ran on the Liberal ticket. He got a lot of credit for New York not going the way of Newark or Detroit or Los Angeles during the riots the year before. But when the big blizzard hit in February of '69 and paralyzed the city, Lindsay took the heat for the Sanitation Department being caught napping, and that was the end of his career.

Every mayor that followed him got the message. New Yorkers will tolerate just about anything on their streets, from projectile-vomiting drunks to mumbling lunatics, but snow is un-fucking-acceptable.

I made my way over to the West Side Highway, rolled north to Ninety-sixth, exited, and looped back, heading downtown. Even at two in the morning, I couldn't be sure I didn't have company—in this city, there's always enough traffic for cover. But I knew a lot of places that would expose a shadow real quick, some as flat and empty as the Sahara, others as clogged as a ready-to-rupture artery.

I opted for density. Took a left on Canal, motored leisurely east, then ducked into the Chinatown maze. Made two slow circuits before I finally docked in the alley behind Mama's joint, right under a white square with a freshly painted black ideogram. My spot. Empty as always—the Chinese calligraphy marked the territory of Max the Silent, a message even the baby-faced gangsters who infested the area understood.

I flat-handed the steel door twice. Seconds later, I found myself staring into the face of a man I'd never seen before. That didn't matter—he knew who I was, and I knew what he was there for.

The restaurant never changes, just the personnel. Like an army base with a high turnover. I went through the kitchen, past the bank of payphones, and sat down in my booth. The place was empty. No surprise—the white-dragon tapestry had been on display in the filthy, streaked front window when I had driven past. If it had been blue, I would have kept on rolling. Red, I would have found a phone, made some calls.

Mama appeared from somewhere behind me, a heavy white tureen in both hands. "Come for visit?" she said.

"For soup."

"Sure, this weather, good, have soup," Mama said. She used a ladle to dole out a steaming portion into a red mug with BARNARD in big white letters curling around the side. Mama is no more a cook than the place she runs is a restaurant, but her hot-and-sour soup is her pride and joy. Failure to consume less than three portions per visit would be considered a gross lack of respect.

I took a sip, touched two fingers to my lips, said, "Perfect!"—the minimally acceptable response.

Mama made a satisfied sound, her ceramic face yielding to some version of a smile. "You working?"

"I was," I said. I told her what had happened. When I got to the part about the shooting, Mama held up a hand for silence, barked out a long string of harsh-sounding Cantonese. Two men in white aprons came out of the kitchen. One went to the front door, crouched down, and positioned himself so he had a commanding view of the narrow street. The other vigorously nodded his head twice, then vanished.

I went back to my story and my soup.

A few minutes later, the front door opened, and the man who had gone back to the kitchen area walked in. He conferred with the man by the window. They came over to where we were sitting. Rapid-fire conversation. I didn't need a translator to understand "all clear."

"So?" Mama said.

"I don't think it had anything to do with me, Mama. The way I see it, whoever this guy was, he was important enough for someone to have a hunter-killer team on his trail. Once the spotter had him pinned, he called in the others."

"We do that, too, now, yes?"

"Right," I agreed. I got up and headed for the pay-phones.

*E*veryone was there in less than an hour. The Prof and Clarence drove in from their crib in East New York. The warehouse where Max the Silent lives with his wife, Immaculata, was only a short walk away.

I'd been on the scene when they first met, on a late-night subway train, a lifetime ago. Immaculata was part Vietnamese, part who-knows? First dismissed as a "bar girl" by Mama, she was instantly elevated to Heaven's Own Blessing when she gave birth to Max's baby, Flower. The moment her sacred granddaughter decided on Barnard College, Mama had personally emptied the school's merchandise catalogue.

Apparently, she considered the sweatshirt she had presented to me last year to be adequate compensation for the fortune she'd extorted from me over the years "for baby's college."

I told the story of my meet, gesturing it out for Max, even though he can read my lips like they were printing out words.

"The boss pay for a toss?" the little man asked, miming a man bent over a victim, rifling through his pockets. Max nodded, to let us know he was following along.

"Didn't look like it, Prof. The shooter plugged him once, then walked over and made sure," I said, gesturing to act out my words. "But I didn't see him search the body, and the other two were already in the wind."

"If he had a silencer, it must have been a semi-auto," Clarence said. The young man usually didn't speak until he thought the rest of us were finished. But when he was on sure ground, he would.

"My son knows his guns," the Prof said, approvingly. "The shooter pick up his brass?"

"Not a chance," I said. "The street was too dark, and he fired at least three times."

"The police, they will know it was an execution," Clarence said, his West Indian accent adding formality to his speech. "If the killers did not search the dead man, he will still have everything with him."

"If the street skells don't loot the body before the cops get on the scene," I said. "That neighborhood, that hour, who's going to call it in, some good citizen? Besides, you couldn't hear the shots, even as close as I was."

"They couldn't be counting on all that," the Prof said. "Even if nobody did a wallet-and-watch on the dead guy, that pistol's in two different rivers by now."

"Somebody spent a lot of money on this one," I agreed. "That means it'll make the papers. We might be able to find out something then."

"The way I see it, whoever this guy wanted you to find, they found him first," the Prof said, leaning back in his chair and lighting a smoke. "That ain't us, Gus. None of our gelt's on the felt."

"My father is right," Clarence said, more for the chance to say "my father" than to add anything. He used to do that all the time after the Prof first found him; now it's only once in a while. "The money you got from that man, whoever he was, there will not be any more."

"Maybe," I told them, putting the jewel-cased CD on the table.

I used my key to work the brick-sized padlock, opened the chain-link gate, and drove my Plymouth inside the enclosure behind the darkened gas station. While I was jockeying the big car into the narrow space, the three pit bulls who live there politely divided up the half-gallon container of beef in oyster sauce I had brought from Mama's. It sounded like alligators tearing at a pig who had wandered too close to the riverbank. If they hadn't recognized me, no bribe would have stopped them. By the time I finished stowing the Plymouth, they were back inside their insulated dog condo, probably watching the Weather Channel on their big-screen.

It was almost four when I walked into the flophouse. There was a man behind the wooden plank that held the register nobody ever signs. He looked up at me from his wheelchair and shook his head, the equivalent of the white-dragon tapestry in Mama's window.

"All quiet, Gateman?"

"Dead as the governor's heart at Christmas, boss."

All cons know what Christmas means—pardon time. Last year, Sweet Joe, an old pal of ours, had sent us a kite, saying he was sure to make it this time. "Finally got my ticket to the door," is what he wrote. His ticket was terminal cancer—the prison medicos had given him six months to live. The parole board responded with a two-year hit, meaning Sweet Joe was going to die behind the walls unless the governor did the right thing.

Sure. When Joe got the bad news, he took it like he had taken the twenty-to-life they threw at him thirty years ago—standing up. He's gone now. Didn't even last the six months.

I climbed the foul, verminous stairs, past signs that warn of all kinds of DANGER! The top floor is "Under Construction"—there's all this asbestos to remove, never mind the mutated rats staring hungrily out from the posters on the walls. That's where I live.

While I was away the last time, my family knocked down every wall that wasn't load-bearing and built me a huge apartment. It's got everything a man like me could ever want, including a back way out.

I never get lonely.

I woke up at eleven, flicked the radio into life, and took a long, hot shower. While I was shaving, the mirror confronted me with the truth. My own mother wouldn't recognize me. That's okay—I wouldn't recognize her, either. A teenage hooker, she had hung around just long enough to pop me out. Then she fled the hospital before they could run her through the system. Decades later, as soon as they unplugged me from the machines, I'd done the same thing.

"Baby Boy Burke" is what it says on my birth certificate. The rest of it is blanks, guesses, and lies. For "father" it says "Unk." It should say "The State of New York." That's who raised me. Raised me to hate all of them: scum who spend their lives looking the other way . . . and getting paid to do it.

Having the State as your father bends your chromosomes like no inherited DNA ever could. You come up knowing that faith is for suckers. The only god I ever worshiped was the only one who ever answered my prayers. My religion is revenge.

That's why, as soon as I escaped the hospital, I went on a pilgrimage. By the time I reached the end, I'd squared things for Pansy.

Getting that done had cost me my retirement fund, and I'd been scratching around for another score ever since—a nice, safe one. I haven't been Inside since I was a young man, and I don't get nostalgic for being caged.

While I was gone, a cop named Morales had found a human hand—just the bones, not the flesh—in a Dumpster. There was a pistol there, too. With my thumbprint on it. Far as NYPD was concerned, that upgraded me from "missing and presumed" to "dead and gone." And the longer I stayed away, the deeper the whisper-stream carried that message into the underground.

I was halfway through shaving when the story came on: Unidentified man found shot to death on the sidewalk, in a quiet neighborhood just a couple of blocks from West Street. The body had been discovered by a building super who had gone out to rock-salt the concrete so his tenants wouldn't break their necks going to work in the morning. A landlord could get sued for that. The announcer said the police were not releasing any details, pending notification to next of kin. Meaning they knew who the dead man was but they weren't telling.

That wasn't news, just a collection of maybes. Maybe the cops found the cash the man in the camel's-hair coat said was in his car. Maybe they divided it up among themselves; maybe they were holding back the info to use as a polygraph key once they had suspects to question. Maybe the money was in the car, but in a hidden compartment, one they hadn't found yet. Maybe it was never there at all, and the guy was just heading to his car to make a getaway. Maybe the cops still hadn't connected him to the Audi. . . .

The print journalists would take a deeper look—they always do—but it would take them longer to come up with anything.

I walked downstairs, picked up my copy of *Harness Lines* and a couple of fresh bagels from Gateman—he's got a guy who delivers every morning—and ate my breakfast while I decided which horses were worthy of my investment. I only bet the trotters. Like me, they haul weight for their money, and they usually earn it after dark.

I smeared a thick slab of cream cheese on the last of a poppy-seed bagel, and held it under the table.

"You want . . . ?" I started to say, before I choked on the words. Pansy wasn't lurking by my feet, waiting for the treat she knew was always going to come.

I thought I had stopped . . . *feeling* her with me. Stopped seeing her looming dark-gray shadow in the corner by the window. Stopped hearing the special sound she always made before dropping off to sleep, like a big semi downshifting to climb a hill.

"This late in the day, you're probably on your third quart of French vanilla up there, huh, girl?" I said aloud.

If you think I'm crazy to be talking to my dog like I do, fuck you. And if you don't get how that's better than crying over her, fuck you twice.

My little sister called a couple of hours later.

"That bar you recommended? Well, baby, let me tell you, it is *beyond* tacky. Imagine, putting ice in a Bloody Mary!"

So the stash we had gotten word about *was* from Sierra Leone. That shifted the risk-reward odds too far to the wrong side for us to take the shot. Stealing a load of "blood diamonds" would be like hijacking counterfeit bills. Sure, we could find someone to take the loot off our hands, but the discount would shred our profit down to cigarette money.

"I thought it sounded too good to be true, the way it was described to me," I said, not surprised.

"Maybe we should open our own place," Michelle said, switching to the liquid-honey voice she earned her living with.

"I was about to," I said. "But the financing fell through."

"That, too, huh?"

"Yeah."

"It's this weather, sweetie. Winter is the suicide season. Like it's raining depression. But it won't last, you'll see."

"Sure."

"All right, Mr. Grouch. Want to buy me dinner?"

"Okay. I'll see you at—"

But I was talking to a dead line.

Driving through Chinatown at night is like riding the subway past one of those abandoned stations. You feel the life beyond the shadows, but all you ever get is a glimpse—then it's gone, and you're not really sure if you actually saw anything. You might be curious, but not enough to leave the safety of your steel-and-glass cocoon to get a closer look.

I was explaining to Max why we might want to consider investing a significant chunk of our betting kitty in a ten-dollar exacta wheel tomorrow night. For seventy bucks, we could have all the possibilities covered, provided this six-year-old we'd been following since he was a bust-out flop in his freshman season came home on top.

With Max, this is never a hard sell. Anytime he falls in love with a horse, he's ready to go all-in. And Max gets there faster than a high school kid in a whorehouse.

This particular horse, a gelding named Little Eric, was a fractious animal who was prone to breaking stride, a move that takes a trotter out of any chance to win. But Max and I had watched some of those races, and we had marked every single time it happened. We decided the breaks weren't because Little Eric was naturally rough-gaited. He couldn't handle the tight turns at Yonkers very well, so he usually spent a lot of every race parked out. He was okay on the outside, but every time he tried for a big brush to get clear, he'd go off-stride. He didn't have the early foot to grab the lead right out of the gate, but he was a freight train of a closer. And he liked the cold weather, too.

The reason I fancied him so much for tomorrow night was that he was moving to The Meadowlands. That's a mile track, with only two turns to negotiate, as opposed to the four at Yonkers. Little Eric could take his time, settle in, and make his move late, down that long stretch. He was in pretty tough, but he could beat that field if he ran his number. And the outside post he drew wouldn't be as much of a handicap at The Big M.

Nothing close to a sure thing, but a genuine overlay at the twelve-to-one Morning Line price; maybe even more if the favorite drew a lot of late action.

Michelle made her entrance in a lipstick-red jacket with shoes to match. She glistened like a cardinal in a snow-covered tree, defying winter to dull her beauty.

"I'm such a sucker," she said, as Max held a chair for her to sit down. "I'm still a young girl, but I've been around long enough to know better."

Max and I put on matching quizzical looks—Michelle sometimes loops around a story like a pilot circling a fogged-in airport.

"You know what's the stupidest thing about racism?" she said.

Max and I shrugged.

"That it's stupid," she said, grinning. "Racism, it makes you think you know a person just because you know his race, see?"

"Sure," I agreed, thinking of some of the bogus wisdom I'd been raised on, passed along by the older street boys I was sure were the smartest people on the planet. After all, they lived on their own. And they never seemed afraid. "Niggers are all yellow inside," they'd counseled me. "In a crowd, they act like they got balls, but get one of them alone . . ."

I got one alone once. We both wanted the same shoeshine corner. He was a little bigger; I was a little faster.

"You didn't run," I told him, a few minutes later. It was hard to talk—my mouth was all bloody, and my tongue was swollen to twice its size.

"You didn't pussy out, neither," the colored kid—I'd already stopped thinking of him as "nigger" in my mind, even though I didn't realize it—said, sounding as surprised as I was.

I guess some older guys had lied to him, too.

"Well, you know the hard-core Jews? The ones who dress like the Amish?" Michelle said, accepting a light for her cigarette—a thin black one with a gold filter tip.

"Hasidim? Like the ones who control a piece of Crown Heights?"

"Whatever," Michelle said, airily. "You know who I mean . . . the ones who handle diamonds. For them, it's all a handshake business, right? No paper. Everyone knows you can trust those guys. It's always been that way."

"So?"

"So the guy *I* trusted, the one who was setting up that job for us? He never said the diamonds were dirty."

"You didn't really trust him, girl. Otherwise, we would just have gone on ahead, right?"

"Oh, I know. But *still*. I mean, who would ever think one of those super-straight Jews would go anywhere near dirty stuff."

"They bought diamonds from South Africa even when the boycott was on," I said. "And uranium, too."

"Mole says—"

"—they just did what they had to do," I finished for her. I've known the Mole since we were kids. By him, Israel drops a nuke on one of its neighbors, it's just doing what they had to do.

You could say it's people like the Mole who keep Israel from finding peace. Or you could say it's people like the Mole who keep it from disappearing. Me, I don't care. The only country I care about is about the size of Mama's restaurant—that's enough space to hold every member of my family.

"This one was going to be so juicy," Michelle said, regretfully.

"Been lots of those," I told her.

By the time the morning light was making a run against the grimy windows, we weren't any closer to a good scheme. This was the third plan that had gone sour in the past couple of months.

Good scams are harder and harder to come by these days. Too many thieves fishing in the same pool of chumps. Colloidal silver for longevity, "form books" for tax evasion, orgasm enhancers for patheticos who think a lap dance is a relationship. Online auctions for collector cars that don't exist . . . and every bidder's a winner. Even some neo-Nazis were going into the penis-enlargement business to finance their operations—skinheads aren't much for paying their membership dues, and the self-appointed Führers are too afraid of their own followers to get heavy about collecting.

I used to do violence-for-money. But the older I get, the less it's worth playing for those stakes. "The gun's fun, but the sting's the thing," the Prof called it, when he first started schooling me.

For lifelong outlaws like us, crime is all about cash. We're not psychopaths—we don't need the action to feel alive. Crime's not about the buzz; it's a business.

Anyone who's been running on our track for long enough has learned a few things. Like, you'll get more time for a gas-station holdup than for taking a few million out of a company pension fund. And a double-nickel jolt for a young man is a very different trip than it is for a guy with a lot of miles on his odometer.

A generation ago, our whole crew got involved with hijacking a load of dope. It was a foolproof scheme. The people we took it from wouldn't run to the Law—they'd just buy it back from us. Nobody gets hurt, we make a fortune, and they chalk it up to the cost of doing business.

The first half clicked as sweet as stiletto heels on a marble floor. Then the wheels came off. If we'd known how deep some NYPD boys were involved with the dope trade back in the day, we wouldn't have gone near the job.

I was the only one of us they caught. In an abandoned subway tunnel, with enough heroin to give a small town a collective overdose. The dope never got vouchered; I got to plead to some assaults, avoiding the telephone numbers a possession-with-intent charge would have brought. And best of all, I got to go down alone.

I'm a two-time felony loser. The Prof has three bits under his belt. If either of us ever falls again, we're looking at the life-without they throw at habitual offenders in this state.

Clarence and the Mole have never been Inside. Max has, but not for long. Just arrests, no convictions. Why plea-bargain when you know the witnesses are never going to show up for the trial?

Michelle was locked up back when she was pre-op. About the hardest time you can do, unless you're willing to whore out or daddy-up.

She spent most of her time binged, in solitary. Not PC, Ad Seg. You go to Protective Custody—aka Punk City—as a volunteer, to keep yourself safe. You go to

Ad Seg—Administrative Segregation, aka The Hole—
when you commit a crime inside. Michelle wasn't big,
and she wasn't fast, but she *would* cut you, and she was
real good at always finding something to do that with.

In our world, showing you can do time counts for
something only when you're young. After that, what
earns you the points is showing you can avoid it.

I spent most of my childhood caged. The rest of the
time, I was on the run—from the foster parents they
"placed" me with, the "group homes" they sentenced
me to, and the "training schools" I'd been destined for
since birth.

In the juvie joints, it seemed like nobody was ever
there for the worst things they did. One guy, he was in
for stealing fireworks. He wanted the cherry bombs
and ashcans to torture animals with. Another guy was
a fire-setter. They caught him doing that a year after
they caught him raping his baby sister. He got counsel-
ing for the rape, but destruction of property, that was
something they couldn't let slide.

Most of the gang kids were there for fighting, but, to
hear them tell it, they'd all gone much further down
the violence road. One little Puerto Rican guy was talking about how he chopped an enemy's hand off with a
machete in a rumble. A white kid laughed out loud at
the story, as deep a diss as a bitch-slap.

The Puerto Rican kid went back to his bunk, came
over to where we were all standing around, and hooked
the white kid to the stomach with a needle-sharp file.

Gutted him like a fish. The white kid didn't die, so, instead of going back to court with a new charge, the Puerto Rican kid got shipped to another juvie joint. With a bigger rep.

It was inside that kiddie prison that I first claimed another human being as family. I told the others that Wesley was my brother. I wasn't worried that anyone would ever ask Wesley if it was true—nobody ever asked Wesley anything. But a kid who called himself Tiger called me on it.

Tiger was twice my size, plus he never walked around alone. So he should have been safe. But, one night, he got shanked in his sleep.

Everyone thought Wesley had done it—that was what Wesley did, even then. But it wasn't him. It was his brother.

"You have anything, honey?" Michelle asked. "Anything at all?"

"Little Eric in the fifth," I told her, just to see her smile.

*T*he noon sun was a throbbing blood-orange blob, pulsating against the mesh screen of a pollution-gray sky. For once, it actually made an impact on my permanently crusted windows. I figured I'd better get it while I could.

"You want something from down the way?" I asked Gateman.

"Which way is that, boss?"

"Diner?"

"Sold. I could really go for some of their bull's-eye meatloaf today."

"Two sides?"

"You're singing my song," he said, grinning. "Make mine mashed potatoes and spinach, okay?"

I got the same for myself, and brought the whole thing back, hot. Gateman and I admired the way the half-cut hard-boiled egg looked embedded in the thick slab of heavy-crusted meatloaf before we dug in.

"Ever wonder how come this is the only good thing they make in that dive, boss?"

"I figure it's what they call a 'signature dish,' Gate. Every restaurant's got one. It's how the chef shows off."

"Yeah? Well, I been in that joint plenty of times, boss. And if they got a 'chef,' I'm a fucking ballerina."

"Got to look past the cover, bro," I said mildly, holding out a clenched fist.

Gateman tapped my fist with his own, acknowledging the mistake more than one man had made about him. Dead men now. Gateman is one of the reasons they have to make prisons wheelchair-accessible. He was a pure shooter, and he could conjure up the pistol he wore next to his colostomy bag like a fatal magic trick.

A couple of years back, the Prof had bet Max that Gateman could drill the center out of the ace of hearts at ten yards. Took a couple of weeks to set up the match, trucking sandbags down to the basement. The lighting down there was so lousy I could barely make out the white card, never mind the red heart in its center.

I should have known something was up when

Clarence put down a hundred on Gateman. The Prof and Max were both hunch-players, but Clarence was a gunman. Still, I faded his action, saying, "No disrespect" to Gateman first.

Gateman braced himself in his chair, holding his compact 9mm Kahr in both hands, turning himself into a human tripod. He exhaled a soft sigh, then he punched out the center of the card with his first shot.

"Got something for tonight?" he asked.

"Just a guess," I cautioned him.

"That's all there ever is, right?"

"At the track, sure."

"It's all a bet," Gateman said. "Everything. All that changes is the stakes, boss."

I started telling him what I liked about Little Eric. By the time I was up to my two favorite trotters of all time, Nevele Pride and Une de Mai, duking it out at the International—I never saw that race; that was the year I spent in Biafra—Gateman's eyes were starting to glaze over. He wanted action, not ancient history.

"On the nose, okay?" he said, shoving a twenty over to me.

*A*s I let myself back into my apartment, one of the half-dozen cell phones I keep on a shelf in separate charging cradles rang. I have each one marked with a different-colored piece of vinyl tape so I don't make a mistake, but I don't really need that system anymore, since I finally figured out how to give each one a different ring tone.

I pushed the button, said, "Lewis."

"It's me."

"Okay."

"You don't sound happy, honey."

"I was expecting another call," I lied. Only one person had the number to the phone I was holding, and she was at the other end of the conversation.

"I won't keep you. I just thought you might like to come over and see me later."

"How much later?"

"In time to take me to dinner?"

"Ah . . ."

"Oh, come *on,* sugar. We all have to eat, don't we? So why can't we do it together?"

"I'm a private person."

"There's plenty of places we can go where you won't—"

"There's no place where *you* won't draw a damn crowd," I said, trying for the soft deflection.

"I won't dress up, I promise. *Please?* You won't be sorry."

I let the cellular silence play over us for a minute. Then I said, "Eight, okay?"

"*Okay!*"

I hung up without saying goodbye. She was used to it.

*T*he easiest person in the world to lie to is yourself. Anyone who's done time knows how seductive that call can be. The Prof warned me about it, back when I was still a young thug, idolizing the big-time hijackers who pulled major jobs and lived like kings until the money ran out. Then they went looking for another armored car.

"You pick up a pattern, it's harder to shake than a hundred-dollar-a-day Jones, Schoolboy. You let motherfuckers read your book, they always know where to look."

I had a few hours before dinner, and I knew I wasn't going to sleep where I'd be spending the night, so I grabbed a quilt and curled up on my couch.

One of the cells woke me. The ring tone told me it was family.

"What?" I said.

"There was a lot on that CD, mahn."

"A lot of stuff, or stuff that's worth a lot?" I asked Clarence.

"A lot of stuff for sure. I cannot tell you about the other, mahn. You probably want to look for yourself, yes?"

I glanced at my wristwatch. Couple of minutes after six.

"Could you bring it by tomorrow?"

"Sure."

I cut the call. Showered and shaved. Put on a pair of dark cords with a leather belt polished with mink oil—a trick I learned from a couple of working girls whose private joke was that I'm a closet dom. A rose silk shirt—I know a sweet girl who gets them made in Bali for a tiny percentage of what I used to pay Sulka—a black tie, and a bone leather sport coat that was pulled out of inventory before it ever got the chance to fall off a truck. Alligator boots with winter treads and steel toes, and I was ready to walk.

I strapped a heavy Kobold diver's watch on my left wrist, fitted a flat-topped ring onto my right hand: a custom-made hunk of silver housing a tiny watch battery that powers a series of micro-LEDs on its surface in random patterns. I slipped a black calfskin wallet into my jacket. It held a complete set of ID for Kenneth Ivan Lewis.

I shrugged into a Napapijri Geographic coat, an Italian beauty like the ones they used in the Antarctic Research Mapping Survey. It's made of some kind of synthetic, with enough zippers, straps, hooks, and Velcro closings to stock a hardware store. Weighs nothing, but it sneers at the wind and sheds water like Teflon.

By seven-fifteen, I was on the uptown 6 train.

I answered the doorman's polite question with "Lewis." He opened his mouth to ask if that was my first or last name, caught my eye, changed his mind.

"I'll be right with you, sir," he said, making it clear he wanted me to stay where I was while he walked over and picked up the house phone.

I couldn't hear his end of the conversation . . . which was the whole point.

"Please go on up, sir."

"Thanks."

I took the elevator. The building was new enough so that it actually had the thirteenth floor marked.

I stood outside the door to 13-D, waiting. I didn't

touch the tiny brass knocker, or the discreet black button set into the doorframe.

"How come you never knock?" she said as the door opened.

"You're going to look through the peephole before you open the door, right? And you knew I—or someone, anyway—was on the way up, so you'd be on the watch."

"What do you mean, 'someone'?" she said, standing aside to let me into the apartment.

"You don't use video in this building. All the doorman had was a name. Anyone can use a name."

"He described you, too," she said, slightly sulky.

"And that description would fit—what?—a million or so guys in Manhattan alone."

"Oh, don't be so *suspicious*," she said, standing on her toes to kiss me on the cheek, right over the bullet scar. "That's how you get lines on your face, being suspicious of everything."

"Then my face should look like a piece of graph paper," I said, putting my coat in her outstretched hands.

"I'm not dressed yet," she announced, as if coming to the door in a lacy red bra and matching panties hadn't been enough of a hint. "Go sit down; I'll only be a few minutes."

She turned and walked down the hall with the confidence of a woman who expects to be watched and is ready for it. I sat down in a slingback azure leather chair and watched tropical fish cavort in the flat-screen virtual aquarium on the far wall. I slitted my eyes against the vibrant pixel display until it became the kind of kaleidoscope you get when you press your fingers against your eyelids. I don't mind waiting; it's one of the things I do best.

The lady I was waiting for was a zaftig blonde without a straight line anywhere on her body, like a pinup girl from the fifties; the kind of woman who turns a walk to the grocery store into an audition. A sweet little biscuit, bosomy and wasp-waisted, with big hazel eyes like a pair of jeweler's loupes. Her idea of foreplay is what she calls "presents," and the right ones make her arch her back like a bitch cat in heat.

I met her in a BMW showroom on Park Avenue. I was there to see a guy who does beautiful custom work . . . on VIN numbers. She was just window-shopping, keeping in practice.

I was dressed for the part I was playing, all Zegna and Bruno Magli. She was wearing white toreador pants, a fire-engine-red silk plain-front blouse, and matching spike heels with ankle straps, holding a belted white coat in her right hand. As soon as she was sure she had my attention, she turned around to caress the gleaming fender of a Z8. Instead of back pockets, the white pants had a pair of red arrows, pointing left and right. I wished she'd get mad at something, and walk away.

Instead, she walked over to where I was standing.

"Want to buy me a car?" she said, flashing a homicidal smile.

"I never buy cars on the first date," I said.

"Ooh!" she squealed, softly.

That's where it started. She doesn't know what I do for a living, but she's sure it's something shady. She's *real* sure I'm married—you wear a wedding ring long enough, when you take it off it leaves a telltale mark a woman like her could spot at a hundred yards.

She's so gorgeous she can show off just by showing up. Keeps a big mirror on her bed, where the head-board should be. Her favorite way is to get on all fours and wiggle a little first. She wants it so that the last thing she sees before she lets go is herself, watching me doing her.

When I pretend to go to sleep afterwards, she vacuums my clothes with a feather touch. She's not looking for money, just information.

She thinks my name is Ken Lewis. She calls me Lew. I never asked her why.

There's a dirty elegance about her. She looks as lush as an orchid, and comes across just about as smart. But that's just another kind of makeup for her. She's got the dumb-blonde thing down so slick that trying to get a straight answer out of her is like cross-examining a mynah bird with ADD.

Her name is Loyal.

I never sleep over.

"Call you a cab, sir?" a different doorman asked, as if getting a cab at three in the morning in that neigh-borhood required a professional's touch.

"Thanks," I lied, "but I'm parked around the corner."

The next day started out like the beginning of a long winning streak. Before I could even take a look at the paper, the TV called to me with a breaking story. A guide dog was walking with his person just before day-break when a couple of muggers descended. Probably junkies who'd spent the whole night trying to score, I thought. The muggers kicked the blind man's cane out of his hand. When he went down, they dropped to their knees to rip at his jacket. Apparently, that was a major mistake. When the cops arrived, the blind man still had one of the muggers in a painful joint lock. The other one got away, but left a lot of blood on the side-walk.

The newscaster said the blind man was a veteran of World War II. They showed a photo of a man who looked vaguely Asian, with a stiff white crew cut and a prominent tattoo on one biceps that I couldn't make out. As the camera panned down, my earlier guess was confirmed: who but a desperate junkie would try to put a move on a blind man whose seeing-eye dog was a Doberman?

I raised my glass of guava juice in a silent toast to the man and his dog.

The day got better when I saw the race results. Little Eric had gotten away cleanly and settled back in the pack, letting the favorite and another horse battle for the lead. The first quarter went in a blistering .28 flat. While the lead horses dueled on the front end, Little Eric moved to the outside, picking up cover just past the half. The three-quarter went in 1:26.2, with Little Eric still two deep on the outside. He made his move at the top of the stretch, going three wide to calmly gun down the rest of the field, nailing the win and taking a lifetime mark of 1:54.4 in the bargain.

He paid $27.40 to win. Even with the two-to-five favorite hanging tough for second, the exacta returned a sweet $89.50. Our seventy-buck investment was going to net well over four hundred.

Damn!

I switched on the bootleg satellite radio the Mole had hooked up for me, and was instantly rewarded with Albert King's "Laundromat Blues," the Sue Foley version of "Two Trains," and, to cap the trifecta, Magic Judy Henske's new cut of "Easy Rider."

Today's the day to play my number, I remember thinking. Then I made the mistake of opening the paper from the front.

MURDERED MAN IDENTIFIED, BUT MYSTERY DEEP-ENS, the headline read. I scanned the article quickly, then reread it carefully, culling the facts away from the adjectives the way you have to do to translate the tabloids.

The dead man was a "financial planner" named Daniel Parks. He was forty-four years old, an Ivy League M.B.A. who lived on a "multimillion-dollar" waterfront estate in Belle Harbor with his wife and three children, the oldest a teenage girl who tearfully told the reporters that her father couldn't have had an enemy in the world.

They hadn't ID'ed him from prints; his wallet—containing several hundred dollars, the reporter noted—had provided a wealth of information. Not just his driver's license and the registration and insurance papers for the Audi, but a permit for the "automatic pistol" they found in his coat.

New York's very stingy with carry permits. There's only about forty thousand active ones at any time— you've got better odds of finding a landlord who voluntarily cuts your rent. Almost all those permits go to celebrities—they're an important status symbol in a town where status is more important than oxygen. Of course, if you're one of those "honorary police commissioners"—the "honor" comes from a heavy annual contribution to some murky "police fund"—you get to walk around with all the iron you want. Park anywhere you want, too—another one of the perks is an official NYPD placard for your windshield.

I didn't like any of that. When I got to the part about Parks being "rumored" to have recently testified before a grand jury investigating money laundering, I liked it even less. If the hunter-killer team had been shadowing him, they might have sent a man inside to see who he was going to meet.

The scenario was bad enough, but it wasn't worst-case. The *federales* aren't the only ones who can tap phones. If the shooting team had a heads-up for where the target had been headed that night, they could have had the place covered for hours before I even showed up. It didn't look as if they had, so I was probably in the clear.

Probably.

Even if they'd had a man inside, I told myself, they wouldn't know anything but my face—and you have to get *real* close to see anything distinctive about it. I didn't think they had seen my car, and even if they had, the license was a welded-up fake. A trace-back on the number I had called Parks from would dead-end no matter how deep they looked.

So I was clear unless . . . unless Charlie had been offered enough cash to stray out of his home territory, take a vacation from the middle. If there was a bounty on the dead man, Charlie would know about it. So, when the target came to ask Charlie to put him together with someone who could help with his problem, Charlie could have sold him.

Bad. That little ferret practiced a dark martial art, the kind that lets you kill a man with a phone call. But if I asked him about it . . . *very* fucking bad. Word gets out you were looking for Charlie, it could make a lot of people nervous. Where I live, it's a lot cheaper to kill the hunter than hide the prey.

I went into myself. All the way down the mine shaft where the only ore is truth and pain. Like when I was a kid, and those words were synonyms.

I had one hand to play. I was holding it in my mind, turning it over, seeing the aces-and-eights full house, the only one my ghost brother ever dealt. Then Clarence walked in the door, and made things worse.

*I*t's a dossier, mahn," he said, holding out the CD I'd given him. "The person who put this together, he had a lot of time on his hands. Spent some money, too."

"Any money *in* it?" I asked, hoping for something to get me back to my winning streak.

"Maybe," the West Indian said dubiously, tossing his cream cashmere topcoat over the back of my futon couch, the better to display a fuchsia satin shirt with black nacre buttons worn outside a pair of black slacks with balloon knees and pegged cuffs. "There's account numbers and all, but no access codes or PIN numbers."

"How do I—"

"Got it right here, mahn," Clarence said, removing a narrow silver notebook computer from a black brushed-aluminum case. "I downloaded the CD to a USB key, so all I have to do is—"

Catching the expression on my face, he clamped down on the geek-speak long enough to hit some keys and bring the machine to life.

The first screen was all vital statistics. Peta Bellingham, DOB September 9, 1972, five foot seven, 119 pounds, and a note to "see photos." Whoever had put together the package had her home and cell phones, fax, e-mail, Social Security number, three local bank accounts—checking, savings, and a handful of sub-jumbo CDs, all showing balances as of a couple of months ago—plus one in the Caymans and another in Nauru, with a series of "????" where the balances should have been. Two cars registered, a Porsche Carrera and a Mazda Miata . . . which didn't make sense, for some reason I couldn't quite touch. A co-op on West End, recent purchase; estimated value a million four, against a seven-hundred-grand mortgage. A one-bedroom condo in Battery Park, free and clear. A mixed-bag portfolio, weighted in favor of biotech stocks, managed by . . . Daniel Parks, MBA, CPA, CFP.

So this woman had—what?—skipped out on a big pile of money she owed to this guy Parks? That didn't add up. Walking away from all those assets would have to cost her a cubic ton more than any commission she could owe a money manager.

I shrugged my shoulders at Clarence.

He tapped a key, and another screen popped up, displaying a whole page of thumbnails. "Put the pointer on the one you want to see, double-click, and it will blow right up, like enlarging a photograph."

The first one was a young woman—hard to tell her age without a tighter close-up—standing next to a fireplace, one hand on the mantel. She was fair-skinned, willowy, with long, slightly wavy dark hair. I couldn't see much else.

I scanned the thumbnails with my eyes, looking for a full-face shot. Found it. Clicked it open.

And went back twenty years.

You know her, mahn?" Clarence said, reading my face.

"Let me look at a few more," I told him, moving the cursor and clicking the mouse.

I flicked past the ones with her in outfits—everything from French maid to English riding costume—and the nudes, which were all posed as if she was sitting for an artist's portrait. It was the close-ups that sealed the deal. Those icy topaz eyes hadn't changed at all.

"Yeah, I know her," I said.

Beryl Eunice Preston had just turned thirteen when she disappeared from her parents' mansion in one of Westchester's Old Money enclaves. It was her father who came to see me, back when I had an office carved out of what was once crawlspace at the top of a building in what the real-estate hucksters had just started to call "Tribeca." I lived in that office, in a little apartment concealed behind a fake Persian rug that looked like it covered a solid wall.

Where I lived may have been the top floor, but it was so far underground it made the subway look like a penthouse. The Mole fixed it so I could pirate my electricity from the trust-fund hippies who lived below me. I used their phone, too . . . but only for outgoing. So long as I made my calls before noon, there was no chance any of them would catch wise. They were on the Manhattan Marijuana Diet—no coherency allowed before lunch.

The narrow stairway that led to my place was on the other side of the building from the regular entrance, and I kept my car stashed in a former loading-bay slot that was concealed from the outside by a rusted metal door.

That was back when I worked as an off-the-books investigator. I could go places a licensed PI wouldn't even know existed, and I found all kinds of things during my travels. One thing I stumbled across had been an address for the building owner's son, a professional rat who was doing very nicely for himself in the Witness Protection Program. The little scumbag had a federal license to steal—he cheated everyone he dealt with, then turned them all over to the law, and got to keep the money, like a tip for a job well done. I found more than just his address, too. I had his whole ID trail . . . and a real clear photo of the new face the Law bought for him.

Hard to put a price on something like that, but the landlord agreed that making a few minor structural changes to his building would be a fair trade. He didn't charge me rent, but it wasn't like he was losing money on the deal.

Pansy lived with me then. We would have stayed in that place forever, but the landlord's son eventually got exposed, and the stupid bastard blamed me for it—as if I'd queer a sweet deal like I had just for the pleasure of playing good citizen.

So the landlord had called the cops, said he had just discovered the top of his building was being illegally occupied by some Arabs. I wasn't there when the SWAT guys hit the building, but they tranq'ed Pansy and took her away. They could have killed her, but they were afraid to just blast through the door, so they sent for the Animal Control guys.

Pansy was as unlicensed as I was, and I knew what happened to unclaimed animals. We had to jail-break her out of that "shelter" they were holding her in.

After that, I called that landlord. Told him he'd made a mistake. Two of them, in fact. One stupid, one fatal.

I'm . . . not comfortable, doing this," Beryl's father had said to me the first time we met, his thin, patrician face magnifying that message.

"You didn't find me in the Yellow Pages," I told him. "And you must have already been to guys with much better furnishings."

"I don't want the police. . . ."

"I don't want them, either."

"Yes. I understand you've had some . . ."

"It's your money," I said, referring to the five hundred-dollar bills he had put on my battered excuse for a desk as soon as he walked in. "It buys you an hour, like we agreed on the phone. You want to spend it tap-dancing around me having a record, that's up to you."

He clasped his hands, as if seeking guidance. Pansy made a barely audible sound deep in her throat. I lit a cigarette.

"My daughter's run away," he finally said.

"How do you know?"

"What . . . what do you mean by that?"

"You said 'run away,' not 'disappeared.' What makes you so sure?"

"Beryl is a troubled child," he said, as if the empty phrase explained everything.

I blew smoke at the low ceiling to tell him that it didn't.

"She's done it before. Run away, I mean."

"How'd you find her those other times?"

"She always came back on her own. That's what's different now."

"How long's she been gone?"

"It will be two weeks tomorrow. If school wasn't out for the summer, it would be difficult for us—my wife and me—to explain. As it is . . ."

"You did all the usual stuff, right?"

"I'm not sure what you—"

"Contacted her school friends, checked with any relatives who might be willing to let her hide out at their place, read her diary . . ."

"Yes. Yes, we did all that. Under normal circumstances, we would never——"

"Does she have a pet?"

"You mean," he said, glancing involuntarily at Pansy, "like a dog or a cat?"

"Yeah."

"What difference would that make?"

"A kid that's going to run away permanently, you'd expect them to take their pet with them."

"Beryl never had a pet," he said flatly, his tone making it clear that, if they had deemed one advisable, her devoted parents would have run out and gotten her one. The very best.

"Okay. What about clothes? Did she take enough to last her awhile?"

"It's . . . hard to tell, to be honest. She has so *many* clothes that we couldn't determine if anything was missing."

"What makes you think she's in Manhattan?"

"One of the private detectives we hired was able to trace her movements on the day it . . . happened. We don't know how she got to the train station—it's about twenty minutes from our house, and the local car service hadn't been called—but there's no question that she bought a ticket to Penn Station."

"Penn Station's a hub. She could have connected with another train to anywhere in the country. Did she have enough money for a ticket?"

"I . . . don't know how much money she had. None of the cash we keep in the house was missing, but we've always been very generous with her allowance, and she could have been saving up to . . . do this. But the last detective agency we retained was very thorough, and they are quite certain she didn't catch a train out . . . at least, on the day she left."

"So you hired this 'agency,' and . . . ?"

"Agen*cies*," he corrected. "Two of them rather strongly suggested we call in the police. The third place we consulted told us about you."

"Told you what, exactly?"

"They said you were a man who . . . who could do things they wouldn't be comfortable doing."

"What makes you think your daughter is with a pimp, Mr. Preston?"

"What?!"

"You didn't want to come here," I said, calmly. "Now that you showed up, you don't like *being* here. You want to waste your money lying to me, that's up to you. But there isn't a PI agency in this town that would have recommended me—they don't even know I exist."

He sat there in silence, not denying anything. Back then, NYPD had a Runaway Squad, and I went back a long ways with the best street cop they had, a nectar-voiced Irishman named McGowan. His partner was a thug with so many CCRB complaints against him that the only thing keeping him on the job was that all the complaints came from certified maggots: baby-rapers a specialty. Guy named Morales. So the Commissioner teamed him with McGowan, and, somehow, they meshed into a high-results unit. Word was, if they had partnered Morales with the devil, it would be Satan who played the good cop in tag-team interrogations.

Years later, when McGowan finally retired, Morales went off by himself. He was an old-school street beast, a badge-carrying brute who'd always pick a blackjack over a warrant. He'd been dinosaured to the sidelines because nobody wanted to partner with a bull who knew every china shop in town.

In his eyes, I was always a suspect—which was nothing special for Morales—but I'd saved his life once, and he hated the debt more than he did me. It was Morales who planted the pistol and the bone hand, calling things square in whatever crazy language he used when he talked to himself.

It wasn't just his feral honor that guaranteed Morales would never change the story he'd made up. When 9/11 hit, he was one of the first cops into the World Trade Center. When his body was recovered from the wreckage, the papers called him a hero. Down here, we know they got the answer right, but had figured it all wrong. Morales had charged into the flames with a semi-auto in one hand, a lead-weighted flashlight in the other, and a throw-down piece in his pocket, like always. The old street roller hadn't been on any rescue mission; he'd been looking for the bad guys.

Jeremy Preston wasn't the first parent McGowan had sent my way. He never came right out and *recommended* me, exactly—he just wove my name into one of his long, rambling accounts of the shark tank that was the Port Authority Bus Terminal then, each newly arriving bus discharging chum into the water, the pimps circling.

We're not talking Iceberg Slim here. The Port Authority trollers were the low end of the scale: polyestered punks with CZ rings and 10K gold, not a Cadillac among them. They didn't turn a girl out with smooth talk and sweet promises. For that breed, "game" was coat-hanger whips and cigarette burns. And gang rape.

I lit another cigarette, watched Preston's derma-glazed face through the bluish smoke. Said, "Well?"

"Look, I don't *know* for a fact that my daughter is with some . . . pimp."

"I understand," I said. "Just tell me what you *do* know, okay?"

By the time he was done, we'd agreed on a price. And I went hunting.

M y first rescue had been an accident. One thing I had learned from my last stretch Inside: steal from people who can't go to the Law. And stick to cash. I had lurked for days, watching for what I thought was a good target. When he made his move, I followed him and the teenager he had plucked off a bus from the Midwest. The derelict building he took her to was a couple of notches below slum, the kind of place where the mailboxes were all wrenched open on check day, and the despair stench had penetrated down to the last molecule. There was no lock on the front door. I followed them up a few flights, listening to the pimp saying something about how this was "just for tonight."

The top floor was all X-flats—cleared of occupants because the building was waiting on the wrecking ball. The pimp had put his own padlock on the door. I fig-

ured he had another one on the inside, so I didn't wait.
I came up fast behind them, shouldered them both into
the apartment, and let the pimp see my pistol—a
short-barreled .357 Mag—before he could make a
move.

"What is this, man?"

"I'm collecting for the Red Cross," I said. "They
take money or blood, your choice."

"Oh," he said, visibly relaxing as the message that
this was a stickup penetrated. "Look, man, I'm not
carrying no real coin, you understand?"

"A major mack like you? Come on, let's see the roll.
And move *slow*—this piece could punch a hole in you
the size of a manhole cover."

The girl stood rooted to the spot, her eyes darting
around the vile room, taking in the stained, rotted mat-
tress in one corner, the white hurricane candle in a wide
glass jar, the huge boom box, and the word "Prince"
spray-painted in red on a nicotine-colored wall.

The pimp reached . . . slowly . . . into the side pocket
of his slime-green slacks, came out with a fist-sized wad
of bills. At a nod from me, he gently tossed it over.

I slipped the rubber band with my left thumb. A
Kansas City bankroll: a single hundred on the outside,
with a bunch of singles at the core.

"Where's the rest?" I said, gently.

"Ain't no 'rest,' man. I'm still working on my stake."

The girl walked over to the closet, head down, as if
some instinct told her not to look at my face. She
opened the door, gasped, and jumped back. I glanced in
her direction. Inside the closet was a single straight
chair. Draped over the back were several strands of

rope and two pairs of handcuffs. On the seat of the chair was a thick roll of duct tape, and one of those cheap Rambo knives they sold all over Times Square.

"Get the picture?" I said to her, nodding my head at the other item in the closet—a Polaroid camera.

"I'm sorry. I'm sorry. I'm sorry."

"What?"

But she just kept saying "I'm sorry," over and over again.

So much for my big score.

"Turn around," I told the pimp.

"Look, man, you don't gotta—"

"I'm not going to shoot you," I said. "I'm a professional, just like you. Thought you'd be carrying heavy coin. Now I've got to get out of here. So I'm going to put those handcuffs on you. Your friends will get you loose soon as they show up."

"I ain't got no—"

"Friends? Yeah, that's right, you probably don't. But you're expecting some company, aren't you, *Prince*?"

"Shit, man," he said, resignedly. He turned around, put his hands behind his back.

The Magnum was a heavy little steel ingot in my right hand. I stepped close to him, tipped his floppy hat forward with my left hand. He was still saying "What you—?" as I chopped down at his exposed cervical vertebrae with all my strength. He dropped soundlessly— his head bounced off the wood floor and settled at an angle that looked permanent.

"Come on," I said to the girl.

She followed me without a word.

On the walk back to the Port Authority, I said, "You know what was going to happen to you, right?"

"Yes. I'm sorry. I—"

"Don't say another word," I told her. "Not until you get back where you came from."

"I don't have any—"

"Where did you come from?"

"St. Paul. I thought I—"

"Shut your stupid fucking mouth," I said.

Inside the terminal, I bought her a one-way ticket to St. Paul, handed her two ten-dollar bills, said, "I'm going to watch you get on that bus, understand? If you ever come back here, you're going to get hurt worse than you ever imagined."

"I'm—"

"I told you to shut up. Don't say another word until you're talking to someone you *know*."

I watched the bus pull out. She didn't wave goodbye.

I never got paid for that one.

*L*ike I said, that was back in the day. In Times Square, you could buy anything on the back streets, from a hooker to heroin, and some of the stores sold magazines with photos so foul you wanted to find the people who took them and make them dead. Today, Times Square is another planet: Disney World.

You can't buy porn from Disney. They're all about family. Of course, they've got no problem hiring a convicted child-molester to make horror movies . . . about kids. Tourists think things have changed. People who live here, they know all that ever changes are the addresses.

But even back then, freaks had to know their way around to find a baby pross. A girl pross, anyway; the little-boy hustlers were pretty much out in the open, working the arcades.

You won't find kids hooking in Times Square now. But it's just like what happens anytime the cops crank up the heat on a drug corner—the traffic just moves to another location. You want an underage girl, there's always Queens Plaza after dark, and dozens of other spots.

A while back, two dirtbags grabbed a fifteen-year-old runaway, raped and sodomized her until she had nothing left, then put her out on the street. She wasn't working back alleys, either. Last arrest was on Queens Boulevard, in a nice section of Elmhurst. They took the girl to Florida for the winter, where the local cops grabbed her . . . and probably saved her life.

Extradited to Queens, the dirtbags got the usual sweetheart deal from the tough-talking clown who calls himself the District Attorney. He threw out the rape, sodomy, and kidnapping charges, let them plead to "promoting prostitution." Now they can prance around the yard Upstate, jacketed as pimps, not kiddie-rapists. When they get out, they won't even have to register as sex offenders. With all the heavy cred they'll have accumulated—what's more max than being a player *and* an ex-con?—they'll probably start their own rap label.

I didn't know where Beryl was, but I had a good idea of where she wasn't. A snatched-up runaway wasn't going to end up in a high-end house. Kiddie sex is a specialized business, and—back then, before the Internet—that meant a lot of risk for the money.

I had the girl's picture, half a dozen different shots. And a one-two punch: not only the promise of heavy coin if you turned her up, but the guarantee that, if you saw her and I *didn't* get word, you better be carrying a lot of Blue Cross.

It wasn't me that scared anyone. It was Max at my side. And Wesley in the shadows. On top of that, the city was full of bad guys who thought kiddie pimps were a disgrace to their good name, and I knew a lot of them.

I was a different man then. I was just making the transition from armed robber to scam artist, and if you pushed me anywhere *close* to a corner, violence was still Option One. I was still learning how to sting freaks: promising everything from kiddie porn to mercenary contracts, never delivering. Once I took your money, good luck finding me. And bad luck if you did.

This part never changes: The best way to track someone down is to plant the word, burying the trip wires under sweet promises. Then you put on a lot of pressure, and wait for whoever you're tracking to stumble over one of them. But when you're looking for a kid who's in the wrong hands, too much patience can be fatal.

So I started in Hunts Point, the lowest end of the scale for working whores, then. They were all turning scag-tricks. Their only customers were truckers who had dropped off their cargo at the Meat Market, or serial killers who liked the odds of a desolate piece of flatland where you could find anything on earth except a cop.

Getting any of that sorry collection of broken-veined junkies to talk was easy—for money they'd do anything you could imagine, and plenty that would give you nightmares if you did—but getting them to talk *sense* was near impossible.

So I just cruised, with the girl's photo taped to my dashboard. I came up empty a few days in a row—Hunts Point was a daylight stroll. Nights, I worked lower Lex, which was racehorse territory then. Fine, young, sleek girls, with much stronger, smarter pimps running them.

I didn't waste time down there, just showed Beryl's picture around, told every working girl who came over to my rolled-down car window about the bounty, and moved on.

Next stop, under the West Side Highway. Back then, it ran all the way downtown, and below Canal was Hookerville. Michelle worked that stroll in those days, when she was still pre-op. She got into the front seat of my car, listened to my story, and promised if Beryl showed she'd make sure she didn't leave until I got there.

That should have sounded like big talk, coming from a small, fine-boned little tranny. But Michelle hated humans who fucked kids as only a kid who'd been fucked could, and she'd learned a lot since prison. Now she was snake-quick with the straight razor she never left home without.

It was almost two weeks before I got word that someone had a girl to sell. Not to rent, sell. Supposedly, an eleven-year-old virgin with a hairless pussy who loved to suck cocks and was looking for a permanent home with the right man.

I called the number I had gotten from a guy who ran a private camera club—"The girls will pose any way you tell them, gentlemen. No film allowed." As soon as I heard the voice on the other end, I knew this could be for real: He was a young guy with a sociopath's chilly voice, talking from a payphone.

"I don't know you, man. All I know, you could *be* The Man, you know what I'm saying?"

"So meet me, wherever you say, and I'll prove I'm a legitimate purchaser," I said, softening my voice as I pictured myself as the seal-sleek, middle-aged man who had told me how much money there was in "un-broken" little girls.

The sleek man had come into my life just after I first got out. I thought he'd be the start of my career as a scam-master. Instead, he turned out to be a still-unsolved homicide. It took me a long time to get still enough inside myself so I could listen to one of his tribe without having to hurt him.

"How you gonna do that?"

"Surely you don't expect me to say on the phone?"

"I— Yeah, all right, I see where you coming from. This number's no good for me after today, man. Leave me one where I can call you, when I got it set up."

"I'll give you a number, but I am rarely there in person. My assistant will always know how to reach me, and I'll get back to you within an hour or two, fair enough?"

I raced back to Michelle's stroll, saw her getting out

of a white Oldsmobile. By the time I closed the distance between us, she had taken a slug of the little cognac bottle she always carried with her, rinsed and spit, and was already snake-hipping her way back toward the underpass. I took her over to Mama's, set her up in my booth, and told her there was a hundred in it for her to just sit there until the last payphone in the row against the wall that separated the kitchen from the customers rang. The line was a bridge job, forwarded from one of the dead-end numbers I always kept for emergencies—the Mole had set it up so I could divert it by calling and punching in a series of tones.

The phone rang while Michelle and I were still having our soup; the dealer was getting anxious to unload his merchandise.

"It's him," is all Michelle said when she came back to the table.

"Quick enough?" I said into the receiver.

"You want to see quick, just fuck with me, and watch how quick you get yourself a problem, man."

"What's all this?" I said, hardening my voice. The kiddie-trafficker whose ticket I had canceled had been steel under the sealskin. Stainless steel. If I acted too intimidated, it would be out of character; might spook the bottom-feeder I had on the end of my line. "I thought we were going to do business," I said, "not sell wolf tickets."

"I ain't selling no fucking tickets, man. I'm just saying—"

"Just say where and when, all right? Then you can satisfy yourself I'm straight up, and we can do what we have to do."

"You know," he said, barely suppressing his admiration for his own cleverness, "this jewelry we talking about, it's expensive, man."

"I heard it was twenty."

"Twenty-*five*, man."

"If it's as fine as you say it is—"

"It's finer. You'll see."

"When?"

"Tonight, maybe. If you check out. I'm nobody to fuck with, man. 'Long as you understand."

The pathetic amateur gave me the address of a vacant lot behind a deserted tool-and-die plant in South Jamaica. That wasn't the amateur part. Telling me about a midnight meet at four in the afternoon, that was.

*B*y the time I pulled into the back lot behind the wheel of a gunmetal Mercedes four-door, Max was dialed into the molecular vibrations of the empty building as if he'd been part of the first concrete poured into the foundation. The Mole had dropped him off, driving one of those Con Ed trucks he seems to be able to "find" whenever he needs one. Probably the same place he had found the Mercedes.

I got out, dressed in a dark-gray suit, a white silk handkerchief in the breast pocket matching the white shirt I wore without a tie. I spotted the target, but acted as if I hadn't. He was lounging in the shadows of the back wall, cleverly dressed all in black. I lit a cigarette and paced in tight little circles, glancing at my watch: 11:51.

He let me wait a few minutes. Not because he was a

pro, but because making people do what he wanted made him feel more like himself.

He rolled up on me out of the darkness, like some movie ninja. I jumped back, fake-startled.

"You got something to show me?" he said, voice swollen with confidence now that he was sure he was dealing with exactly what he expected—a nervous man with a heavy fetish and a heavier wallet.

"Sure," I said, keeping my voice soft.

"I got to search you first," he said. "You know the routine."

"What do you—?"

"Oh, fuck it, man! Just turn around, assume the position. I got a piece, see?" he said, holding up some little pearl-handled popcorn-pimp special. "You do anything stupid, and—*pow!*—that's all they is for you. Way out here, nobody find your body for a month."

"Listen," I said, standing with my arms extended away from my sides, "just take it easy, okay?"

His pat-down was just like him—rough and stupid.

"All right, man. You can turn around."

"Can I see her now?" I said, a little too eagerly.

"You know what I got to see first, right?"

"Sure, sure. I brought it."

"You brought twenty-five K *with* you?"

"Yes. I didn't want to . . . drag this out. You're not going to rob me, are you?"

"I fucking *should,* dumb as you are, man. Show it to me."

"It's in the trunk. I put it in a briefcase, so you could—"

"Well, open it, motherfucker."

"Sure. Just don't—"

I unlocked the trunk. As it slid up, I stepped aside, and the nose of the Prof's double-barreled sawed-off went jack-in-the-box on the pimp.

"Surprise!" the little man said.

"Hey, man. I—"

Max had him by then. The little pistol dropped from the pimp's nerve-dead hand.

The Prof climbed out of the trunk, the sawed-off never wavering from the pimp's midsection.

"I think we should talk now," I said.

*I*nside the building, I used my pencil flash to illuminate a clear spot. Max crooked his left forearm around the pimp's neck, grabbed his own right biceps, and curled his right hand over the top of the pimp's head.

"All he has to do is squeeze now," I said. "You understand?"

"Look, man—"

"Sssh," I said, gently. "There's nothing for you to be worried about. I kept my word, didn't I?"

"I—"

"Ssssh," I said again. "You know I'm not a cop now, right?"

"Yeah, man. I was—"

"But you, you *do* have the girl, right?"

"Nah, man. I was just trying to run a game, you know?"

"If that's true, you're a corpse," I said, not raising my voice. I brought my thumb and forefinger together.

Max tightened the noose. The pimp's eyelids fluttered. I moved my fingertips apart. The pimp gasped a few times.

"Want to try again?" I asked him.

"It ain't what you think, man. I swear! It was all *her* idea."

"*This* 'her'?" I said, showing him the photo with my flashlight.

"Yeah! She came up to *me,* man. This whole thing—"

"That's enough," I told him. "We don't care how it happened. Some people put up a hundred grand for her. So we want her, and we want her right now. It's worth the twenty-five we promised, you turn her up, okay?"

"She ain't here," he said.

"We know that," I said, barely above a whisper. "That's not the question you were asked." I held up my thumb and forefinger again, letting him see the gesture.

"No, no, man! Listen, I prove it to you, okay? She's at my woman's house. Few minutes from here. But she ain't tied up or nothing, she just sitting there, watching TV. How's that?"

"That's real good," I said, soothingly. "Now let's go pick up the package."

*T*his place where your woman has the merchandise, is it an apartment or . . . ?" I asked him. I was behind the wheel, the pimp seated next to me, Max behind him, the choke hold back in place.

"It's a private house, man," he said, a wire-thin

twist of pride in his voice. "You know where Union Hall Street is? You just—"

"I know where it is," I told him, keying the ignition.

Hey, man, this ain't the way to—"

"Just relax. Be *very* calm. You know the payphone down that way?" I said, pointing with my whole hand, so the sparkler on my finger would calm him. "A few blocks past the boulevard?"

"That one? Man, that one hasn't worked for years. It's all ripped out and—"

"It works now," I promised him. "I'm going to pull up right next to it. We're going to get out, all of us. What you're going to do, you're going to call your woman, understand? You're going to tell her everything went down just like you planned. What you need her to do is bring the girl outside. Nice warm night, let them sit on the front stoop, so you can see them when we pull up. Soon as we're sure it's the right girl, we hand you this," I said, making a gesture with my right hand. The Prof handed over a hard-sided attaché case. "Look for yourself," I told the piece of toxic waste sitting next to me.

He unsnapped the case on his lap. "Damn!" he whistled. "You for *real,* man."

"This is just business, like I told you all along. Maybe a little different than you thought, but it's the same payoff, right?"

"Right!" he said. "Look, man, you don't need this noose around my neck, okay? I'm a businessman, just like you."

"Maybe you're right," I said, making a sign. Max released his hold. "We'll trust you that much. But hand the money back over; we're not going to have you jump out and run."

"I wouldn't—" he started to say, then interrupted himself to hand over the attaché case. I casually tossed it into the back seat, where the Prof caught it deftly.

"You ever get more like her?" I asked him.

"Me?" he said, slyly, a man who had just figured things out for himself. There was no reward for the girl he was holding. We weren't working for her father. That was all cover; we wanted the girl as merchandise, and we expected to get a lot more than twenty-five grand when we retailed her. "Sure! A man in my line of work, I gets all kind of—"

"Then maybe we can do business again, if your stuff is together enough."

"What you mean, together? Didn't I—?"

"This place where you're holding the girl, you said it was a private house? You mean one of those up-and-downs, or are you the only one there?"

"Just me. And my woman, like I said. It's perfect, man. Nice and quiet."

"Your woman, she got any kids?"

"Yeah, man. She got a couple, but they ain't around; the Welfare took 'em away."

"So you and her, you're the only ones who live there?"

"Yeah, man. Why you asking all this?"

"Because we have . . . packages we sometimes like to have watched for a few days at a time. Before we can move them, you understand?"

"Yeah," he grinned. I was disappointed he didn't have any gold teeth.

"Okay," I said, pulling up to the phone. "You call her. Tell her what you'll be driving up in. She brings the girl to the curb. You get out of the front seat; the girl gets in, we drive away with her, you *walk* away with the twenty-five, and that's all there is. Got it?"

"How I know you won't—?"

"We already have the address," I said, patiently. "Like you said, that building you brought us to, nobody would find a body there for a month. I think we can do business again. We're not risking a murder rap for a lousy twenty-five G's."

I attached the telephone receiver the Mole had given me with a set of alligator clips. The pimp dialed a number, holding the phone so I could hear both ends of the conversation.

Hey, man," he said, on the way over. "Soon as you know it's the girl you want, I just get on out, right?"

"Right."

"So how about I hold the money? I mean, make it nice and smooth, so you don't have to hang around."

I thought it over for a couple of seconds, then said, "Give it back to him," to the Prof.

Two figures were standing by the front door to the house, turned into silhouettes by a lamp glowing inside the front window. When the taller one saw us, they both walked down toward the street. I didn't see any sign of force or restraint.

The pimp got out, the attaché case in one hand.

"Get in!" he ordered the girl. "The man wants to look at you."

She climbed in docilely, a tentative smile on her face.

"Hello, Beryl," I said.

Her mouth opened in a silent "O" of surprise. The pimp slammed the door behind her, and we took off. The pimp had about thirty seconds of triumph left . . . if it took him that long to open the attaché case, an identical twin of the money bag we'd switched it for.

*T*he Con Ed truck was waiting where the Mole said it would be. I pulled over, and the back seat emptied out. In a few minutes, the Prof would dial the number Preston had left with me. When he heard a voice, he'd press the button on the little cassette player, and Preston would hear me say: "I've got her. We're on the way. Sit tight and don't make any calls."

I slipped the soft-riding sedan through the streets, heading for the Van Wyck. At that hour, the Whitestone Bridge was my best bet.

"My father sent you," the girl said to me. It wasn't a question.

"That's right, Beryl," I told her. "You'll be home in an hour or so."

She didn't say another word all the way.

s soon as the Merc's headlights cut across his driveway, Preston bolted out the front door. He was tearing at the passenger-side door handle before I came to a full stop.

"Beryl!" he half-sobbed, clutching at her like she was about to go over a cliff.

The girl turned, gave me a look I couldn't interpret, then surrendered to her father's embrace.

The two of them walked back toward the house, his arm wrapped protectively around her shoulders. I followed, keeping my distance.

A woman's backlit shape filled the doorway. Preston passed the girl to her like a baton in a relay race. The girl was pulled into the woman's shadow. By the time I crossed the threshold, the shadow had vaporized.

"Come on in," Preston said, gesturing with his hand to show me where he meant.

It was either a den or a library—hard to tell, because the walls were mostly bookshelves. I'm no appraiser, but the desk looked like a piece of one-off cherrywood, and the dark-burgundy leather chair hadn't come out of a catalogue, either. Blond parquet flooring, with some kind of Navajo blanket used as a throw rug.

"Sit, sit," he said, pointing to a tufted armchair that matched the other furniture. For what it must have cost, it should have been more comfortable. The plate-sized brass ashtray on a wrought-iron stand next to the chair encouraged me to light a smoke.

Preston closed the door, then walked over and

seated himself behind his special desk. He fiddled with a pipe—something uncharitable in me guessed it was cherrywood—until he got it going. "Tell me all about it," he finally said.

"That wasn't our deal," I told him.

"Well . . . I guess it wasn't. But surely you understand that I'm—"

"You wanted your daughter back. The reason you came to me was because you thought I might be able to do that. You never asked me how I was going to do it. I figured that was no accident—that was you being smart, protecting yourself."

"You mean, there's things I wouldn't want to know?"

"I'm not saying that. I'm just saying we had a deal, right? Cash on delivery. And here I am, delivering."

"I'm not disputing that. I just thought . . . I guess I thought you, what you do, it isn't just about money."

"I don't know where you got that idea," I said.

"From the—"

"I wasn't asking."

"Oh. I . . ."

His voice spooled out into silence until he finally accepted that I wasn't going to say anything more. "Here's your money," he said, putting a neat stack of bills on the top of his desk. Probably dug it out of a safe somewhere in the house as soon as he heard my tape-recorded voice on his phone. I wondered how much he usually kept in there.

I couldn't tell if making me step over to his fancy desk to get the money was a little bit of nastiness because I wouldn't give him the gory details, or because he was back to being himself already—a boss, paying off a worker.

As I pocketed the cash, he answered the question. "Berry will tell me all about it," he said, self-assured.

I found a lot of kids back then. Sometimes it was the parents who paid me. Sometimes it was the people who I took them back from. Sometimes both. Every so often, neither.

I hadn't told Preston the truth. Not just because he was a citizen, and lying to citizens was one of the first things my father—the State—had taught me, but because of something Wesley told me once. "You can't ever give them any reason but money," the iceman whispered one night. "They think there's something else in it for you, they might want to do you down on the price."

"I set the price in front," I replied, a little hurt that Wesley would think I'd be such an amateur.

"But you don't get it *paid* in front," he said. "And this thing you got about kids, it's a marker. A way for people to find you."

"People know where my—"

"Not know your address," the iceman said. "Know *you.* They know that, your address don't matter—they can get you to come wherever they need you to be."

That was a long conversation for Wesley. He had the same one with me, over and over again, right up to the time he checked out of the hotel he had hated from the moment the State had booked his room.

I might have kept going like I was: working the

edges of the fringes, a poacher on rich men's estates, a liar, con artist, thief . . . and, sometimes, a man who found kids and brought them home. But after I shot a pimp, McGowan stopped recommending me. And the people who started coming to me for tracking jobs after that weren't looking for rescue work.

I might have kept going anyway—my lifestyle didn't require a lot of income—but things kept . . . happening.

I thought I was done with things like that.

W hy did you give me this?" I asked Mama. I held up my cup of soup as if I was toasting an audience, so there wouldn't be any doubt about what I was saying.

"You don't like soup?" she said, ominously.

"I don't like *this* soup. I mean, it's not terrible or anything, but it's not yours."

"Ah!" she said, expressionlessly. "No time last night. Cook make soup himself."

Every year or so, Mama tests to see if I recognize the one thing in that restaurant she makes herself. It would never occur to her to question that I love her, but she occasionally needs some reassurance that I love her soup.

I bowed slightly, brought my fingertips together. She removed the steaming tureen and my Barnard cup without another word.

"Prawns today," she said. "Cook fix them good, okay?"

"I'm not hungry, Mama."

"Max coming?"

"Should have been here already."

"Okay," she said, getting up and walking over to her post by the front register just as Max loomed up behind me.

As soon as he sat down, I made a gesture of ladling out a cup of soup, taking a sip. Then I made a face to indicate the soup was lousy today. Max nodded his thanks—Mama wasn't going to waste a bogus pot of hot-and-sour without testing it on more than one of us.

I was in the middle of regaling Max with Little Eric's monumental triumph over the Forces of Evil— that's the Morning Line, for all you hayseeds—when the Prof strolled in with Clarence at his side. He slid in next to me, spoke out of the side of his mouth in a barely audible prison-yard whisper: "What's with the old woman, Schoolboy?"

"What do you mean?" I said, charitably not mentioning that the Prof himself was older than corruption. Or that I knew why he was keeping his voice down.

"She tells me it's cold out, maybe I want some soup. It's the off-brand stuff today, am I right?"

"On the money."

"Damn, son. You'd think she'd stop trying to gaff us with that tired old trick after all these years."

"You want her to think up a new one?"

The little man turned and gave me a look.

"Where is my little sister?" Clarence asked, looking at his watch.

"Michelle's not in on this," I said. "Not this *part,* I mean."

"I thought there was green on the scene," the Prof

riffed. "Something my boy found in that computer thing."

"There *was* money," I said. "All over that CD Clarence looked at, sure. But—"

"Right!" the Prof interrupted. "So—we did the scan, now we need a plan. And if we're going to go in soft, we need our girl to walk point, don't we?"

"The money on that CD, it belongs to the girl the guy who hired me was looking for."

Max pointed his finger, ratcheted his thumb in the universal gesture of a hammer dropping.

"Yeah," I said. "The guy who got smoked. And, it turns out, he was some kind of money man. Other people's money."

"So he wasn't looking for the girl, he was looking for her stash?"

"I . . . I don't think so, Prof. But we can't start looking for either one without some answers."

"But you know the girl, mahn," Clarence put in. "That is what you said."

"I know who she is. But the last time I saw her, she was just a kid. You saw her, too, Prof. You, too, Max," I said, miming the last sentence.

The waiter brought a tureen of the booby-trap soup. Mama left her register just in time to see Max spit out a mouthful. He lurched to his feet, bowed an apology to the waiter.

"What's up with this stuff?" the Prof said, pointing to the tureen. "You serving us tourist food now?" He wasn't faking the annoyed look on his handsome face— if there's one thing the Prof hates, it's being upstaged.

"Oh, sorry," Mama said. "Big mistake, okay?"

"This isn't Mama's soup," I explained.

Max pointed an accusing finger at me, for not warning him.

Mama's lips twisted—whether with pleasure at her family's immediate recognition of the impostor, or in admiration of Max's drama-queen performance, I couldn't tell.

As soon as she left, I told Clarence about the time we had rescued Beryl Preston, watching the recognition flash in Max's face, hearing the Prof say, "Oh yeah. *That* one," next to me.

"Her name is different now," the West Indian said. "Why would that be?"

"I don't know," I said. "She *came* from money, that much we know. If only her last name was different, maybe she got married. But . . ."

"What's the front name she's using now?" the Prof asked.

"Peta."

"And it was, what, Sapphire or something?"

"Beryl."

"Middle name, maybe?"

"Nope. The girl we pulled away from that pimp, her middle name was Eunice. This one—on the CD— didn't have a middle name at all."

"Maybe the guy who wanted you to find her, he didn't know it."

"No, Father," Clarence told the Prof. "There was a wealth of information there. Very, very detailed. If the woman had a middle name, it would have been there, I am sure."

"And the guy who hired me, I don't think it was

money he was after," I added, more sure of myself than when the Prof had first asked, even though I couldn't say why.

Max responded to my rubbing my first two fingers and thumb together and giving a negative shake of my head with a "What then?" gesture.

"I don't know," I told them all. "He *did* have a whole lot of financial information on that CD, but if he was her money manager, he'd have known all that, anyway. And those photographs . . . that's personal, not professional. It's like the only reason he had all the financials listed was just to help whoever was going to look for her."

"You think she played the player?" the Prof said.

"That would fit. He wouldn't be the first manager to get himself managed. But let's say she did—why would she just disappear after that? If the stuff on the CD is true, she had loads of assets in her own name. Legit, aboveground stuff. She gets in the wind, she can't get her hands on any of that. Who gets to steal so much that they can afford to walk away from millions?"

"This guy, the one who hired you, *he* had money, right?"

"Looked like it, sure. But I only saw him that one time; it could have all been front."

Max clasped his hands in front of him, then slowly pulled them apart. His fingers made a plucking gesture, one hand taking from the other. The looted hand balled into a fist as the thieving hand fled.

"They were a partnership, maybe working some kind of paper scheme, and she ran off with all the cash?

Could be," I acknowledged. "That'd make him spend time and money looking for her, sure."

"And if she really had all that coin, she could buy herself major muscle," the Prof said.

"But now that the man who was looking for her is . . . out of the picture, would she not come back to her own home?" Clarence asked.

"Maybe he wasn't the only one looking," the Prof said, lighting a cigarette.

"Right," I agreed. "We don't know anything about the shooters. If they were working for her, that's one thing. She's got that kind of protection in place, making too much noise looking for her is a good way to get ourselves dead. But if they were looking for her themselves . . ."

"Yeah," the Prof rode with me. "Same thing. But we can't go nosing around the dead guy's life. The cops would get on that like a priest on an altar boy."

"I'm not worried about that end of it," I said. "Not now, anyway. If she stole from the dead guy, she's got the money. Finding her, that's what we have to do. But I'm not even going to start looking until we know one thing: How did the shooters know where the guy who hired me was going to be that night? That's the only way to know if I'm in the crosshairs, too."

Nobody said anything for a few minutes.

Finally, Max got up. He returned with a handful of objects he had pulled off other tables. Identifying each one with gestures, he constructed a triangle on the tablecloth: the guy who hired me, the girl, and the shooters. Then he built another: the guy who hired me, the shooters, and me. One more: the guy who hired me, the shooters . . . and Charlie Jones. Using chopsticks, he built a matrix. When he was done, a wooden arrow pointed right at the ferret.

"Charlie tipped off the shooters?" the Prof said, touching Max's chart.

Max shrugged his shoulders.

"Even if he did, he would not have to bring Burke's name into it, would he?" Clarence said.

Now it was the Prof's turn to shrug. "Who we gonna ask?" he said. "We don't know who the shooters are. And *nobody* knows where Charlie cribs."

"If he's kept the same place he had years ago, *we* might know," I said.

"How?" the Prof asked. But his voice was already tightening against what he knew was coming.

"The book," I told them, gesturing to Max at the same time.

*T*he book was Wesley's once. Mine now. It had shown up in one of my drop boxes after Wesley had canceled his own ticket. What the media called his "suicide note" was a confession to a whole string of paid-for homicides. A couple of those had been mine. Wesley knew how things worked: If he left the cops enough to clear those cases, it was the same as clearing me.

But Wesley hadn't told them everything. *That* was in the book he had mailed to me. The killing machine had recorded it all, the details of every hit: who got done, who paid for it, and how much. That was my legacy, a Get Out of Jail Free card, but I could only play it once. I hoarded it tight, my most valuable possession.

I knew Charlie Jones had to be in that book. He'd never put a penny in Wesley's hand, but he was a bridge to plenty who had. And the iceman always covered his back trail.

"Mama," I said, when she came over to where we were sitting, "could I have the book?"

I didn't have to say anything more. Her eyes narrowed, but her expression didn't change. Mama was our family's bank, and Wesley's book was in what passed for a safe-deposit box. Only, in Mama's house, you never say the iceman's name out loud.

"Now you want it?"

"Please."

"Order food. I get it, okay?"

Meaning: The book was buried somewhere in the catacombs under the building that housed the restaurant, and it would take a while for her to dig it out.

"Bring me some duck for luck," the Prof said to one of the white-coated hard men who passed for waiters in Mama's joint.

*I*t was almost an hour before Mama came back. She put a thick notebook about the size of my hand on the tablecloth and walked away, as if afraid it was going to explode. The book was bound in oxblood leather, with a gold ribbon page-marker, its fine linen pages almost three-quarters full of Wesley's tiny, machinelike printing. I always wondered where he had found such a book, and what he would have done when he ran out of pages.

I'd been through the book plenty of times before, but every time I opened it, there always seemed to be more than I remembered, as if my ghost brother was still making entries from wherever he was. There was no real organization or index, but it moved in rough chronological order. From looking at the first date, I could tell Wesley hadn't started his book when he'd started killing. That would have been a long time earlier, back when we were kids.

I felt the book throb in my hands. Not like a beating heart; like an oncoming train. I opened it, and started reading.

I took a drag off the cigarette I hadn't remembered lighting, put it back in the ashtray that hadn't been on the table when I'd started reading. "I've got him," I said.

The Prof and Clarence came back to where I was sitting. I looked up and there was Max, right across from me; he had never left.

"Charlie hired Wesley four times," I said. "Not directly, but he made the matches."

"Everything go okay?" the Prof asked. He wasn't asking if the hits had gone down, that was never a question; he was asking if Wesley had been paid. The one time we knew he hadn't been, the iceman had turned the whole city into a killing ground.

"Yeah," I said, still thinking about one of the jobs I'd run across in the book. Looked like Charlie Jones had known some politicians.

"Must have followed him home," the Prof said. "No way my man pays anyone for info."

"It doesn't say. But he's got an address here, all right."

"Where was the little weasel holing up back then?" the Prof asked, frankly curious.

"Over in Queens. Briarwood."

"Briarwood?" the Prof jeered. "In that neighborhood, Charlie'd stick out like the truth in Jesse Jackson's mouth."

"He might," I said, my finger on the page where I'd found him. "But Benny Siegel wouldn't."

*T*hat boy is big-time slick," the Prof said, his preacher's voice garnished with admiration. "You got to give it to him. Folks been trying to pass ever since there *was* folks, but that's a one-way street—people trying to move up, not down. Charlie got to be the first time I ever heard of anyone trying to pass for Jewish."

"You know how Wesley worked it," I said, looking over my shoulder to make sure Mama wasn't close by. "You wanted work done, you never got to see him face-to-face. You hired a voice on the phone, sent the money to wherever he told you. But it was a different number and address for every job. So Charlie, he had to know a way to find Wesley. Or to leave word for him, anyway."

"Do you think they ever met?" Clarence asked. He

was the only one of us who hadn't known Wesley, but he'd been hearing the legend since his early days working for a Jake gunrunner in Brooklyn. He always wanted to know more, but he had to balance his curiosity against the Prof's disapproval.

"You mean, like, were they pals?" the little man said, bitterly. "Forget that. Wesley, he was about as friendly as a cobra with a grudge."

"But if he and Burke—"

"We came up together," I said, hoping to cut off the young man's questions before we had a problem.

"Still. If he was as—"

"Look, son," the Prof said, gruffly. "Wesley was the mystery train. You never knew where he was going, but you always knew where he'd been—dead men be all over the tracks. Nobody knows why he picked Burke out when they were little kids. Ain't no point talking about it. Nobody knows. And nobody ever gonna know, okay?"

"Your father's right," I told Clarence, gently guiding him away from the edge. "When it comes to Wesley, you ask a question, the answer's always the same: Nobody knows. But I can tell you this for sure: He wasn't friends with Charlie Jones. He wasn't partners with him. That wasn't Wesley. He was always one up. If Charlie knew where to leave a message for Wesley, then Wesley had to know where Charlie lived; it's as simple as that. Wesley wasn't a gambler. The only way he'd play is with a marked deck."

"He has been gone a long time, mahn."

"You mean, the address might be no good now?

Sure, that's true. But if Charlie went to all the trickery and expense involved in a complete ID, he could still be there. Remember, we know one thing—he never crossed Wesley."

"How could we know that, then?"

Nobody answered. It only took the young man a few seconds to catch up.

F or some places, a cab is the perfect surveillance vehicle. You can circle the same block a dozen times, go and come back, even park close by and eat a sandwich, and nobody pays attention. A leaf on a tree, a bird in the forest.

But that wouldn't work in Briarwood, a community of upper-middle-class houses and even higher aspirations. The only Yellow Cabs you see in that neighborhood are making airport drop-offs, the cabbies seething at the "shortie" trip. For the drivers, waiting on an airport line is a dice-roll. A Manhattan run is a soft six. A carful of Japanese tourists who don't have a firm grasp of the exchange rate is a natural. Briarwood, that's snake eyes.

Walk-bys would be even riskier. In that neighborhood, people were peeking out from behind their curtains decades before anyone ever heard of Neighborhood Watch. The population is aging and house-proud, the kind of folks who keep 911 on speed dial. Nobody hangs out on the corners at night. And the community has enough political clout to ensure for-real police patrols, too.

But this is still New York, where info is just another peach to pick. If you can't reach the branches, you have to know how to shake the trees.

Some do it with research, some do it with subpoenas. People like me do it with cash.

There's two kinds of bribes—the ones where you get asked, and the ones where you offer. A building inspector looking for *mordida* knows he has to make the first move—too many DOI stings going on today for an experienced slumlord to take the chance. But the pitch is always so subtle you have to be listening close to catch it.

That kind of bribe, it's just the cost of doing business, an everyday thing. But if you want someone to go where they're not supposed to, it's a lot trickier to put a deal together. The phone company's wise to employees selling unlisted numbers; the DMV knows what the home address of a celebrity is worth; and there's always a bull market for Social Security numbers. So there's all kinds of safeguards in place: You access the computers from inside the company, you're going to leave a trail. You say the wrong thing on the phone, someone could be listening. Somebody's always watching, and they're not anyone's brother.

Computers make it a lot easier to check on what your employees are doing. But putting all the information in one place is a party where you have to screen the guest list. Not all hackers spend their time trying to write the ultimate virus or crack into a secure site. Some of them are people like me. Working criminals.

The best tools to unlock an account are a Social Security number and a date of birth. We didn't have either one for Charlie Jones, but we had the name he had been living under and the address where he lived at the time. If that info was dead, so were our chances.

I know a few cyber-slingers, but I don't trust any of them enough to let them work a name when its owner might wind up deceased. So I had to go to people who don't trust me.

*P*epper is a sunburst girl. She's got more bounce than a Texas high-school cheerleader, and a smile that could make Jack Kevorkian volunteer to teach CPR. She probably likes everybody on this planet, except . . .

"It's me," I told her, on the phone.

"Okay," she answered, warm as a robbed grave.

"I want to buy a package."

"She's not going to meet you."

Pepper was talking about Wolfe, the warrior woman who headed up their operation. Back when she was still a prosecutor, she had let me hold her hand for a minute. But then the road we were walking divided, and I took the wrong fork. I did it knowing she'd never follow, hoping she'd wait for me to come back. When I did, she was still in the same spot. But she wasn't waiting for me. She was doing what she always did—standing her ground.

Not many men get a second chance with a woman like Wolfe. I was probably the only man alive who could have blown them both.

"This isn't about her," I said. "It's not about me, either. I need a package, that's all."

"Say where and when."

"The cafeteria? Tonight? Anytime after eight?"

"Bring it all with you," she said, and disconnected.

She came in the front door, beamed a "Hi!" to Mama, and breezed over to my booth. Mick was a couple of paces behind her, like he always is. He clasped his hands, bowed to Mama, who returned the gesture of respect.

Mick's a big man, broad-shouldered, with a natural athlete's build. His face would be matinee-idol material if it ever had an expression. Pepper once told the Prof that Mick had gone to one of those colleges where the football coach makes more than the whole science department, but he got disgusted with it and left. Made me curious enough to do a little research. Apparently, fracturing the coach's jaw was enough to get your scholarship canceled.

Mick glided behind Pepper so he was standing beside her as Max and I got to our feet. Mick bowed to Max as he had to Mama, caught the return, then gave me mine. Pepper was still smiling . . . at Max. We all sat down.

"Oh, could I have some of that special dish we had last time, please?" Pepper said, as Mama came to our table.

"Sure, okay," Mama said, and disappeared into the back.

"I *love* fortune cookies," Pepper said, turning around

agilely and swiping a small metal bowl from the table behind her.

"You don't want those," I told her.

"Why not?"

"They're for tourists, Pepper."

"So?"

"So Mama doesn't like tourists."

"Oh, stop!"

I exchanged a look with Mick. He made a "What do you want *me* to do?" gesture with his eyebrows that might have been one of Max's.

Pepper delicately cracked one of the cookies open. "Oh, ugh!" she said, tossing the tiny scrap of paper onto the table.

Max picked it up, twisted his lips, and handed it to me. *Life is the road to death. All you choose is your speed.*

"Told you," I said.

"Are they all like that?" Pepper asked, curious despite herself.

"Pretty much," I assured her. One of Mama's proudest boasts was that no tourist visited twice.

"But the food here is *wonderful*!"

"That's not customer food," I said. "It's just for . . . people Mama knows."

"Then why does she even—?" Pepper started to say, before a look from Mick cut her off.

A waiter came out with a huge, shallow bowl of . . . whatever it was that Pepper had eaten the last time she'd been there, I guessed.

We ate in silence. Mick was a kung-fu man, and it looked like he was questioning Max about some sort of praying-mantis technique. Or maybe he was just practicing his nonverbal conversation skills. Pepper watched, fascinated. One of the prettiest things about her is how interested she always is in things. I wish she liked me.

The waiter took away our dishes. Max lit a cigarette. Pepper frowned. I reached over and took one for myself. Mick shook his head sadly at my immaturity.

"I've got a name," I said to Pepper. "Two names, really. We don't know if either one's legit. One address, but it's real old."

"What else?"

"White male. Between five eight and five ten, slim build. Brown eyes, brown hair. Looks to be somewhere in his fifties."

"You think he's on paper somewhere?"

"No. Far as I know, he's never taken a fall."

"And you want what exactly?"

"I want to know where he lives. If he's still at the same place, that would be good enough. If not . . ."

"You've seen him personally, or are you just working off that vague description?"

"I know him."

"So you want a picture? Of him at the address?"

"Yeah. That'd do it."

"All right," she said, all business. "You know we can't give you a price until we know how long it's going to—"

"I know," I said, grinding out my cigarette. "Be careful, Pepper. This guy's no citizen."

"How could I have guessed?" she said, smiling. At Max.

Want to go someplace with me?" I asked Loyal, later that night.

"Someplace nice?"

"Afterwards."

"Do I get to dress up?"

"You're always dressed up."

"Yeah?" she said, deep in her throat.

This isn't so much fun," she said later, doing it in baby talk to take the sting out.

"I thought you loved acting."

"Well, I *do*. But this isn't . . . I mean, all we're doing is driving around."

"*Why* are we driving around?"

"We're tired of paying a fortune to rent in Manhattan, and co-op prices are just ridiculous. We heard this neighborhood has real *value* in it," she said, in the bored tone a schoolgirl uses to tell you, yes, she *did* do her homework.

"That's good!"

"It's only good if someone *asks* us," she said, pouting. "And who's going to ask us *anything* if we just keep driving around?"

"I was thinking a cop."

"A cop? You mean . . . Oh my *God*! Are we, what do you call it, *casing* someplace to rob? Is that what you really—?"

"I don't do things like that," I said, my tone indicating that a criminal of my stature didn't do manual labor. "We're just . . . scouting, okay? You know what eminent domain is, little girl?"

"Yes!" she said, suddenly interested. "I once had a . . . friend who was a lawyer. A real-estate lawyer, in fact. He told me all about how it works."

"Good. See all these houses?" I said, turning my head from side to side to indicate I was talking about the whole area. "They've gone up in price like a rocket, the past couple of years. Nobody knows where the top floor is. Everyone here thinks they're sitting on a gold mine, okay?"

"Okay. . . ." she said, interested despite her pose.

"What if the rumor got started that the city was going to cut a big swath right through this area, to sell to some private developer? The Supreme Court says they can do that now."

"The government never pays fair market value," she said, firmly.

"Right. And . . . ?"

"And people would want to sell before the word got out so that . . . Oh!"

"Yeah."

"That's the kind of thing you do?"

"One of them."

"I hate these seat belts," she said, crossing her legs and taking a deep breath. "They make me feel all . . . restrained, you know?"

I eyeballed the house," I said. "Nice size, solid, set close to the sidewalk."

"Look like anyone was home?" the Prof asked.

"Couple of lights on, behind curtains. And one out front, but that was more for decoration."

"My man got burglar bars?"

"In that neighborhood? They'd probably run him out of town for messing up the decor."

"Might be going electronic."

"Sure."

"Could you see the yard?"

"In front, there isn't much of anything at all. I got some old City Planning maps of the neighborhood. Near as I could tell, if those houses have back yards, they're postage stamps."

"He could still have a hound on the grounds."

"Yeah."

"I've been thieving since way before you was born, Schoolboy. Any crib can be cracked. But that one's in a bad neighborhood for B-and-E. If Charlie's holed up there, it's a mortal lock that he's got the place wired."

"I'm not thinking about going in, Prof."

"Then what's with all the—?"

"I'm not thinking about going in," I repeated. "But I *have* been thinking. If Charlie's there, he's been there for a long time. He might have a wife, kids, who knows? But, whatever he's got set up, he's got a big investment in it."

"How does that help us, mahn?" Clarence said.

"Motherfucker's not bringing his work home," the Prof announced, holding a clenched fist out to me. I tapped his fist with mine, acknowledging that he'd nailed it.

"I do not understand," Clarence said, without a trace of impatience.

"Charlie's been at this forever," I told him. "If he's still at the same place, it means he went to a lot of trouble to keep one life separate from the other. Charlie never goes hands-on, remember. He probably leaves his house to go to work, just like everyone else in his neighborhood. Which means . . . ?"

"He has an office, somewhere else."

"Good!" the Prof said to his son.

"And if *that's* true, what?"

"Then his home would be sacred to him, Burke."

"Yeah," I said, slowly. "This is starting to look less like a muscle job every minute."

"If your man's info is still good," the Prof cautioned.

*T*he next morning, the sun came out of its corner swinging. It didn't have a KO punch in its arsenal—not this time of year, not in New York—but it came on hard enough to drive the Hawk back against the ropes. My breakfast was a hot mug of some stuff that Mama gives me to microwave. It's almost as thick as stew, and smells like medicine, but it unblocks your nasal passages like someone went in there with a roto-tiller.

I checked the paper to see if there was anything new on the dead man, and came up empty. Some half-wit—or, maybe, bought-and-paid-for—columnist had a piece about how the Bush administration was finally winning the war on drugs. Seems all that money poured into Colombia was paying off. Or maybe God really is on his side.

The writer had an orgasm over how the number of acres under coca cultivation was down 75 percent. That's like dipping a yardstick into the Atlantic and reporting back that it's three feet deep.

There's only one way to measure how "the war" on any contraband is going—street price. When the Taliban was running Afghanistan, they banned poppy farming. No more opium, on pain of death. Being such devout Muslims, they were strictly against the evils of heroin. Sure. Poppy production dropped like a safe off a building. Only thing was, the street price of H didn't trampoline in response like you'd expect—it stayed as steady as a sociopath's polygraph needles.

You didn't need a degree in higher mathematics to figure out what was going on. The Taliban banned poppy farming because they already had huge stocks on hand. Same way OPEC gets together and reduces oil production—to keep the barrel price high . . . and stable.

Colombia doesn't have one gang ruling the country, so there's no price-fixing. Both the pseudo-liberation guerrillas and the right-wing death squads run on money, so they were all madly pumping product, widening the pipeline. How could I know that? Because the street price for coke—grams to kilos—was even lower than it had been years ago.

The only war on drugs the sanctimonious swine are winning is the one to keep old folks on fixed incomes from filling their scrips in Canada or Mexico. And Ray Charles could see who was making out on that deal.

Why was I even bothering with the damn newspaper? It was a chump play to keep looking for Beryl. I wished I could just walk away. That job Charlie Jones had brought me was turning out to be the worst kind, the kind where you end up spending money instead of making it. No choice, though: I had to pay whatever it cost to make sure Charlie hadn't been the one who put the man in the camel's-hair coat on the spot. Because that might mean the shooting team knew about me, too.

The dead man wasn't going to pay me to find the woman he knew as Peta Bellingham anymore. And even if she really had all the money showing on that CD, that didn't necessarily add up to a dime for me.

I don't like looking for my money on the come, but that's where I was stuck now.

I sipped some more of Mama's brew while I thought it through again. All that money didn't mean anything by itself. Her father had been a rich man—maybe it was from an inheritance.

But what would have made her disappear? If the dead man had been stalking her, there would have been other ways to deal with that problem. For a woman as rich as she was, anyway.

I used to do a lot of that kind of work, about the same time I was looking for missing kids. I didn't have much finesse back then. And even less self-control. But I learned.

I got schooled good the time a soft-spoken man in an undertaker's suit came to my office. I didn't know him, but he had a message from a guy I'd done time with. A solid, stand-up guy who wasn't ever coming home. The soft-spoken man told me this guy had a little sister. And the little sister had a husband.

The husband turned out to be a big man, with a bad drinking habit and a worse temper. That made it easy.

The celluloid crunch of his boozer's nose brought both his hands up to cover his face. I hooked to his liver with the sap gloves, and he was on his knees in the alley, vomiting, bleeding, and crying at the same time. I leaned down quick, before he passed out, said, "Next time you beat on your wife, we'll snap your fucking spine."

When the soft-spoken man came back with the other half of my money, he was shaking his head apologetically.

"What?" I said.

"We've got a problem."

"We?"

"The girl. Our . . . friend's sister. She saw her husband in the hospital and she just went off. Started screaming."

"So?"

"So she's the problem."

I didn't say anything.

"Your . . . friend, there's nothing anyone can do to him, okay? But your friend, he's *our* friend, too, understand?"

"No," I said, lying.

"Then let me spell it out for you," the man said. "The sister, she knows more than she should. Instead of . . . appreciating what her brother wanted to do for her, she's decided that her husband is this innocent victim. So she made a phone call."

"To the cops?"

"To my boss. But her next call *will* be to the cops, unless things get made right."

"Which means . . . ?"

"An apology. And some money."

"So apologize. And pay her the money."

"It's not her," he said. "Him. He wants ten large to forget the whole thing."

"Why tell me all this?"

"Because you didn't do the job right."

"I did what I got paid to do."

"You got paid to fix it so he stops using the girl for a punching bag, not to bring heat down on my boss."

"It's not me who's doing that."

"Exactly," the man said, soft-speaking the threat.

I lit a cigarette. Watched the smoke drift toward the low ceiling. Pansy shifted position in her corner, the movement so slight it might have been the play of light on shadow. The soft-spoken man was trapped. But nowhere near as bad as I was.

S he's my only sister," the man on the other side of the bulletproof glass said to me through the phone. "I'm sorry about that," I told him. "But I didn't pick the people you sent to me, you did. And it's me they're putting in a cross."

"I can talk to them," he said.

"You already did that," I told him, guessing, but real sure of the guess. "It's *her* you have to talk to."

"She missed her last two visits," he said. "And she didn't answer my letter, either."

"Call her."

"I did. She wouldn't accept the charges. She never did that before."

"You understand what they asked me to do?"

"I can figure it out," he said.

"I'm not doing it," I told him. "But there's plenty who would."

"What if . . . ?"

"If she went as far as she already did behind what happened, what do you think she does if something heavier goes down?"

"Yeah."

"So?"

"I only wanted to help her," he said, shaking his head sadly.

I thought I had more time, but I was wrong. While I was visiting the prison, the soft-spoken man's boss was making a phone call. To Wesley.

Husband and wife went together. Two surgical kills the papers called "execution-style." The apartment had been ransacked. That made it "drug-related."

I was sad about everything. But I learned from it.

*J*ust because I'm good at waiting doesn't mean I like to do it. I'd been good at doing time, too.

It took me another three full spins through the CD before I snapped that, for all the info this "financial planner" had put together on his target, he had nothing from her past. If he didn't know her birth name, he didn't know where she had grown up.

I'd met Beryl when she was a runaway. Now, maybe, she had run back home.

People with records learn not to *keep* records. I've got a memory so sharp and clear that, sometimes, I have to wall off its intrusions before they finish the job the freaks started when I was a little kid.

Every one of us feels those spidery fingers sometimes. There's no magic pill. Therapy works for some of us. Some self-medicate: everything from opiates to S&M. Some of us go hunting.

I knew I could find Beryl's house again. I probably couldn't give directions, but, soon as I started driving, the sense impressions would flood my screen and guide me, the way they always do.

The Plymouth wasn't the correct ride for where I had to go. Clarence had what I needed—an immaculate, restored-to-new '67 Rover 2000TC, in classic British Racing Green. Just the kind of expensive toy someone in Beryl's father's neighborhood would have for Sunday drives. But Clarence was as likely to allow his jewel out in this weather as Mama was to file a legitimate tax return.

I could get something out of the Mole's junkyard, but he specialized in shark cars—grayish, anonymous prowlers that no witness would be able to recall. Except that what blended into the city would stand out in the suburbs.

Renting was always an option, but I hated to burn a whole set of expensive ID just for a couple of hours' use.

So I made a phone call.

"Hauser," was all the greeting I got.

"It's me," I said.

"Whatever you want, the answer is—"

"You still leave your car at the station when you take the train in to work?"

"Yeah . . ." he said, warily.

"I'd like to borrow it. Just take it out of the lot, use it for a couple of hours, put it right back."

"Use it for what?" Hauser demanded. I've known him a long time; it wasn't so much that he gave a damn, it was that being a reporter was encoded in his genes, and he always needed to know the story.

"I have to visit someone tomorrow. Not in your neighborhood, but close by. I'm looking for a runaway." Only the very best liars know how to mix a heavy dose of truth into their stories. And which buttons to push. Like I said, Hauser knew me going all the way back. And he has a couple of teenage sons.

"It'll be there when I get back?"

"Guaranteed," I promised. I'm the rarest of professional liars—unless you're the one I'm playing, my word is twenty-five-karat.

*T*he next morning, I was riding the Metro-North line, one of a mass of reverse-commuters heading out of the city. The car was about three-quarters full. I sat across from a scrawny, intense-looking man with short, carelessly cropped, no-color hair, indoor skin, and palsied hands. A pair of tinted trifocals dominated his taut, narrow face. Behind them, his eyes were the color of a manila envelope. He looked me over like a junkie who's afraid of needles, his need fighting his fear.

The two of us were probably the only ones in the car not jabbering into cell phones. The fool next to me, clearly annoyed that the racket might actually render his own conversation private, compensated by damn near shouting the "Just checking in!" opening he'd already used half a dozen times in a row. Some of the howler monkeys tried to sound businesslike, asking if there had been any calls—apparently *not*—but most of them dropped the pretense and just blabbered what they thought was important-sounding crap. They weren't talking, they were fucking broadcasting—using volume as signal strength. We were all captives.

I caught the paranoid's eye, made a "What can you do?" face. He studied me for a split second, then nodded down at the thick briefcase he had across his knees and twisted his lips a millimeter.

The fool next to me said, "Hello. Hell-*o*!" before pushing a button on his phone to disconnect. He hit another button—my money was on "redial"—then stared blankly at the little screen, as if it would explain some deep mystery. All over the train car, people were shouting into their phones but not getting a response.

"Dead zone," I heard someone say, smugly. "We'll pass through it in a minute."

I locked eyes with the paranoid across from me long enough to realize that the smug guy had it all wrong. Portable cell-phone jammers are expensive—good ones go for a couple of grand—but they're a reasonable investment for a lunatic who wants to make sure nobody watching him can report back to HQ. I would have offered the jammer a high-five, but I suspected that would start him suspecting me. So I leaned close, whispered, "You should carry a phone, too. Just in case one of these morons ever looks around and does the math."

He nodded sagely. After all, I wasn't one of Them.

Who says therapy doesn't work?

*H*auser's car was waiting just where he promised— a dark blue ten-year-old Lexus ES300 with a spare key in a magnetic box under the front fender. It had Westchester tags, with registration and insurance papers in the glove box, plus a today's-date note on the letterhead of the magazine Hauser works for, saying that Mr. Ralph Compton was using the vehicle with his permission.

I never felt more like a citizen.

I didn't remember exactly what Beryl's father did for a living—if he'd ever actually told me—but I figured the odds on my finding someone home at the residence were good, even if it was only the maid.

The Lexus was front-wheel drive, but I didn't need that extra safety cushion—the roads had been precision-plowed, and it was too sunny for black ice to be a problem. I drove around until I found a reference point, then went the rest of the way on autopilot, guided by the signals from my memory.

I get those a lot, and I always trust their truth. For most, I wish I didn't.

The house was a three-story mass of wood and stone that had been built to look like a carefully preserved antique. No cars in the circular drive, but the door to the detached garage was closed. The place felt like someone was home.

I couldn't spot a security camera, but that doesn't mean much today, not with tiny little fiber-optic eyes everywhere. I parked at the extreme end of the drive, at an angle. Anyone who wanted the license number would have a long walk to get it. I strolled up the driveway, casual.

A pewter sculpture of a bear's head was centered in the copper-painted door. I saw a discreet silver button on the right jamb, pushed it, and was rewarded with a sound like wind chimes in a hurricane.

The click of heels on hardwood told me whoever was coming to the door wasn't the cleaning lady. I felt myself being studied. The door opened—no security chain—and a tall, too-skinny woman regarded me for a second before saying "Yes?" in a taking-no-chances voice. She was way too young to be the wife I'd never met, but maybe Preston had gotten a divorce, and picked up a trophy on his next hunt.

"Ms. Preston? My name is—"

"Oh," she said, smiling. "We haven't had anyone asking for them in quite a while."

"You mean they—?"

"Moved? Yes. At least . . . well, *we've* owned the place for . . . it'll be eight years this summer."

"Damn!" I said, shaking my head ruefully. "I haven't seen Jeremy since I moved to the Coast. I just got back, so I thought I'd drive out and surprise him. That's what I get for not staying in touch."

"Oh, I'm sorry," she said, putting more sincerity into it than I expected. "I know the house was on the market for some time before we bought it. If we had known how prices were going to go through the roof, we never would have bargained back and forth for so long, but my husband . . ."

"I'm the same way," I assured her. "You wouldn't know where they moved to, by any chance?"

"I'm afraid not. We never met them, actually. Everything was done through brokers and lawyers. You know how that is."

"I do. Well, sorry to have bothered you, then."

"Oh, that's all right."

I turned to go.

"Mr. . . . ?"

"Compton," I said, turning back toward her.

"Would you like to leave a card? I don't think there's much hope, but I *could* give the broker a call, and see if she has any information. . . ."

"I'd be very grateful," I said. I took out a business card for Ralph P. Compton. It had a midtown address— I've got a deal with a security guard who works there; I slip him a hundred a month, and he slides any name I tell him into the building's directory—and a 212 number that would dump into one of the cell phones at my place.

She took the card, held my hand a little too long. I knew where that came from; one of the worst things about being locked up is how boring it gets, even in a mink-lined cell.

I returned the Lexus, took the near-empty train back to Grand Central, grabbed the subway downtown.

The car I picked was densely packed, but there was an empty seat on the bench at the end of a row. I started for it, but the woman sitting in the next spot pointed at a suspicious puddle on the gray plastic seat, warning me off.

Three stops later, when she thought no one was looking, the woman reached into her handbag, took out a small bottle of water, and freshened the puddle.

That held off all applicants until a guy wrapped in about seven layers of coats and an even thicker odor stumbled in. The woman frantically pointed to the puddle on the seat next to her. The homeless guy took that as an invitation, and plopped himself down. The woman jumped up like he'd hit the other end of her seesaw.

The homeless guy had an empty seat next to him for the rest of the time I was on the train.

Many paths to the same door.

I stopped by a deli on my way home, planning on grabbing a sandwich to go. But the tuna looked suspicious and the egg salad looked downright guilty, so I passed.

I looked a question at Gateman as I stepped through the doors.

"All good, boss."

"You have lunch yet?"

"Yeah. I had the Korean kid from down the—"

"Okay, bro," I told him.

"I got the paper, you want to check last night's Yonkers."

I hadn't bet anything last night, but I took his copy of the *News* anyway.

N o messages waiting.

I had roasted almonds and papaya juice for lunch, idly going through the paper by habit, a soldier scanning the jungle even when there's been no activity reported in the area.

If I hadn't gone cover-to-cover, more to kill time than anything else, I would have missed it. The gossip column had an unsourced item: "What financier's wife had filed for divorce just weeks before he was gunned down on the streets of Manhattan?" Then some stuff about how the wife had charged him with adultery, naming a "Ms. X" as the co-respondent.

I went back through the paper. Nothing. Which meant the cops had already talked to the wife, and knew a lot more than they were releasing.

I wished I was one of those private eyes in books; they've all got a friend on the force. I didn't, but I knew someone who did.

She's not going to meet with you," Pepper said, letting a drop of vinegar into her sweet voice. "Nothing's changed. And it's not going to."

"I just want to ask a question. Not of her, okay? A question I want her to ask one of her pals."

"Ask me," Pepper said, unrelenting.

By the time I remembered that I had a date with Loyal that night—worse, that I had promised to take her somewhere special, somewhere she could really dress for—it was edging into five o'clock.

"Davidson," the lawyer's bearish voice growled into the phone.

"It's me," I said. "You still repping the guy who owns Citarella?"

"The stores or the restaurant?"

"The restaurant."

"Josephs by Citarella, yeah. Who wants to know?"

"An old pal, who desperately needs a reservation for two."

"So call and make one. They're open to the public."

"Uh, it's for tonight."

"Christ. Business or pleasure?"

"Business."

"Then you won't need the window."

"Come on."

"This worth me using up a favor?"

"I'll make it up to you."

"Call me back. Half an hour. And, Burke . . ."

"What?"

"Make sure you order the fish—that's the specialty of the house. And there's no apostrophe in 'Josephs,' so don't make a fool of yourself telling them there's something wrong with their sign."

T he hostess at Josephs treated me like royalty, proving she wasn't just a pretty girl but a damn fine actress.

"Oh, this is *gorgeous,*" Loyal said, tapping her foot as she tried to decide between sitting with her back to the window and missing the glittering view along Sixth Avenue, or facing the window and making everyone in the restaurant miss their view of her.

The hostess immediately tuned to her wavelength. "The corner is perfect," she advised.

Loyal seated herself, glanced to her right out the window, to her left at the other tables, and, finally, across at me. "You're so right," she said to the hostess, flashing a megawatt smile. "Thank you."

I still had the image of Loyal's little foot in the emerald-green spike heels, tapping a toe so pointed it looked as if it would deform her foot.

"How do you get your feet into those shoes?" I asked her.

"What?" she said, sharply. My sister's voice rang in

my mind like an annoyed gong. *You are a hopeless, hapless idiot.* Her refrain, when it came to me and women.

"No, no," I said, hastily. "I meant the *toes.* They're so . . . radical."

"Oh, don't be so silly," she said, shaking her head at my stupidity, but mollified. "They're just for show."

I'm no gourmet—Davidson is, even though every meal I'd ever shared with him was sandwiches in his office—but I could tell the food was world-class. Loyal did her trick of appearing to really chow down, but only picking at her food as she moved it around her plate. I didn't mind.

"Lew," she said, looking up from her perfectly presented crusted arctic char, "you know a lot about money, don't you?"

"Who really *knows* about money?" I said, positioning myself for a deflection move.

"Oh, stop! You know what I mean. I've got a problem, and I wanted to ask your advice."

I heard the Prof's voice in my head. We were back on the yard, and he was explaining women to me. *If all you want is gash, all you need is cash. But if you want a woman's heart, you gotta do your part. One way or the other, there ain't no such thing as free pussy, Schoolboy. There's always a toll for the jellyroll.*

So I was on all-sensors alert, but all I said was, "Sure, girl."

"Well, you know what the real-estate market has been like, right? I mean, it's just *insane.* Even *studios* are going for half a million in some parts of the city."

"It's a bubble," I told her, with more confidence than I felt.

"That's what people say," she said, nodding as if to underline the words. "But if it's a bubble, when is it going to burst?"

"If I knew that . . ."

"I know. But I feel like I have to do *something,* before I miss out."

"But you already have a—"

"That's exactly it!" she said, excitedly. "I bought that apartment *ages* ago—well, not *ages,* of course," she interrupted herself, not being old enough to have done *anything* too long ago, right?—"but it *feels* like that, the way the market keeps rising and rising."

"I still don't see a problem."

"Well, *I* do," she said, emphatically. "I could get . . . well, a lot of money for that place, if I was to sell it now. In two or three years, it could be worth a lot more . . . but it could also be worth a lot less. If I sold now, I'd have a big pot of cash."

"You'd *need* a big pot of cash if you wanted to keep living in this town."

"That's just it," she said, regretfully. "But if I had a place to stay, I could do it. I'd only need a couple, three years here, working, then I could go back home . . . with enough to live on forever, I bet."

"Where's home, Wyoming?"

"No, silly. I'm from a little town in North Carolina. I haven't been back since—oh, I don't even remember—but my daddy left me a little place when he passed on. There's people living there now. Renters, I mean. It's not a big house, but it's got some land around it. I could be happy there . . . especially after this city. I know I could."

"I never picked up an accent," I said.

"Well, you better not, all the voice lessons I paid for," she said, turning her bruised-peach lips into a practiced pout. "When I came to the city, I was just a girl, not even old enough to vote. I was going to be an actress. Everyone back home told me I was a dead ringer for Barbara Eden—when she was Jeannie, I mean—and I was dumb enough to listen."

"You do favor her," I said, gamely.

"You're sweet, Lew," she said, not diverted. "But I know that's not going to be for me, not now."

"Things didn't work out?"

"I didn't have any talent," she said, soft and blunt at the same time. "This so-called agent I had told me to change my name—the only part I was ever going to get with a name like Loyal Lee Jenkins was if they remade *The Beverly Hillbillies*—so I did. A little. But that didn't make any difference. Casting directors would see my pictures—oh, did I have to work to pay for *those*—and I'd get calls, but as soon as I opened my mouth, that was it."

"Your accent?"

"Well, I *thought* it was my accent, but I ground that rock into powder . . . and that *still* didn't change anything. I tried and tried for years until I got the message. You know what it comes down to, baby? I'm not fashionable anymore."

"You? Come on!"

"You're thinking of the shoes, aren't you? There's a

lot more to being fashionable than buying things, Lew. You know those jeans everybody's wearing now? They're not built for girls like me. I work out like a fiend, but I can't change my shape."

"Why would you want to?"

She turned her big eyes into searchlights, scanning the terrain of my face for a few seconds. Whatever she found must have satisfied her, because she nodded as if agreeing with something. "I remember, once, this man who wanted me to pose for him," she said. "He told me I had the classic American hourglass figure. I was thinking about that just this morning, looking in the mirror. And you know what, Lew? No matter how tiny the waist of an hourglass, the sand still drops through it. Running out. I have to start thinking about my future."

"Your apartment."

"My apartment," she agreed. "Now, I told you some truth about myself, even if it was embarrassing. So can I ask you a question?"

"Sure."

"Are you married?"

I had been expecting that one for weeks. "No," I told her. "Well, I guess that's not a hundred percent. I've been separated for years, waiting for her damn lawyers and mine to get together on some financial issues."

"You have kids?"

"No."

"And that one *is* a hundred percent?"

"Oh yeah," I said, shrugging my shoulders to show she was being absurd.

"When you say 'separated,' you mean physically, too, don't you?"

"Well," I said, seeing where she was headed, trying to block the exit before she got there, "it's not that simple. I own a brownstone. That is, *we* own a brownstone. The lawyers made it clear that the one who moves out is the one who gets the short end of the stick, so we're both still there. We live on separate floors, so we're not even roommates. Sometimes I don't even catch sight of her for weeks. But I've got so much of my money tied up in that place, I'm not leaving. And neither is she."

"So you sleep there?"

"Uh-huh."

"And that's why you can't bring me to your place? Because that would be, like, adultery, right? And that would make your wife's case better."

"That's right," I said, wondering how Loyal was such an expert on the topic . . . for about a second.

"But if you had a friend who let you stay at their place anytime you wanted, for as long as you wanted, I'll bet you'd like that just fine."

"I guess."

"I mean, a friend who'd just clear out and disappear. So, say, if your *girl*friend wanted to spend some time with you . . ."

"I guess I never really thought about it."

"Well, you *should*. Because it could solve both our problems in one jump," Loyal said. Breathlessly, because all her breath had dropped into her cleavage.

"I'm not following you," I said. Stalling, because I was.

"You wouldn't want to rent an apartment in your name," she said, leaning forward and licking a trace of something off her lips. "But _I_ could rent one, couldn't I? Then I could rent out my co-op, have a place to stay while I keep my eye on the market, and you'd have the best setup in the world, too."

For three grand a month, I could have a lot of things, I thought, but kept it off my face. "That could get tricky," I said, still looking for an opening.

"You mean you would have to go back to your place and spend the nights? That's no big deal, honey. That's what you do now, anyway. If I had my own place, like we're talking about, I could be ready for you anytime you wanted."

Like you're _talking about,_ I thought. "There might be a way," I said aloud. "But it would depend on some things working out."

"I'll do anything," Loyal said, lips slightly parted in abject sincerity.

I met Pepper the next morning, in the lobby of an "I'm cool, but are _you?_" hotel on West Fifty-second. It's perfect for a man in my line of work. The people who hang out there put in so much mirror time that their observational skills have atrophied from disuse. And the doorman doesn't come on duty until after dark, when his outfit works better.

"What?" Pepper said, as she sat down on one of the quasi-sofas artfully scattered near the revolving door. Mick stood behind her right shoulder.

"Daniel Parks . . . ?" I began. Got a blank stare for my efforts, kept going: "He was gunned down a little while back. Made the papers. First he wasn't ID'ed.

When they released his name, there was nothing else, except for the usual filler. Then I read in a gossip column that his wife had sued him for divorce just before it happened. Named another woman."

Pepper turned and shot Mick a look that would have terrorized a gorilla.

"The gossip columns have trollers," I said. "They root through the bins in Supreme Court, looking for celebrities' names. Lawsuits, restraining orders, divorce filings—stuff like that. This guy's name wouldn't be on their hit list until he *got* hit, which is probably why it didn't make the columns before now."

Pepper rolled her eyes dramatically in a "Tell me something I don't know" gesture.

"That's one possibility," I said, unfazed. "The other is that a cop leaked the info. Some of them have a standing arrangement with the gossip boys."

"So?"

"So I need to find out what was in the actual complaint, Pepper. Supposedly, the wife named the other woman—they called her 'Ms. X' in the column, which means either they don't know or she's not famous—and that's info I need. Plus anything else she charged him with—"

"Like?"

"Like, especially, anything to do with money."

"Why can't you just go down to the courthouse and—?"

"I guarantee that's all sealed up by now. And if it's not, it's a baited trap, and the cops will be all over anyone who goes looking."

"So you want *us* to do it?"

"Pepper, I know you don't think much of me, but I'm sure you don't think I'm stupid, okay? Wolfe—"

Mick made a sound somewhere between a grunt and a threat.

"I know *she* still has friends on the force," I went on, nothing to lose.

"Friends do favors for friends," Pepper said, flatly. "What you want, it's not that sort of thing."

"I know what you're saying. I know money won't do this. All I'm asking you is to ask *her,* all right?"

"Don't call us," she said, getting to her feet.

Mick glided out behind her, his broad back covering her like a steel cape.

*T*he calendar said spring, but instead of blossom-bringing showers, the city stayed mired in dry cold. I never considered trying the co-op on West End. Parks was the source of that address, so he'd already worked it over long before he asked Charlie Jones to find him a tracker. Anyway, the info CD he had given me didn't say anything about the girl I had known as Beryl Preston being married, or even living with someone, much less having kids.

A three-bedroom in that neighborhood would fetch a fortune for the owner—if the co-op board in her building allowed owners to rent out their units. But the Battery Park apartment was a condo. It wouldn't have a board. Or a doorman.

Getting around this town isn't complicated. You

need to go north-south, there'll be a subway someplace close, get you there quick enough . . . on days when its crumbling innards aren't showing their age. You want to go east-west, you're better off walking. I could spot most crosstown buses a couple of avenues and still catch them before they got to the next river. Battery Park is a nice walk from where I live, but not in bitter weather. And not when I'm working.

All I had for the pits who guarded my Plymouth was a few sawdust-and-pork-products wieners I picked up from a street vendor, but the beasts went for them like they were filet mignon. Or an enemy's throat.

Every time I came, I got another micromillimeter closer to patting one of the females, an orca-blotched beauty who had begun twitching her tail at my approach a few months ago. "Hi, sweetheart," I said to her. She's the only one I ever talk to. She cocked her head, gave me a look I couldn't read, then went back inside her house.

The Plymouth fired right up. I let the big pistons glide through the engine block on their coat of synthetic oil for a couple of minutes, waiting for the temperature gauge to show me signs of life. Then I motored over to the West Side Highway and turned left.

The ride lasted just long enough for James Cotton's cover of the immortal Slim Harpo's "Rainin' in My Heart." Blues covers aren't the bullshit "sampling" rappers do, stealing and calling it "respect." When a bluesman covers another artist's song, he's not just paying dues, he's paying tribute. From the moment I'd caught Son Seals live in a little club in Chicago years ago, I'd wished he would cover "Goin' Down Slow," following the trail of giants like Howling Wolf and Big Bob Hite. But before that ever happened, he went down himself. Diabetes, I heard.

I found the complex easy enough; it was only a few blocks west of the blast zone from where the Twin Towers had fallen. Supposedly, the air around what tourists call "Ground Zero" is still full of microparticles from the atomized glass of all those exploded windows. I don't know what effect stuff like that has on your lungs, but it hadn't changed the asking—and getting—prices for lofts in the neighborhood. In this city, you could build apartments on top of a nuclear reactor and they'd be full by the weekend.

The gate to the parking lot wasn't manned. A speaker box sat on a metal pole at the entrance. I hit the button, told the distorted voice coming through the grille that I was William Baylor, EPA, there to do some ambient atmosphere sampling.

I couldn't tell if they understood a word I said, but the gate opened. I backed the Plymouth into the far corner of an open lot and climbed out. I was just taking a six-dial meter with two carrying handles and "EPA" stenciled across its side out of the trunk when a short, broad-chested Latino in a dark blue private-cop uniform strolled up.

"You're the guy from . . . ?" he said.

"EPA," I answered, holding up the meter like it was an ID card.

"*That's* what they give you to ride around in?" he said, nodding in the Plymouth's direction.

"Nah. That one's mine. If you use your own, you

can make out like a bandit. Even with gas the way it is here, at forty-point-five cents a mile, you come out way ahead."

But the guard wasn't interested in the finer points of government reimbursement. "Is that righteous, man?" he asked, pointing at my car.

"Nineteen sixty-nine Roadrunner," I told him, proudly. "All steel and all real."

"Damn, it's fine," the guard said, strolling around the Plymouth like he was examining a prize horse.

"It's gonna be, when I get all done with her."

"It's not a hemi, is it?" he asked, hopefully.

"It was once," I lied. "But by the time I got it, the whole thing was in pieces. I'm running a 528 wedge."

"That's a crate motor?"

"Yep. Pulls like a train, and ticks like a good watch when it's done."

"What are you going to do for rims?" he asked, looking at the dog-dish hubcaps on the Roadrunner's sixteen-inch wheels like you'd look at a potato sack on Jayne Mansfield.

"I haven't decided yet."

"A ride this size, you could run dubs, bro."

"Maybe . . ."

"It would be awesome sick, man. Awesome."

I looked around the near-empty lot. "You want to try it out? I know you can't leave your post, but just a couple of laps . . ."

He stole a quick glance at his watch. "Oh, *hell,* yes!"

I handed him the keys, got in on the passenger side, putting my bogus measuring device in the back. He sat there for a second, taking it all in. Then he fired it up. "Oh, man, you can *feel* it."

He pulled the shift lever into D, delicately eased off.

"No burnouts," I warned him, keeping my voice light so he'd know I wasn't taking him for an idiot.

He maneuvered around the lot, barely off idle, steering carefully. He wasn't timid, just feeling his way.

"When we turn at the end, give it a little down the straight. But watch out—this sucker's got mad torque."

He didn't say anything, concentrating. Made the turn, carefully straightened the front wheels, and gave the throttle a quick stomp. The Roadrunner squatted and launched, pinning us back in our seats. The guard stepped off the gas. We both listened to the sound of the monster V-8 backing off through the twin pipes. The muscle-car signature, as American as the blues.

"Oh, you one lucky hombre, esé," the guard said.

*U*nit 229 was a townhouse, the last one in a row of immaculate, white-fronted look-alikes. Pushing the doorbell triggered some ethereal quasi-Asian music. I tucked the meter under one arm and waited, not hopeful.

The man who opened the door was a compact blond, with delicately precise features. He was wearing a thin black mock-turtleneck pullover that had to be cashmere tucked into cream-colored slacks with elaborate pleats. His pale hands were as neat as a surgeon's.

"Yes?"

"Uh, I was looking for Peta. Peta Bellingham?"

"I think you have the wrong address," he said, politely.

"No, I don't," I said, letting a current of concern into my voice. "I've been here before. To see—"

" 'Peta.' Yes, I understand. But that must have been a while ago."

"Not *so* long ago," I said, taking the risk.

"Ah," he said. "You must mean whoever lived here before I did."

"I . . . guess. I mean, I always thought this was her own place. But I could be . . ."

"Well, I don't think so," he said thoughtfully, one hand on his hip. "Not with the way the owner has things set up."

"Damn."

"You haven't seen her . . . Peta . . . in quite a while, have you?"

"I've been away," I told him, watching his eyes to see if it registered.

"You're not some stalker, are you?"

I shook my head sorrowfully. "No, I'm not a stalker," I said. "I'm a professional disappointment. Peta's not my girlfriend; she's my sister. Maybe if I'd ever answered her letters while I was . . . away, I'd know where she is now. She's the only one in the family who stuck by me. I figured, let me . . . finish what I had to do by myself, not drag her into it, you know?"

He studied me for a long minute, making no secret of what he was doing.

"Do you think the owner might have a forwarding address for her? You know, where to send the security deposit and all? All I want to do is send her a letter, tell her I'm . . ."

"That wouldn't be much help, I'm afraid."

"Maybe not. But it would be worth a try. I've got no one else to—"

"No, I mean . . . Oh, come in for a minute, I'll show you what I'm talking about."

I followed him into a living room that looked like a Scandinavian showroom, only not as warm.

"Just sit down anywhere," he said. "I'll be right back."

I found a metal-and-leather thing that I guessed was a chair, right next to a wrought-iron sculpture—another guess—and a plain black cylinder that seemed to be growing out of the hardwood floor.

He came back into the room, a purple file folder in one hand, a black-and-white marble ashtray in the other.

"You smoke, don't you?" he said.

"Yeah, I do," I lied. "How did you know?"

"I'm good at things like that," he said, just this side of smug. He placed the ashtray in the precise center of the black cylinder—at least now I knew what it was for. I took out a pack of Barclays, tapped a cigarette free, and fired it up with a wooden match.

He seated himself on a severe-looking bench the same color as his hair, and handed me the file folder.

"This is why I don't believe the owner would be of any help to you," he said. "I've never met him. Take a look at the lease. Did you ever see anything so bizarre?"

I opened the folder. It looked like a conventional lease, on a preprinted form. On the last page, just above the line for the tenant's signature, was a paragraph in large bold type. It specified that the rent was to be paid via wire transfer to a numbered account in Nauru; the tenant was to authorize auto-debit from his own account no later than the third day of each month. Then, in big red letters:

THIS CLAUSE IS DEEMED TO BE AND SHALL BE THE ESSENCE OF THE AGREEMENT. IT IS UNDERSTOOD AND AGREED THAT ANY VIOLATION OF SAID CLAUSE CONSTITUTES A WAIVER OF ALL TENANT'S RIGHTS TO OCCUPY THE PROPERTY, INCLUDING BUT NOT LIMITED TO THE RIGHT TO CONTEST IMMEDIATE EVICTION PROCEEDINGS.

"My attorney told me that's all nonsense," the blond man said, as if to calm my anxiety over the prospect of him being evicted. "Absolutely unenforceable. But, as you can see, it's all so very mysterious, isn't it?"

"Sure is," I agreed. Thinking, *Here's something that wasn't on your little dossier, Mr. Certified Financial Planner.*

"I'm truly sorry," the blond man said. "I wish I could have helped you."

"You did," I told him, grinding out the cigarette I'd allowed to burn down in the ashtray. "If you know a room's empty, saves you the time of knocking on the door, right?"

"Well, *my* door . . . I mean, if you think of something that I might be able to help you with, please come back."

"I just might," I lied, again.

Patience. I knew I had to wait for Wolfe's crew to get back to me with something—like a solid confirm on the address Wesley had for Charlie Jones, or whatever was in the police file on the divorce papers filed by Daniel Parks's wife—before I made my next move. There wasn't any point working the rest of the info on that CD. If Beryl still owned the condo in Battery Park—and it felt like she did—she'd had it all locked and loaded way before she got in the wind.

I was spending money like I was actually working for Parks, but he was never going to settle his bill. In my world, that's just wrong. But I had a writhing viper by the back of its neck, and I couldn't just drop it and walk away until I was sure it wasn't me it wanted to bite.

I stayed low, waiting. Every time Loyal called, I told her I was trying to put a deal together, and it needed all my attention.

"Has it got anything to do with . . . what we talked about, baby?"

"It . . . it *could,* is the best I can say now, little girl."

"Well, are you sure you can't come by? Even for an hour or so? I'll bet you'd work better if you got your batteries recharged every so often."

"I'd work happier," I said. "But not better. When

you're on top of a deal like this, you can't take your eye off the ball, or it gets dropped."

If she knew that was all deliberately vague snake oil, she didn't let on.

Nobody call," Mama said, in response to a question I hadn't asked.

I made an "It's out of my hands" gesture.

Max looked down at his own hands, a pair of oversized slabs of bone and sinew, each with a horned ridge of callus along the chopping side, the first two knuckles as dark and bulging as ball bearings.

I shook my head No. With nobody to answer our questions, it didn't matter if we came on sweet *or* sour.

The Mongol's face settled into lines of calm. He reached inside his jacket and took out a deck of cards, still in the original box, and put them on the table between us, raising his eyebrows.

"Let's do it," I said.

Out came Max's score pad. Probably Volume 90— we started our life-sentence gin game a million years ago. When we had gotten bored with the steady diet, I taught him to play casino. Now we alternate randomly.

But it didn't matter what game we played; we always kept score in dollars. At one point, Max had been into me for six figures, built up over a decade. He was lousy at cards to start with—a hunch-playing, omen-trusting, logic-hating sucker to his core—and Mama's incessant-insistent kibitzing made him even more incompetent. Then, one day, he caught a streak gamblers only fantasize about. Before we stopped—Max wouldn't let me walk while he was on his prime roll—it was more than thirty-six hours later, and he was just about even.

Took me another few years to get it all back.

I opened the pack of cards as Mama, smelling an opportunity to screw things up for Max, drifted over from her register. Mama worships numbers. Adores them. She can work her way through the toughest sudoku puzzle faster than the Prof can pick a lock—"*Not* Japanese!" she had hissed at me the first time I noticed her doing one. "Chinese invent, Japanese copy. Like always"—and she keeps three sets of books in her head. But when she gambles, the fever burns up the abacus in her brain like it was dry-twig kindling.

I held up both hands, fingers splayed, asking if Max wanted to try gin. He shook his head, held up four fingers.

Okay, casino it was.

I shuffled and dealt. The flop was the queen of spades, ten of clubs, ace of clubs, and seven of diamonds. I was holding a king, a pair of nines . . . and the deuce of spades, a money card.

Max studied the table. Mama pounded on his arm with a jeweled fist, hard enough to raise a bruise on a two-by-four. Max ignored her, concentrating.

Max took the queen with one of his own. I'd given up trying to teach him to count cards and spades; when it came to gambling, Max was a Taoist.

I dropped my king.

Max threw the jack of spades.

That left me with two choices: throw my Good Two on top of the seven, building nines, or put one of the nines, a club, on the table, in case Max was holding a ten. But if Max had been holding the ten of diamonds, he would have snatched the club ten off the table with it in a heartbeat. The ten of diamonds is worth two points; they don't call it the Big Ten for nothing.

Or would he? I knew Mama would have; maybe that's what she was beating on him about. . . .

I threw the nine of clubs.

Max slowly and deliberately turned to face Mama. She looked away as the Mongol dramatically produced the Big Ten. He showed it to me, scooped the nine of clubs and the ace of hearts plus the ten of clubs into his hand. Three points, four cards, one move.

I bowed, and put the Good Two on the seven.

Max threw down the four of diamonds, and bowed to me as I took in my build.

Mama looked disgusted.

One of the payphones rang.

*P*olice girl call," Mama said, a minute later.

"You mean Pepper, Mama?"

"Police girl," she repeated, adamantly.

I must have gone blank for a minute. Next thing I heard was, "Burke! You want number?" I nodded. "Police girl" is what Mama always called Wolfe, even years after the beautiful prosecutor had gone on TV to denounce a sweetheart deal the DA was giving to a bunch of frat boys who'd raped a coed.

Wolfe's pale, gunfighter's eyes had been chips of dry ice, the white wings in her dark hair flaring as if in anger. She knew this was going to cost her more than

just being Bureau Chief of City-Wide Special Victims:
She'd never work as a prosecutor again, anywhere.
But she never took a backward step.

After that, when every legit door closed in her face,
Wolfe had gone outlaw, running the best info-trafficking
cell in the city. But to Mama, there's lines you can't
cross. To her, Wolfe would be "police girl" for life.

I grabbed a throwaway cell, dialed the number
Mama had given me.

"That was quick." Wolfe's voice.

"Anytime you—"

"This isn't about me," she said, softly but with no
warmth. "Not about you, either. I have half of what you
asked for—the half I had to do myself."

Meaning she had to ask a cop. Ask him personally. I
wondered if it was the same sex-crimes detective who
was so in love with her that he'd committed a half-
dozen felonies to protect her when Wolfe had been
false-arrested a while back. Sands, that was his name.

I don't know what he got for going out on that limb
for her. Me, I went a lot further out than he did. And
when it was over, all she had for me was a goodbye.

"How do I get it?" I said.

"I don't know where you are now," she said, not expecting me to tell her. "You know the short piece of
Park Lane, on the northeast edge of Forest Park? Not
Park Lane South, or Park Lane North, the little connecting piece, just up from Queens Boulevard?"

"Yeah. I was—"

"Can you get there in an hour?"

My watch said ten-twenty. "Give me to eleven-
thirty?"

"Okay. Look for a light-colored Chrysler 300."

"Finally traded in that old wreck of yours—" I started to say. But she had already cut the connection.

Forest Park was in Wolfe's home territory, just up the hill from the courthouse-and-jail complex on Queens Boulevard where she'd once had her office.

At that hour, I didn't play with side streets, just grabbed the BQE to the LIE to the Van Wyck to the Interborough. When I exited at Union Turnpike, I was only a few blocks from the meet, twenty minutes to the good.

The big Chrysler was sitting at the curb next to the park, steam burbling from its tailpipes. I drove past, glanced over to my right, saw a bulky male shape behind the wheel. Wolfe might still have her old car somewhere, but she sure had a new friend.

I spun the Plymouth into a U-turn, crawled along back the way I'd come until I found a place to pull over. I got out, started walking toward the Chrysler. The passenger door opened, and Wolfe stepped out into the spray of light. She was wrapped in a grape-colored coat with a matching toque, moving toward me quickly, as if to keep me from getting too close to the Chrysler.

I let her make the call, stopped in my tracks. She closed the ground between us, as sure-footed in spike heels as a Sherpa on sandpaper.

"It's too cold to stand around out here," she said. "Let's sit in your car."

I did an "after you" gesture. She strolled over to the

Plymouth, let herself in. By the time I got behind the wheel, she had lowered her window and fired up a cigarette.

"You've got something for me?" I said, matching her all-business posture.

"Not with me. Pepper has it. I told her to bring it over to that restaurant of yours by one."

"One in the morning?"

"Yes."

"That's not a lot of time for me to—"

"You'll have plenty of time," she said, dragging on her cigarette. "This won't take long."

I didn't say anything, not liking it already.

"That other thing you asked for? It's not going to happen."

"Why not?"

"It's not what we do," she said. Her voice was gentle, but hard-cored. "Information, that's what we deal in. You know that. I won't put my people in risk situations."

"All I wanted was—"

"You wanted my people to get you a photo . . . or some other kind of confirm on a certain person at a certain address."

"Right. And what's so—?"

"You think I don't know what Charlie Jones does, Burke?"

"He's just a—"

"What? A 'businessman'? I don't think so. And the only reason a man like you would be looking for him is if he put you into something and it went wrong."

"A man like me?"

"A man like you," she repeated, turning to face me. "You used to be . . . something else, once. When we first met. You had, I don't know, a . . . code of some kind."

"I still do."

"Is that right?" she said, snapping her cigarette out the window. "Remember that first time, what you were doing? Why you were doing it? When's the last time you worked a kid's case?"

"I'm working one now," I said, hurt in a place I didn't know I had.

"No, you're not," she said, sadness thick in her voice. "That's not the kind of stuff Charlie Jones deals in."

"Do you want me to tell you about—?"

"No. I don't want you to tell me anything. I came here to tell *you* something, and I want you to listen. Listen good, Burke. This is the last time you put my people in harm's way, understand? You think I don't know what you brought Mick into last time you went off the rails? From now on, it's like this: You want information, you can buy it from us, like anyone else. But no side deals, or you're cut off. Are we clear?"

"Yeah," I said. "I got it. No matter how careful I wipe my feet, I'll never be good enough to walk on your carpet."

"You want to feel sorry for yourself, go for it, Burke. You can't be a mercenary and expect to be treated like a patriot."

I stared straight ahead as she got out. I felt the door close behind her.

I was back at Mama's by a quarter of. At one, Pepper walked through the front door, Mick looming behind her right shoulder. She came over to my booth, studied my face for a second, then said, "You didn't expect her to come herself, did you?"

"No."

She sat down across from me. Max was having an animated conversation with Mick, using playing cards to make some kind of point.

Mama brought Pepper a plate of assorted dim sum, and a pot of tea. They spent a few minutes trying to out-polite each other. Then Pepper slid a dark-brown nine-by-twelve envelope over to me.

I thumbed open my sleeve knife.

"It's not original," Pepper said. Meaning, don't worry about opening the envelope delicately.

Inside was a sheaf of photocopied court documents. Mrs. Daniel Parks—née Lois Treanor—charged her husband with separate counts of adultery and "cruel and inhuman treatment." The meat of the complaint was the wife's affidavit. "Upon information and belief," Parks had been maintaining a "long-term illicit relationship" with a woman "whose specific identity is not, at this time, known."

The key word was "maintaining" . . . and as I read through the affidavit I could see why the cops were sitting on this one. According to his wife, Parks had been systematically looting the assets of the private hedge fund he managed, "with estimated diversion of no less than seven million dollars."

That didn't sound like a lot—hedge funds charge a percentage of assets under management as their fee, so Parks wouldn't have come close to emptying the vault with those numbers. But then came the kicker: The complaint charged that Parks had stolen the money to "artificially inflate the management results for his paramour." Like a Ponzi scheme, where you pay dividends to old investors with new investors' money, syphoning off the cream until the pyramid collapses. Only this one wasn't set up to benefit the manager; according to the complaint, it was set up to "impress and fascinate" one of the investors.

"Ms. X" was a siren, all right.

I read it over a couple of times. Most of it was lawyerese: lots of heavy adjectives bracketing slender facts. Whoever drew it up was careful not to accuse "Ms. X" of being in on the scam with Parks. Stripped to its core, it came down to this: Some guys will use presents for seduction, trading a piece of jewelry for a piece of ass. But *this* guy's idea of a present was way off the charts; he was pumping himself up as a financial-management genius by pumping cash into the mystery woman's account.

I went over the chronology. Parks had been served with the papers on Valentine's Day—the kind of touch lawyers who keep press agents on staff think is very, very special. By the time Parks had gotten desperate enough to ask Charlie Jones for a referral, over a month had passed.

There was no indication that Peta Bellingham had been subpoenaed as a witness. And neither she nor

Parks had been charged with a crime. Not yet, anyway—the forensic accountants would have to pick through the paper first.

And it wasn't the cops who'd been looking for Peta; it was Parks.

I read through the papers again, but it was like trying to buy a Big Mac in a health-food store. Whatever I needed, I wasn't going to find it in there.

Why would Peta Bellingham get in the wind? Even if Parks *had* diverted funds to her, she could always claim she was just an investor who thought her money manager was doing a great job . . . especially if she paid taxes on the gains, and had her *own* CPA do the returns. Plus, even if all the skimmed money really went to her, she had walked away from damn near that same amount in assets she left behind.

Or had she? Anyone with the contacts and connections to set up banking in Nauru might have been getting ready to vanish for years. Co-ops can be sold through agents, money can leave one account and appear in another without any human hands touching the cash.

And who had the hunter-killer team been working for when they X-ed out Daniel Parks?

Wolfe's package was full of info, but it was a mutant hydra, birthing five new questions for every answer it disgorged.

"Thanks, Pepper," I said, looking up.

She was nowhere in sight. I must have gone somewhere in my head—that happens when I hyperfocus.

I looked at my watch. Damn. Almost three in the morning.

"Where's Max?" I called over to Mama.

"He go back home. Friend go with him."

Friend? "Mick? The big guy who was here with—?"

"Sure, sure."

I knew Max trusted Mick—the big man had been on the scene when we canceled the ticket of the guy who had made up the case against Wolfe—and I knew Mick was a kung-fu guy, but I never imagined the two of them working out together, especially in Max's temple.

"Did Pepper go with them?"

"Little girl, big smile?"

"Yes, Mama," I said, patiently. "You know who Pepper is."

"No. She stay with me, we have tea."

"So where is she now?"

Mama pointed instead of speaking. She doesn't like the way the word "bathroom" sounds in English.

When Pepper came back out, she glistened as if she'd just bounced out of a shower.

"What are you so happy about?" I asked her.

"Well, you may find this hard to believe, Burke, but Mick doesn't make friends easily."

"A charmer like him?"

"He's *very* charming when he wants to be. He just doesn't like . . ."

"People?" I filled in, helpfully.

"Oh, stop that! You know what I mean. Anyway, he and Max are, like, real pals now. I told them I'd just wait here until they were done working out, or whatever it is they do. You know, the karate?"

"Yeah."

"And I had a *great* time talking with Mama! Did you know her husband was an architect?"

I answered her with a noncommittal facial gesture— I didn't know Mama even *had* a husband.

Max floated in behind me, Mick at his side.

"Did you have fun?" Pepper asked, brightly.

Mick and Max exchanged looks. "Yes," Mick said. Yeah, I could see where all the charm came from, all right.

"We have to go," Pepper told me, holding out her hand, palm up.

"How much?" I said.

"She said there was no charge," Pepper said, lifting my heart a little. "But I have to take everything back with me," she finished, putting it back where it belonged.

*B*y the time I got up the next morning, every channel had some version of the same story: Some young kid, a reservation Indian out in Minnesota, had walked into the local high school with a shotgun, a pistol, and a bulletproof vest. He killed a bunch of people at random—a security guard, a teacher, and a lot of students—before he took himself out.

The kid had been "troubled." I guess that's the new word for a born-to-lose with a father who committed suicide, a mother who was severely brain-damaged, raised by a grandmother who constantly called him a "human mistake" when she wasn't beating him. The kid became a Nazi—in his own mind, anyway. He preached racial purity to anyone who would listen—no one ever did, but he was used to that—and posted endless shrieks to his personal blog, too. At school, he wore black clothes and eyeliner, as if to make sure nobody ever forgot he was an outcast.

Producers spun their Rolodexes, and the lucky winners got to be on television, "analyzing" what happened. None of them went near the truth. I knew that truth. The kid was a member of a bigger tribe than you could ever find on a reservation. My tribe. The Children of the Secret. We know.

The experts droned on about "communication" and "reaching out" and "peer rejection." But this kid hadn't flown under the radar. Everyone around him knew he was buried in despair. They probably figured they knew the outcome, too—the suicide rate on reservations is right up there with the alcoholism level.

That kid was just another of the invisible ones—bullied, beaten, and belittled every day of his marginalized life. If anyone had the slightest idea that he might be a danger to someone other than himself, they would have unleashed a snowstorm of "services."

Suicide, well, kids do that kind of thing. Homicide— now, *that's* serious.

Every high school in America has them, the invisible ones. They all silent-scream the same warning: *If you won't see us, you'll never see us coming.*

But nobody ever starts the analysis until after the autopsy.

One of the cell phones trilled. I looked at the label on its holster: Ralph P. Compton. I'd only given that number to . . .

"Compton," I answered, in a brisk, businessman's voice.

"Mr. Compton? My name is Sophia . . . Sophia Ginsberg. You were at my house looking for—"

"Oh, I remember you," I said, my tone of voice telling her she'd made a reverberating impression.

"Well, you'll be glad I called, in any event. I did speak to the broker, and I got an address for Mr. Preston. I don't know if it's still a good one, of course. But it was certainly good at the time we bought the house."

"That's great," I said. "Let me just grab a pen. . . ."

"Oh, I can give it to you tomorrow," she said, quickly. "I'm going to be in the city, and I thought you might like to buy me lunch."

"It would be my pleasure."

"Oh, good! I didn't want to come off as too—"

"I would have called you anyway," I told her. She took the lie like a deep-tissue massage. I gave her the address of a midtown bistro where I knew Michelle could get me treated right, even on short notice.

I don't see where she gets her attitude from, after what you did for—"

"Let it go, honey," I told Michelle, gently. Knowing she wouldn't. Ever.

"You don't need to know the reason to feel the season," the Prof said. "Wish the weather was better, but . . ."

"I could be a Bible man again," Clarence volunteered. He had a door-to-door routine down pat, came across as a bright, sincere young man on a mission to spread the Word.

"Wrong neighborhood," I vetoed.

The Prof walked out of the room without ceremony. Came back with a chilled can of Red Bull and a small bottle of blueberry juice. Michelle poured the two together over a tall glass of shaved ice, sipped it delicately. My sister had a new personal drink every week, but the Prof and Clarence never strayed from their Red Stripe. I went with pineapple juice and seltzer.

We all sat in silence for a few minutes.

"Charlie's a night man," I said, finally. "How about I just pick a day, around noon, okay? I walk up to his front door and ring the bell, ask for Mr. Siegel?"

"I don't like it," the little man said. "What if he's not home? What if his wife—got to have one, if he's been there that long, I'm thinking—says he's a traveling salesman, been on the road for months? He don't come to the door himself, in person, we're not making him pay to see our hole card, see?"

"It would be the same thing if I went there," Michelle said. "It's all chance, all luck."

"Couldn't you reach out for him, Burke?" Clarence asked.

"Anyone ever *asked* to meet with that motherfucker, he'd take off like a hellhound was on his trail," the Prof said. "That's not the way Charlie works it. He knows where to find *you;* you don't never know where to find *him.*"

"That's the truth," I agreed.

"Next time he has a job for you, we follow him to his home?"

"That play won't pay, son," the Prof told Clarence. "One, could be months—years—before Charlie calls Burke again. Two, odds are, he don't *go* home when a meet is over. Strike three, no way to shadow a man like Charlie Jones. Takes more than skill to do something like that; you got to have powers."

The Prof and I shared a look. Wesley had powers. He was as relentless as obsession itself, a remorseless land shark. Not a great white, or a mako—no, Wesley was a bull shark, the deadliest of them all. A bull shark can work the deep ocean or shallow fresh water. It can take prey even in knee-high depths. And it's the only shark with a memory.

It hit me then, why Wesley was the consummate shadow. He was one of the Invisibles. And nobody had ever seen him coming.

"Could we ask the Dragon Lady?" Clarence said, hopefully.

"To do what?" Michelle said, a slight tinge of sharpness in her voice.

"Hack the Con Ed records," I answered for him. "Or Brooklyn Union Gas. Charlie probably never makes a call from that house, but he has to have the utilities turned on."

"So, if this 'Benny Siegel' guy is still there . . ."

"Yeah. It won't pin him down, but it might tell us if we're wasting our time."

"Or we could ask the Mole," Michelle said.

"Ask him what?" said Clarence, retaliating.

"Oh, I don't *know*," she said, in a "don't be dumb" tone. "He's only the most brilliant scientific genius in the whole world, that's all. If anyone can figure out how to—"

"We can take a ride out and see him," I offered. Quickly, before the fuse burned down to the TNT.

No point in telling the Mole we were coming. He's got a phone, but he never answers it if he's working, and he's just about always working.

Michelle fumed at me all the way. She'd been building her mood from the moment I told her we didn't have time to stop at her place to let her change outfits, and hadn't let up since. I ignored her—easy enough, since she was putting so much effort into ignoring me.

I slid one of my custom CDs into the slot, and let the music drift over us, tugging at the buried blossoms. Chuck Willis, "Don't Deceive Me." Johnny Shines swearing "My Love Can't Hide." Sonny Boy's "Cross My Heart." Timothea's "I'm Still Standing." Champion Jack's version of "Goin' Down Slow," the one he called "Failing Health Blues." By the time the CD got to the lush black velvet of Charles Brown's "Early in the Morning," my baby sister was back to herself.

"That young boy"—she meant Clarence, who was a long way from that now but, being younger than her, had to be a teenager, at most—"just wanted an excuse to see that woman," she said, smiling now.

"The Dragon Lady? She's married."

Michelle's the only woman I ever knew who can make a snort sound feminine.

"Fine," is all I had in response.

"Burke, you know Mole will come up with something."

"It's not that, girl. No one respects the Mole's stuff more than me. I was just thinking of something Wolfe told me."

"Her? What would you even—?"

"Enough, okay? Just listen," I said, as I wheeled the Plymouth off the Bruckner onto Hunts Point Avenue, heading for the badlands. "I thought I had a deal with her crew. Do a little surveillance on the address we had, see if they could get me a photo. Or anything that would lock it down as Charlie's address. Then Wolfe pulled them off. She said it was because they just do paper stuff, no agents in the field. But there was something else going on, and I think I know what it is. Charlie Jones might not be much on his own, but anyone who tightropes over an alligator pit for a living gets to know the alligators pretty good after a while."

"That's right. I wouldn't want him . . ."

"I know it, honey. *That's* why I didn't go running to the Mole right away, see?"

"Yes," she said, crossing her legs. "I'm sorry. Maybe this wasn't such a good idea."

"It's fine," I soothed her. "We'll just . . . consult him, okay?"

Her smile was a floodlight.

We rolled through the badlands, while I thought about how it was probably the last piece of real estate in New York that hadn't been gobbled up for new construction. Not yet, anyway. With the tidal wave of property-greed crashing over the city, some Trump-oid was going to find the money—other people's money—to renovate the barren prairie sooner or later. As we made the turn to the Mole's junkyard, I pointed out a prowl car, parked in the shadow of what had once been a building.

"ROAD officers," I said to Michelle.

"What are those?"

"Retired on Active Duty," I told her. "It's a good spot for cops like that. Plenty of crime, but no citizens to report it. They need something for their activity sheets, they can always bust one of the prosties working the trucks out of the Meat Market."

"Very nice," she said, stiffly. Michelle had worked the streets for years, when she was still pre-op. She still had a working girl's mind: hated the cops, feared the johns.

I'd known my little sister since we'd been kids. I was older; she was smarter. I was stronger; she was quicker. The only times we were apart was when I was Inside, or she was. She'd been distance-dancing with the Mole for years before they ever got together.

What finally pushed them over the bridge to each other was the same thing that got Michelle off the streets and onto the phones. Love. Not the love they had for each other—that had been there since the minute they met, arcing between them like electricity, searing the air. No, this was love for a kid. A little kid who'd been turned out before he ever got to kindergarten. I'd snatched him from a pimp in Times Square, back when that part of town was a festering pus pit.

I hadn't thought things through, just did what I used to do all the time back then—hurt the pimp, took the kid. But this wasn't a kid I could take back to his parents: That's who the pimp had bought him from.

While I was still running through options in my head, Michelle had already adopted the boy, pulling him to her in the back seat of my car. She hadn't let go since.

Terry was her boy—hers and the Mole's. The kid had his father's nuclear mind and his mother's titanium delicacy. His *real* father's, his *real* mother's.

I nosed the Plymouth against the rusting barbed wire that wound through the chain-linked entrance to the Mole's junkyard like flesh-tearing ivy. I knew the motion detectors would have already set LEDs flashing where the Mole could see them.

Maybe there was a hidden dog whistle, too. The pack assembled like it always did, moving with the slow and easy confidence of an inexorable force. I looked for Simba, feeling a needle poised above my heart. The ancient warrior was about a hundred years old; one day he wouldn't answer the bell for the next round. Just as I felt my throat close, I spotted his triangular head cutting through the mob like a barracuda parting a school of guppies. The pack was silent except for a couple of yips from the young ones who hadn't learned how to act yet.

"Simba!" I called out. "Simba-witz!"

The old beast looked at me, white-whiskered face as impassive as ever. His eyes were filmy with age, but one shredded ear shot up as he tracked my voice, ran it through his memory banks. He gave out a short half-bark of greeting just as the Mole lumbered up and began unlocking the back part of the sally port.

The Mole drove from the gate back to his bunker. I wasn't worried about letting him behind the wheel of my Plymouth: The tiger-trap potholes would keep his speed down to a crawl, and he could see well enough in daylight, even with the trademark Coke-bottle lenses covering his faded-denim eyes.

Simba and I walked back together, the pack at a respectful distance.

"We've still got it, don't we, boy?" I said.

Far as I was concerned, he nodded.

As usual, the Mole was miserly with his words. But he listened good. When I was done, he said, "Why does he matter?"

"Charlie?"

"Yes. Either he is no danger to you, or he does not know where to find you."

"Because, if he was a danger, he would have already moved on me?"

"Yes."

"Charlie middlemanned a meet between me and this guy who wanted me to find a woman. The guy left to get something from his car. A team boxed him in, and just gunned him down. They didn't ask any questions, didn't even search the body. They knew who they wanted, and what they had to do."

"So?"

"So maybe Charlie's found himself another line of work."

"As a Judas," Michelle said.

"Even if that is so, it wasn't Burke he betrayed," the Mole said, reasonably.

"There's a hundred other possibilities," I said, lamely. "I just want to talk to him."

The Mole gave me a look.

"You have a photograph?"

"I've got nothing," I told him. "And a physical description wouldn't do any good—it'd fit a million guys. All we've got is that address I told you about. If it's still good, he spent a long time building that nest. That'd give us something to bargain with."

"So you *want* a photograph?"

"Exactly."

"Couldn't you hook up some kind of—?" Michelle started to say, but I cut her off with: "No, honey. Now that I think about it, Wolfe's right. Surveillance isn't the way to go. No way we could put a stranger into a neighborhood like that, it's too—"

It was the Mole's turn to interrupt. "I know," he said.

We were all quiet for a couple of minutes. Fine with me. I liked sitting out there in the fresh sunlight, my hand resting on the back of Simba's neck.

"You have one of those new phones?" the Mole asked Michelle. "One that takes pictures?"

"Mais oui," she said, insulted that anyone would think she was a fraction of an inch off the cutting edge . . . of anything.

"Everybody has them now," the Mole said, as if Michelle had just made his point.

"So it wouldn't make Charlie nervous, seeing one," I said, picking up the thread.

"No," the Mole said in a voice of finality. Then he launched into a string of Yiddish. The only word I recognized was *landsman*.

The bistro was called Le Goome. Before I could say a word, a guy who looked like he should be bouncing in a waterfront dive—except for the lavender satin shirt with the first three buttons undone to display a hairless swatch of chest—walked over, said, "Mr. Compton, yes?" His voice was right out of a cellblock.

"That's me," I told him.

"Michelle is very special to us," he said, making it sound like a warning. "We have a lovely, private table for you, away from the window, yes?"

"That'll be great."

"And the lady?"

"Her name is Sophia. She's tall, with—"

"She'll ask for you, yes?"

"Yes."

"I'll bring her to you, sir," he said, about as servile as a bull elephant during mating season.

I'm sorry I'm late," she said, as I got up to greet her.

"Don't give it a thought."

The waiter was androgynous, of no apparent age, wearing a lavender satin shirt. Maybe it was a theme.

"I always feel guilty in a place like this," she said. "I eat so little, and they charge so much."

"Food's just fuel," I told her. "People come to places like this for the experience."

"Oh, that's just right!"

I made a toasting gesture with my glass of vitamin water, telling her I was glad she agreed, but I was done talking. . . .

She got it as if I'd spelled it out in neon. "I know you must want this," she said, sliding a folded piece of paper across to me.

I opened it. One glance and I knew it was a dud. Jeremy Preston's last known address was care of a law firm in Manhattan. They might know where he was now, but they wouldn't be telling if they did.

"I'm sorry," she said, telling me she knew what she'd given me was useless.

"That's okay," I told her. "I might be able to work with this. My company's no stranger to lawyers."

"It was just an excuse," she said, looking down at her French manicure.

"I'm glad," I said, lying.

*B*y early evening, the Ralph P. Compton number had been nuked, the phone itself sledgehammered and tossed into a vacant lot. A new name was in the slot at the office building. Michelle's lavender-shirted pal would respond to any questions with the blank look he'd probably learned in reform school.

And if I'd guessed wrong on the range of security cameras at Sophia's house, and Hauser ever got a call about his license number, he'd pass a polygraph that he'd left the car at the station that morning, and it was right there waiting for him when he returned.

But all of that was reflex—I knew Sophia wasn't going to be looking for me. Just the opposite. She'd had her sad little adventure; Ralph would get the message when she never called again.

Of course, she couldn't be 100 percent sure that Ralph wouldn't come looking for her. Get angry, demand an explanation, insist on seeing her again. That would have frightened some women, but not Sophia. Action like that would have buzzed her neurons. She was a junkie who needed a risk-fix every so often. And Ralph Compton had disqualified himself.

"You know what I always wanted to do?" she'd said, walking around the hotel room like she was thinking of buying it.

"This?" I guessed aloud, giving her the chance to pretend this was her first time with a stranger, if she wanted it.

She didn't. "Did you ever do it outside?"

"You mean, like, in a car? When I was—"

"No. No, that's not outside. I mean, like . . . we came up in the elevator, but there's stairs, too, aren't there?"

"There have to be. In case there's a—"

"We could go out there," she said, leaning back against the wall. "It would be so . . . exciting. Why do you think I wore this skirt? I could just . . ." She slowly turned her back, tugged at the hem. By then, I wasn't surprised to see she was naked beneath it.

Part of me wanted to tell her I never had sex indoors until I was a grown man. Alleys, cars, rooftops—that's where kids like us got it on. One girl I had was so much shorter than me that I used to stand her one step higher on the stairs, come into her from behind.

I didn't tell Sophia that. And I didn't tell her about the sex I didn't want. When I was small, when I couldn't stop them from doing whatever they wanted with their property. Not their property, actually—I belonged to the State. But the State was always very generous about loaning out its possessions.

No, I just told her doing it outside the hotel room was too much for me. She'd almost walked out then, disgusted. But I guess she figured she'd already made the trip, so . . .

*T*hat night, I paid another installment on the malaria I'd bought with my stupidity so long ago. Fever dream. They come when they want to, but less and less over the years. Usually, they're just jungle visions: running, pieces of earth blowing up in chunks, blood in the ears so thick you can't hear the gunfire, fear rising like ground fog, clouding your eyes and imprisoning your mind. Sometimes the location shifts. I'm not always in a jungle. But that ground fog is always there, hungry.

I was my old self in the dream. I mean, I looked like I did before my face got rearranged. It was years ago—I knew that because I was in the downtown meatpacking district at night, and it was deserted. So it had to be before the place turned itself into Clubville, like it is now.

I parked my car—my old car, a 1970 Plymouth four-door sedan so plain it made vanilla look exotic—off Gansevoort Street and started walking. It was as if I was watching from behind myself—I could see with my eyes, but I couldn't see my face.

There was no music to the movie. It was like watching a man in an aquarium.

"You looking for a date, mister?"

I saw a girl's face, peeking around the corner like she was playing hide-and-go-seek. Not one of the tranny hookers who had made the area their personal stroll; this was an XX-chromosome package. I remember thinking, *How do I know that?* But I never answered my own question.

She was under five feet, way short of a hundred pounds. Wearing a baggy pink sweatshirt over jeans and pink sneakers. Her hair was in pigtails. A teenager, trying to look even younger.

"Maybe," I said, to bring her closer. "Would it be an expensive one?"

"That depends on what you want to do on your

date," she said, biting her lower lip and looking a question at me in the darkness.

"You have a place?" I asked her.

"It's a nice night out," she answered, as if she'd been expecting the question. "And back here"—she shot an unrounded hip in the direction of the alley she'd come from—"it's real private."

"I don't . . ."

"Oh, you'll *love* it, mister. You don't have to get undressed or anything." She stepped closer. "Just let me take it out. A man built like you, I'll bet you've got a *big* cock."

I had her then, left hand clamped on the back of her neck.

She didn't panic. "All I have to do is scream," she said, calmly. "My man's back there, and he's a real—"

"Scream," I said, pulling my .357 Mag loose.

"Oh God!" she said, very, very softly. "You're a cop, aren't you? Please, please, please, please, please."

"Just come with me," I said, watching the mouth of the alley.

"Please, please, please." She was crying with her voice, but her eyes were dry.

"Please what?"

"I can do it in your car. I'll suck your cock until it *explodes*," she whispered against me, groping with her hand.

I turned slightly, guarding my groin.

"No, no, no, mister. I just wanted to show you how good I can be. Come on, *please*. I always wanted to suck off a cop. You see how good I am, you'll come back, right? Anytime you want, I'll be right here."

"Come on," I said, clamping down a little tighter to get her moving.

"*Please!*" she hissed at me. "It doesn't have to be like that. I'll do anything, mister. I'll take it in the ass, if you want. Anything."

"You're not being arrested," I told her. "I'm just going to take you—"

"No!" the girl begged. "*Please.* I never did anything to you, did I? And I'll do anything you want. *Anything.* Just don't take me back."

"Back where?"

"You know," she said, accusingly. "Back home."

I woke up coated in sweat. I felt a white-hot wire somewhere in my brain, writhing like a stepped-on snake.

*U*nless Beryl's father was deep underground, any of the Internet "public records search" services would turn him up in an hour. Their best customers are stalkers, and they cater to their clientele with a wide variety of options. They'll give you access to DMV records—there's an extra charge for states where that's against the law—tax rolls, employment history, student-loan databases. If you want, they'll even send you some photos of the target's house.

You don't have to be a celebrity to make the list. There are humans who worship property rights. *Their* property. Some of them see therapists with their "abandonment issues." Others visit a gun shop.

All stalkers have one thing in common: a profound,

overwhelming, all-encompassing sense of entitlement. Leaving them is worse than an affront; it's an act of deadly aggression, a threat to their core. Punishment is required.

Most people who flee don't have the resources to really get gone. They have to work for a living. Open a bank account. Rent an apartment. Get a driver's license.

Ex-cons talk about "getting off paper," meaning no wants, no warrants, no detainers, no parole, no probation. But the one paper nobody ever gets off is a stalker's "to do" list.

For some disturbos, the relationship they think was "broken off" never existed in the first place. A true erotomaniac can construct the illusion of reciprocated love out of a celebrity's autograph, a form-letter answer to fan mail, a "shared moment" during a public appearance. Or from secret messages the victim sends in a magazine interview, a line he writes in a novel, a gesture with his hand during a TV show. Messages only the "special one" can decode.

There's nothing so dangerous as an armed narcissist, but the gun's no good without an address. That's why the highest level of threat assessment is reserved for the ones protection experts call "travelers." Some stalkers get their rocks off writing letters; travelers always deliver their messages in person.

The search services never ask customers what they intend to do with the information they buy. After all, people are entitled to their privacy.

When I was in high school, girls got a name for what they'd do. Or wouldn't do," Loyal said.

"It was a small town?"

"That's right. But I don't see why that would make any difference. When I was in school, if you ever went all the way with a boy, just once, every other boy in school would expect you to do the same with him."

"How old were you when you figured that out?"

"I didn't have to figure it out; it all got explained to me."

"By your mother?"

"Nope. Not my father, either. They didn't talk about things like that. It was my brother, my big brother. Speed told me—"

"Your brother's name was Speed?"

"Yes, it was," she said, hands on hips, as if daring me to make something of it.

I held up my hands in surrender.

"Speed told me how boys talk. See, I always thought it was just girls who did that. I remember him saying it: 'There's some things I can't protect you from, sis. Talk like that, once it gets out of the bottle, you can never put it back in.' I never forgot that."

"He was a good protector, your brother?"

"Oh, he was just the best! Some of the boys I went to school with, they could get a little rough, be too free with their hands, especially when they'd had some liquor in them. But none of them wanted to get Speed mad. He wasn't the biggest boy in the school, but he was just so . . . willing. Do you understand what I'm saying?"

"Sure. I came up with guys like that. You might be able to beat them, but they'd *make* you do it. Cost you something to try, too."

"That's him exactly!" she said, clapping her hands. "It's like you knew him."

"Maybe I will, someday."

"No," she said, shaking her head. "Speed's gone. A year after I left, he was killed in an accident over to the mill. About killed my mother, too. She didn't ever seem to get over him dying. She kept saying it wasn't right— the parent is supposed to go first.

"In the beginning, she was just plain mad. Mad at everyone and everything. Stopped going to church. Told the preacher if taking Speed was part of God's plan she didn't want any part of it. Or Him. Then, one night, she went to sleep and never woke up. Never let anyone say you can't die of a broken heart, Lew. Because my momma did, sure as I'm standing here today."

"Didn't you want to go—"

"Home? Well, sure, I did. I mean, I *did* go, for Speed's funeral, and to stay with my mother for a bit. But it was her, her and my father, who got me to leave. They said Speed would have wanted me to try. I knew, the minute they said those words, it was true. Speed was always willing, and I had to be, too. Because I loved him so much."

"He'd be proud of you, Loyal."

"For trying? Yes, I guess he would be. Even if I didn't succeed, I tried and tried."

"You make it sound past-tense, girl."

"It kind of is," she said, as if really considering the idea for the first time. "Remember what I was talking to you about? My apartment?"

"Sure."

"Well, that's kind of my exit line. I *am* going back home. And I guess I could, you know, just sell out and go. That other plan—the one I told you about?—that's only a good one if there's a reason for me to stay."

"You mean, like, a part or something?"

"More like a 'something,' " she said, looking up at me through the veil of her long lashes.

S pring came in like treachery," the precise-featured man next to me said. We were sitting on an outdoor bench on Central Park West. "It popped up like a mugger out of the dark, pounced, and stole away with the cold. Get it?"

"Nice," I said. He was wearing a black quilted jacket, left open to display a turquoise turtleneck jersey over black narrow-cuffed slacks and black slip-ons just a half-glisten less shiny than patent leather. I knew four things about him: he went by "Styx," he was a writer, and he was plugged into a bunch of data banks.

The other thing I knew about him didn't matter to me, and *that* mattered a lot to him.

All he knew about me was that I get paid for what I do, and I pay for what I want.

"You ever hear of Surry, New Hampshire?" he said.

"No," I told him. Talking with this guy, the less words the better.

"There's no 'e' in it. You spell it like it was 'Furry,' only with an 'S' in front, all right?"

"Sure."

"If there was an 'e' there, it would be like those hansom cabs in the park. You know, a 'surrey with the fringe on top.' "

"Ah."

"It's not far from Keene . . . ?"

"Is that anywhere near Hinsdale?"

"Hinsdale? What's up there?"

"Used to be a racetrack. They closed it down a few years back."

"You mean, like, for racehorses?"

"Yeah. Trotters, not Thoroughbreds."

"Oh." He half-yawned. A mugger must have stolen his interest. "Anyway, that's where your man lives. Surry, New Hampshire."

"Preston, that's a common name. You sure you got the—?"

"If he's the same Jeremy Preston who sold the house in Westchester you told me about, he's the one you want," the man said, a little huffy that I could be questioning his skills. He's a very sensitive guy. I guess writers are like that.

We got up and started walking through the park. He lives on the East Side; we'd part company where the traverse gives you the Fifty-ninth Street option.

A jogger passed us. He was wearing a white bodysuit with orange fluorescent bands around the sleeves and thighs. On his back was embroidered: "Runner Carries No Cash."

"My mistress says to say hello," the writer said. I

guess this was one of those days when he wasn't allowed to say her name.

"Back at her."

We walked some more, watching spring descend all over the park.

"I'm working on a novella now," he said. "I'm calling it 'Sub Plot.' What do you think?"

"Very strong," I assured him.

*I*t took Clarence only a few minutes to computer-map me a route to Surry, New Hampshire. Close to a straight shot: 95 North to New Haven, 91 all the way across the border into Vermont, take Exit 3, and then follow the directions I had taped to the dashboard.

I'd be running in the seam—it was too late in the season for the ski crowd, and too early for the foliage freaks. Even at cop-avoidance speeds, probably no more than four hours.

I would have liked company on the drive, but Beryl's father had known a man with a different face, and I didn't want to spook him any more than I had to. Or let him think anybody but me knew his business.

Once, I would have taken Pansy with me. She loved to ride, and she was a better conversationalist than she looked.

I walled that one off. Quick, before it took hold. Bad dreams are one thing; somewhere down in that darkness, you *know* they're dreams. But invasive memories are ice-pick stabs that bring their own darkness. Waking up won't help you. The best you can do is hold them off until they get tired and fade. Until the next time.

I rolled out at four in the morning. Even at that hour, the city's never empty, but there was nothing you could call "traffic," and I cruised all the way to the bridge without stopping for anything but the occasional light.

The Roadrunner was contemptuous of the speed I held her to, the tach loafing at around two grand. I switched between the all-news stations, listening for anything about the investigation into the death of Daniel Parks, but all I heard was the usual putrid stream of packaged press releases, endless sports scores, some breathless celebrity-watch crap, and a lot of commercials.

I switched to talk radio. People were still foaming at the mouth about some woman in Florida who'd been brain-dead for over a dozen years. She was way past a coma—"persistent vegetative state" is what the doctors called it. A feeding tube in her stomach was all that was keeping her body from rotting—to some, a lifeline; to others, a harpoon in dead flesh. Her husband said she had told him if she was ever in that kind of situation she'd want to go. Her parents said that was all a lie.

Her husband had the final say, and that probably would have ended it, except that the anti-abortion crowd decided this was some kind of "right to life" issue, and they lit a fire under their lackeys. The governor of Florida—a passionate believer in capital punishment, because that's what the Bible told him—stuck his God-fearing nose in, personally passing a law that stopped the husband from disconnecting the feeding tube. When the courts said he couldn't do that, his brother, Big Christian, took over. Once that happened, the same Congress that hasn't been able to come up with a national health plan in twenty years took about twenty minutes to pass a law that sent the whole thing back to the courts.

The TV stations had all been running footage of the woman. Her eyes were empty, lips drawn away from her teeth in a permanent rictus her parents said was a smile of grateful love.

One caller said the husband should be on trial for attempted murder. Another screamed he was a "confessed adulterer," since he was openly living with another woman. Someone else calmly recited that he was going to get "millions" from the lawsuit over what had made his wife brain-dead in the first place.

Fair and balanced.

When she's finally allowed to go, I figure they'll fight over the remains. If the parents win, my money's on cryogenics.

No matter which station I switched to, there was the same topic. One degenerate said the woman was still smarter than his ex-wife had been—probably had worked on that line for days, in between popping Viagra so he could get his money's worth out of his porno DVDs. Then there was a panel of medical experts, who went on about "loss of upper-cortical function," and a bunch of other stuff nobody was listening to or cared about.

The only honesty I heard was from a brimstone-voiced woman who warned, "When America finally becomes a Christian country, cases like Terri's won't be decided in any court. The Lord will rule."

I shivered like it was winter inside the car.

*O*nce I got onto Route 91, I had to break my vow to stay at the speed limit if I wanted to avoid calling attention to myself. I inserted the Plymouth into a clot of cars and let them pull me along with them. Our pack was running a little over eighty when a red Mustang shot past on the left. The driver gave me a hard look, like he'd just backed me down from a challenge. Probably practiced it in his rearview mirror whenever he was stuck in traffic.

When I left the highway, I was only about twenty miles from my target. The Plymouth blended right into a thin stream of mixed vehicles, everything from working-class trucks to luxo-SUVs, with a seasoning of anonymous Japanese sedans and the occasional kid's jacked-up Camaro.

My ID said I was James Logan, who lived in a building in the Bronx that hadn't gotten a mail delivery since a drunken squatter kicked over a kerosene heater a few winters back. License, registration, and proof of insurance all matched the plates. Jim Logan had taken early retirement from his job as a manufacturer's representative, selling restaurant supplies. His hobby was restorations. The Plymouth was a work-in-progress, and now he was looking for an old farmhouse he could bring back to life, too. Friends had told him that southern New Hampshire had a lot of wonderful possibilities, but he preferred to look around on his own first, before dealing with brokers.

There was snow in the fields, but the roads were crisp and clean. A few flakes may be enough to paralyze cities like Charleston or Atlanta, but up here even a major blizzard wouldn't slow things down for long. It's always easier handling what you're used to—that's why people with my kind of childhood do so well in prison.

The town didn't have a lot of street signs, and I wasn't carrying a premarked GPS, so I just meandered around, getting a sense of the place as I searched for the address.

I passed it twice before I pulled over and checked what I had written down. The number matched, but my expectations didn't. Instead of the semi-mansion and fancy grounds I'd expected—and I'd driven past enough of those to know the little town didn't lack for upscale housing—it wasn't a lot more than a cottage, set off to the side of an unpaved driveway.

I drove back, thinking maybe I'd been looking at a guest house, or some kind of artist's studio, and the real thing was somewhere behind it. But the only other building I could see as I went up the driveway was a small garage, sided the same as the house, with a matching roof. The house itself was bigger than it had looked from the road, but no more than a couple of thousand square feet, I guessed. If you transplanted the whole thing to Westchester, probably cost you three-quarters of a mil. Up here, maybe a third of that? I didn't know enough to even guess.

I parked the Plymouth at the end of the drive, jockeyed it around until it was facing out the way I'd come, and walked across a patch of ground to the front door. Before I could raise my hand to knock, it opened.

"Yes?" said a gray man. I blinked twice, and the gray man turned into Jeremy Preston. Or whatever was left of him.

"Mr. Preston," I said, confidently, "my name is Logan. James Logan. I'm here about a matter my brother handled for you, quite a number of years ago. I've driven a long way, and I'd sure appreciate a few moments of your time."

"If it's about the business, that was closed when—"

"No, sir," I said, politely. "It was a private matter."

He stared into my face, nakedly searching. Came up empty.

"Look, Mr. . . . Logan, is it? I don't know any—"

"My brother's name was Burke, sir. And the matter he handled for you concerned your daughter. Do you think we could . . . ?"

*I*nside, the cottage looked like a lot more money than it had from the road. The peaked ceiling must have gone up fifteen feet, with massive beams running across; a series of skylights cut into one side flooded the room with pale northern sun. The furniture looked like it was wall-to-wall antiques, but, for all I know about stuff like that, it could have been a collection of three-dollar bills. A serious-looking woodstove occupied one corner, the cast-iron ducting showing it was used to actually heat the house. The stone fireplace that took up most of one wall must have been put there for entertainment.

"Coffee?" he asked.

"No, thank you."

"Tea? Hot chocolate?"

I could see he wasn't going to engage unless I gave him time to put himself together. "Hot chocolate sounds great, if it wouldn't be too much trouble," I told him.

"Nothing to it," Preston said, leaving me alone in the living room. I could hear the sounds of glass and metal in what I guessed had to be the kitchen.

Enough time passed for him to have called the cops, if that was what he was going to do. But I didn't think so; he wouldn't have let me in if he didn't want to hear what I had to say first.

"How's that?" he said, handing me a heavy white china mug.

"Smells perfect."

"It's store-bought," he said apologetically, as if I had been expecting him to produce something more authentic.

"Just about have to be, right? I've never been up here before, but I can't believe the cocoa bean would survive this climate."

"Yes," he said, seating himself in a rocking chair covered by a white horse-blanket with red diagonal stripes. "Now, can you explain the whole thing to me, please? I'm a bit confused as to what you're doing here"—smiling to take the edge off his words.

"My brother and I had different fathers," I told him. "His name was Burke."

The expression on his face told me he was ahead of me, but I went on, a man explaining his mission.

"We weren't close," I said. "Different lives, different coasts. So, when I learned I had been appointed the executor of his will, I admit I was surprised. I flew in from Portland—Oregon, not Maine—and the lawyer who had handled the will gave me an envelope. Inside, there was a list of my brother's cases—apparently, he was some sort of private detective—and, well, I suppose you'd call them a list of last requests. Things he wanted me to do."

"He wanted you to finish his cases?"

"Nothing like that," I said, smiling to show how absurd the idea was. "I'm not a private detective, I'm a small businessman. *Very* small—I own a motor court on the coast, me and my wife. What Burke wanted me to do was, well—I'm not sure how to say this—kind of, maybe, check on how his cases turned out. It seems most of them involved children. I guess he wanted to know they came out okay. In the long run, I mean."

"Why do you call him that?"

"Call him . . . what?"

" 'Burke.' It seems strange to call your brother by his last name."

"Oh," I said, chuckling. "I see what you're saying. Well, that's what I always called him—a private thing, just between us. He always called me 'Logan.' "

"I always called him Mr. Burke."

I shrugged, as if to say my brother's ways were a mystery to me.

He rocked gently in his chair. "So your brother's records indicate he did some job for me?" he said.

"That's right. There isn't a lot of information there, but, whatever he did, it concerned your daughter. Beryl, right?"

"I had a daughter named Beryl," he said, planting his feet to stop the rocker from moving. "But you're going back a very long time. She's a grown woman now."

"So everything turned out for the best?"

"That's what your brother wanted to know?"

"I *guess* so. He left . . . bequests to several of the children on his caseload. Not very much," I said, holding up my hand as if to disclaim any big-bucks potential, "but . . . Well, like I said, we weren't close. I couldn't begin to tell you what was in his mind. He left some property he owned to me, and his car—that's it, sitting out there in your driveway—too. But all the rest of his estate, and, like I said, that wasn't much, he wanted divided up among five people. From the instructions he left, I could tell they were all old cases of his."

"And you started with my daughter?"

"Actually, I'm *finishing* with your daughter. The other bequests have all been disbursed."

"Well, as I said, Beryl's not a child anymore. So why not just go straight to her?"

"That is what I did, for the others," I said. "It took me a while—I don't have to be a private detective to know that some women change their names when they get married. And the only addresses I had were for the parents, anyway."

"I haven't lived at the address Mr. Burke had for me for many years."

"I found that out when I tried to visit. Luckily, your number was listed."

"So why didn't you just call?" he said, a flash of color showing under his grayness.

"I don't believe this is the kind of thing people would take seriously if they heard it on the phone. With all the con men and scam artists running around today— you'd be amazed at what you learn, managing a motel—how would *you* have reacted if a stranger called and said he had money he wanted to give to your daughter?"

He nodded, but didn't say anything.

I took a sip of the hot chocolate. "I couldn't find a Beryl Preston in any phone book—I used the Internet to search. So I thought I'd drive up, answer any questions you have, and you'd tell me how to get in touch with her."

He cupped his mug closely, as if warming his hands. A minute passed.

"You think I'm nothing now, don't you?" he said.

A beam of sunlight bent itself through the skylight, standing between us like the third rail on train tracks.

"I don't understand," I said, buying time.

"This house, the land it sits on, the furniture you see here, it's mine. Truly my own. I never knew what that felt like, back when I was . . . back when I first met you."

"Me? I—"

"I wasn't just a dog on a leash," he said, bitterness etching his thin voice like vitriol on glass. "Not just an actor playing a role, either. I *ran* the company, even if I didn't own it."

"I don't know what—"

"You know what my strength always was? My secret strength? I was a good listener. I paid attention. A person's voice, it's like an instrument. You can hear if it's out of tune, whether it's under stress. The FBI even has machines now, for listening to voices. It's supposed to be better than a polygraph. I'll bet it is."

I sat back on the couch, waiting for whatever he was going to come at me with.

"Feel free," he said, pointing at a shallow brass bowl on a coffee table made from a cross-sectioned piece of timber, varnished to a high gloss. "That's an ashtray."

"I don't smoke," I said.

"Gave that up when you had the plastic surgery, did you?"

I didn't say anything.

"Your voice," Preston said, two fingers on his chin in a smug, pedantic pose. "It's completely distinctive. I'd know it anywhere. I couldn't be sure at first; maybe not smoking changed it a bit. But there's a special . . . timbre to it. As if every word you say is wrapped around a threat."

"You're the one doing all the talking," I said, just barely loud enough to carry across the room.

"Perfect!" he said, happily vindicated. "That's it. That's it, exactly."

S he always blamed me," he said, an hour and a half later. "And she would never tell me what I'd done wrong."

"When did that start?"

"I . . . don't know, exactly. It seems it was ever since she was a little girl. It was so . . . bizarre. I mean, I loved her so. She had to know that. No matter what she did, I always forgave her. The way she talked to me sometimes! My wife said I should put her over my knee, for being so disrespectful, but I never did, not once."

I didn't like the way his face morphed when he said "my wife," but my own face showed him nothing.

"She was in trouble all the time?" I guessed.

"*All* the time," he agreed, misery and mystery swirling in his voice. "She was smart; my goodness, was she smart. Her teachers said she could be anything she wanted, but she never applied herself, not to anything."

"She went to public school?"

"*And* private school. *And* a residential facility . . . for troubled teens. Nothing made a difference."

"That time I brought her back . . . ?"

"She just ran away again. Not from us, from that . . . program we sent her to. The last resort. When she ran from there, she just disappeared. Fifteen years old, you wouldn't think she would have the wherewithal to survive on her own."

"Why didn't you—?"

"What? Hire a man like you again? What good

would it do? Beryl made it clear that she was *not* going to stay with us. A lawyer told us we could have her locked up—have her declared a 'person in need of supervision,' I think he called it—but that would just mean a state facility instead of a private one."

"You never saw her again?"

"Oh, certainly I did. I'll never forget that day. It's an easy date to remember: nine, nine, ninety. Her eighteenth birthday. She drove right up to the house—the one in Westchester. Actually, I don't think she drove herself; I had the sense that someone gave her a ride, and was waiting for her outside."

"Did she—?"

"I asked her how had she managed to be on her own for all that time. She laughed at me. It was a nasty laugh. I can *still* hear it: 'You think I was the only one to run away that night, Daddy?'"

"I didn't know what she meant, and it must have shown in my face. She told me she ran away with one of her teachers. I hadn't heard—nobody told me about any such thing. She thought that was hilarious. 'She didn't run away from school, Daddy,' she said. 'She ran away from her husband.' "

He sat there, his expression stunned, as if hearing Beryl's words again.

"I couldn't . . . believe it for a minute," he finally said. "What my daughter was telling me."

"That she was gay?"

"No! I would never have cared about such a thing. Beryl knew that. We used to have very frank discussions. I talked to her about all the things I was supposed to: sex, drugs, drinking. . . . It wasn't that Beryl was gay, it was that she *wasn't,* do you understand?"

"She was just using that teacher to support her while she was on the run?"

"Yes," he said, his voice trembling at the memory. "Using her, that's right. And Beryl was proud of it, like it was a new game she had learned, and she was already the best at it."

"That's all she came to tell you?"

"No. That just came out," he said, looking down at his lap. "What she came all that way to tell me was that I was a spineless coward."

"Because . . . ?"

"I don't *know,*" Jeremy Preston said, wretchedly. "When I asked her what she was talking about, she just laughed that nasty little laugh of hers again."

Why are you really looking for her?" he asked, later.

"I ran across some information—more like a rumor, actually; I can't speak for its accuracy, considering the source—that she might be in danger. This was in the middle of another case, nothing to do with her. Or you. But I remembered her from that time when I brought her back. And I thought . . . I'm not sure what I thought. I guess I just wanted to be sure she was safe."

"So why did you come here with that story of yours?"

"She's changed her name," I said, flatly. "There's a lot of reasons people do that. But in my business it usually means they don't want the family's brand on them."

"You mean, you thought *I* was the reason?"

"No way to know," I said, shrugging my shoulders.

"I didn't know she changed her name. What does she call herself now?"

"Peta Bellingham," I told him, watching his face for a tell.

"What kind of name is that?" he said, almost angrily. "I mean, it doesn't connect to . . . anything I know."

"I can't tell you. Not yet, anyway."

"You thought I might know where she is . . . but that I wouldn't want to tell you?"

"Right. I thought she might be . . . aware of the situation. That the rumor I'd heard had some truth to it. I thought she might be staying underground until things got straightened out. Maybe staying with you, I don't know."

"You wanted to help her?"

"Yeah. Yeah, I did. I still do."

"Because . . . ?"

"I don't have a good answer for that one. Maybe I'm just chasing down things I did when I was young."

"Things you did wrong?"

"I don't know," I said. "I couldn't know that until I talk to her."

"Bringing her back to me!" he said suddenly. "*That's* what you thought you might have done wrong."

I didn't deny it.

"I don't know where she is," Jeremy Preston said. He stood up, paced in front of the cold fireplace for a minute, then turned to face me. "I don't know where she is," he repeated. "But I'll pay you to find her."

"Why?"

"Because I want the answer to your question, too, Mr. Burke. A lot more than you ever could."

*P*reston told me he met the woman who would become his wife when he'd been a student at Harvard—"That's right," he interrupted himself, sharply, as if I had challenged his words. When I didn't respond, he visibly relaxed, then went on again. All ponderous and pedantic, like a celebrity twit being interviewed.

"Those were tumultuous times. Not just Vietnam. The civil-rights movement, feminism, music . . . When they talk about a 'counterculture,' that's very accurate. I was a senior, my wife was a sophomore. At BU, just across the river. I met her at a teach-in. Later, she told me that she wanted to marry me from the minute I stood up and . . . well, made a little speech, I guess.

"We had an understanding. A contract, even. We weren't going to be dropouts, we were going to be . . . participants. Change-agents. Not by living on some commune, or marching in protests. It's all very well and good to talk about the inevitable rise of the proletariat, but we knew revolutions need financing to move forward, the same way a car needs gas.

"Her father brought me into his company, but I was never the son-in-law," he went on, as hyper-vigilant to attacks on his credentials as an abused child is to a subtle shift in a parent's voice tone. "I hadn't studied business in college—I don't think *anybody* studied business back then—but I had an aptitude for it, and it came to the surface quickly. Before I was thirty, I was virtually running the company. And when my father-in-law died—heart attack; he wasn't a man who ever listened to doctors—the segue was as natural as if I'd been groomed for the position since birth."

"But your wife was the actual owner? Is that what you meant earlier, when you said—?"

"That this was mine?" he said, sweeping his hand in a gesture meant to encompass the whole house. "Yes, that's exactly right. When we divorced, the prenup—I remember us laughing when I signed it: just a piece of paper her bourgeois father insisted upon, it was never going to matter to *us*—kicked in. There was never an issue of child support. Beryl had been gone quite a while, and she was no longer a minor, anyway."

"Beryl was an only child?"

"Yes," he said. "I wanted more kids. Especially later, when Beryl started to . . . act out. I thought, if she had a little brother or a little sister, it would be . . . I don't know, a good experience for her. For them both, I mean."

"Did she ever have a pet?" I asked. Remembering that she hadn't when her father had first come to me, wondering if they'd ever tried that.

"You mean, like a dog or a cat? No, my wife was highly allergic."

"She couldn't be around animals?"

"Well, she could tolerate them in small doses. Like when we visited a friend's house and they had a dog, she would pat it and everything. But to have one in the *house,* well, that would have been impossible for her."

I shifted position to show I was listening close, said, "You were still together when Beryl came back to visit you, that last time?"

"Together? We were still married, yes. But the life we planned for ourselves had already disappeared."

"You never got to be bankrollers?"

"Oh, we certainly did *that.* You wouldn't believe some of the people who were guests in our home. That was part of what we wanted from our . . . contributions, I suppose. For Beryl to be exposed to the finest thinkers of our generation. The best minds, the best causes. And she was. My wife and I funded some *major* initiatives. And plenty of them weren't tax-exempt, either."

"Did you attract government attention?"

"Oh, I'm sure we did. Everyone in our circle was under some form of surveillance—it came with the territory."

And made you feel like a real player, too, I thought, but kept it off my face.

"By the time Beryl was, oh, I don't know, maybe eight or nine years old, it seemed like the revolution was dying. You know, the Age of Reagan and all that. The country changed . . . and so did our . . . raison d'être, you might say. Oh, we still contributed—the Southern Poverty Law Center, for example—but we weren't dealing directly with the principals anymore. Instead of sitting around our living room, being in on the strategy, we were going to galas and writing checks.

"If you study history, you come to understand that everything changes in cycles. A wave crests, breaks, and the water is calm again. I knew, eventually, we would return to a time of . . . involvement, I suppose you'd call it."

Good fucking luck, I thought. But my expression told him I was paying attention to every word he spoke.

That's technique. Professionalism. And it's going out of style. If America is a nation of sheep, TV is the shepherd. Jurors think *CSI* is a documentary. They'll vote to acquit even when three witnesses saw the defendant shoot the victim, because there were no fingerprints on the recovered pistol—the one with checkered wood grips. Defense attorneys sum up in child-molestation cases by shrieking, "Where's the DNA?" at juries who just *know* every human contact leaves traces a lab can detect. After all, the TV told them so.

Cops get infected with the same virus. They overdose on *Law and Order* reruns and end up thinking they have to "win" every interview. It's not about the information anymore; it's about the repartee.

I don't care what side of the law you work: You *never* want to confront your subject while he's still talking. In fact, you don't want to interrupt him at all. Threats are for amateurs; verbal dueling is for fools. A pro knows there's no reason to get your man talking if you're not going to listen.

Good interrogation is like panning for gold. You let everything the other guy says pass through the mesh of your attention, encouraging him to keep it coming, knowing that the little nuggets won't be obvious until you're done sifting.

There's a rhythm to it. When the flow slows, you have to tap the right nerves to get it moving again.

"You don't think that Beryl . . . I don't know . . . felt let down when things changed around your home?" I probed. "When you stopped . . . participating so actively?"

"Beryl? She was hardly 'political' at that age. And, the truth is, she never seemed to care. Oh, she got along well enough with the people we had over, and she understood why her mother and father were so committed to social change. She knew racism was wrong. She knew Vietnam had been an ongoing war crime, perpetrated against innocent citizens. She knew about the grape boycotts. About apartheid. About . . . well, a whole *range* of progressive movements. And she seemed, if not enthusiastic, at least supportive. But it was never her passion.

"She had a wonderful collection of . . . mementos, I suppose you'd call them. Special little gifts that people who came to visit would bring to her." He gestured toward a chest-high shelf hung on two wrought-iron brackets, standing against the wall to his left. The shelf was crowded with small objects, a random sprinkling of wood, metal, and stone. I wasn't close enough to see more.

"She never took them with her," he said, sadly. "Even that last time."

"So when you and your wife stopped . . . ?"

"It was fine with Beryl," he said. "She had plenty of activities. Piano, dance, art lessons, horseback riding— I let her do anything she wanted to try. Except that karate. That was going just too far. I mean, we were all for young women growing up with self-confidence, but the only place she could have gone for classes was run by a man my wife said made her very nervous. People didn't talk about it back then, but we all knew some . . . pedophiles deliberately put themselves in a position to have access to children."

"Did you ever meet the guy?"

"Well, I did, actually. Beryl was just so insistent, and I could never really say no to her, so I drove over there myself one night. Frankly, I couldn't see what my wife had gotten so worked up about—the instructor seemed like a perfectly innocuous individual."

"Was he Asian?"

"That's right," Preston said, defensive again. "But that had nothing to do with my wife's decision, I assure you. His English wasn't all that . . . precise; I guess that would be an accurate assessment."

"He didn't try and sell you anything, then?"

"You mean for Beryl? No. In fact, he said he personally didn't teach the children's classes. But he did suggest I might want to study with him myself."

"You?"

"Yes. Do you find that so strange?"

"Not at all. I was just wondering if you listened to him."

"How do you mean?"

"The way you explained it to me when I first got here. How you've got a gift for—"

"I didn't say it was a gift," he cut me off, somewhere between aggressive and defensive again. "I said it was a technique, listening for qualities in a person's voice. And that I discovered I had some aptitude for it."

"Okay. So when you were talking to the sensei . . . ?"

He closed his eyes, going back there. I could *see* him listening then.

"No," he said, slowly, dragging out the syllable. "There wasn't anything there I would . . . mistrust."

"But your daughter never did go for lessons?"

"No. As I said, her mother was opposed. And she was entitled to her own instincts. I always respected that."

Are you still in touch with your wife? Your ex-wife, I mean?"

"She knows where I live. I know where she lives. That's about the extent of it. We're not enemies or anything, but there's really nothing left between us. Nothing to talk about."

"Where does she live?"

"In Virginia. Not too far from Washington, D.C."

"Did she ever remarry?"

"Not to my knowledge," he said, not faking his lack of interest. "But she could have, for all I know."

"Did she ever resume her maiden name?"

"Oh yes. Summerdale is her name now. Beryl Summerdale."

"Your daughter was named for—?"

"Yes," he said, adding a dash of unhappiness to his depression cocktail. "But she always had my name, too. Beryl Preston."

"Look," I told him, "all I wanted to do was to see if she's doing okay. Don't ask me why. Maybe I'm just getting older, and I wanted to . . . look back, see if I ever really accomplished anything back then."

"You don't do that sort of work anymore?"

"I . . . do. But not very much of it. I don't know if I could find her—"

"But you'll try?"

"Yeah. But if I do, she's an adult now. I'm not bringing her back."

"I understand," the gray man said. "I want the same thing you do, Mr. Burke. Just to know she's all right. That's worth something to me. It always has been."

I spent another couple of hours there. Half a dozen cups of coffee for Preston, another couple of hot chocolates for me. I kept panning until I was sure there wasn't another nugget in the riverbed.

He offered me money. I told him that if I *did* turn something up, it would be the same as last time: COD.

Darkness was dropping by the time I left. It didn't feel like city night to me. There wasn't a hint of menace in it. Softer, like a blanket of comfort.

I knew better than to trust it.

I knew how to run different programs in my head at the same time way before anyone heard of "multitasking." Any kid who's been tortured learns how to do it. You can call it splitting off. Or compartmentalizing. Dissociating, if that makes you happy. It all comes down to the same thing: not being there while it's happening. You watch them doing . . . whatever they want . . . to you, but you don't feel it.

Not physically, I mean.

Not every kid learns it the same way. Some learn it so good that pain loses all meaning. It just doesn't register. Prison guards call guys like that "anesthetics." When they go, they go. Clubs bounce off their heads; they wear mace like it was a coat of sweat; they pull stun-gun wires out of their bodies and strangle you with them.

You can't hurt them. It takes death to stop their pain.

Other kids split off for good. When it's happening to them, they're not there. It's not that they *go* somewhere else like the splitters do; they *are* someone else.

There's names for them, too.

I found another way. When it was happening, I watched it. Watched them, watched me. And in a little corner of my mind, a place they could never go, I was watching another movie, on a different screen.

That's where I found my religion, watching that other screen.

I prayed and prayed. No one answered, but I never lost faith. I *had* to believe my god was true. Because I knew, if there was no god for kids like me, if the real God was the one the people who beat me and raped me and hurt me for fun had pictures of in their houses, I was lost.

I was still trying to understand when Wesley found me.

We were both just kids, locked-up, powerless kids. But where I had fear, Wesley had hate. I cried; Wesley plotted.

One night, he showed me how to do it.

Years later, I finally had something to show him, too.

I had a family. One I made for myself. They chose me; I chose them. I wanted him with us. But it was too late for Wesley. He never came close to the campfire. He watched from the shadows until the day he checked out.

I know Wesley loved me, in the only way he could. When he crossed over, he left me the only thing that ever had meaning for him in life: a weapon.

I drove on autopilot, rerunning the session with Preston in my mind, looking for a loose thread to pull.

Beryl's mother wasn't hiding; she had a listed phone number. If I could just 411 her, Daniel Parks could have, too. A man like him would have exhausted every possibility before he ever went near the places where you could find a Charlie Jones.

But the CD Parks had given me hadn't had a single line of info about parents. He knew where *Peta* lived, where *Peta* kept her money, where *Peta* shopped. He had to have been close with her. Intimate, anyway— those nude photos of her didn't look commercial.

Daniel Parks had known a lot about Peta Bellingham. But he hadn't known Beryl Preston. Not even that she existed.

By the time I got the Plymouth docked and walked over to the flophouse, it was too late to do anything but check in with Mama.

"Gardens," she answered the payphone, the way she always does.

"It's me, Mama."

"Baby sister say you call her, okay?"

"Thanks."

"Sure."

I t's me, girl."

"You took your time," Michelle said, indignant without asking for my reasons.

"That's me," I said.

"Don't you be sarcastic with me, mister. I knew you'd be anxious to get what I had, that's all. And I didn't want to leave anything on a tape."

"Okay, honey. I'm sorry."

"My boy says his father wants to see you."

"Now?" That was plausible. A man who lives underground doesn't use a sundial.

"No. Tomorrow. In the afternoon."

"I'll be there."

"You'll pick me up first," she ordered.

"Two o'clock?"

"Very good," she said, back to being sweet-voiced. I'm not smart with women, but I wasn't stupid enough to tell her I had finally snapped to why she hadn't just left a message.

T he next morning, I dipped into my cache of dead-ended cell phones and dialed the number I had for Beryl's mother. Three rings, a click, then . . .

Sounds of a baby, gurgling happily. Laid over it, a woman's pleasant voice: "Hi. This is Elysse and her mommy. If you have a message for either of us, we'd love to hear it. Have a wonderful day."

Nothing so unusual—a lot of people think it's precious and special to have their kid record the outgoing message on the answering machine. But Beryl's mother had to be in her early fifties. And her father said Beryl had been an only child. . . .

A grandchild? *Beryl's* child, being raised by the mother? That happens. Girl finds herself pregnant, but can't find the father. Or doesn't know who he is. Or does, and wishes she didn't. So she comes home with the baby—"just until I get on my feet." Sooner or later, she makes tracks, leaving the baby for her mother to raise. Goes back to the life that put her in that trick bag to begin with.

If you think that only happens in ghettos, get yourself tested for cataracts. Rich folks may live on never-touching parallel tracks, but the same train runs on both of them. For some unwanted kids, there are "state homes." For others, boarding schools. Some humans dump their children on the grandparents. Some sell them.

If that baby was Beryl's, could Daniel Parks have been the father? Is that why he was diverting cash to her?

I went back to the CD, using the search function Clarence had shown me. Not even a hint that Beryl might have a child, much less that Parks might be the father.

Was Beryl Summerdale the mother *and* the daughter? Had Peta Bellingham just gone back home, with her child, and taken her mother's maiden name as her own? Hiding in plain sight, separating herself from whatever mess Daniel Parks had gotten himself into, waiting for it to blow over. Or for him to be blown away.

You got pals in D.C., don't you, honey?" I asked Michelle, on the trip up to Hunts Point.

"Good pals," she assured me.

"Good enough to lend a car to a stranger?"

"Oh, please," she said, waving away such pettiness. If Michelle called them *good* pals, they'd drive a man in a ski mask to the nearest bank . . . and wait outside, with the motor running.

"That's some outfit," I said, not lying. She was wearing a lilac business suit over a plum-colored silk blouse trimmed in black around the collar. Her ankle-strapped spike heels were the same color as the blouse. So were her nails. A jet-black pillbox hat with a half-veil completed the picture, and it was a box-office smash.

"Well, I'm glad *someone* noticed."

"Girl, how can you get on the Mole's case before he even gets a chance to drop the ball?"

"Why wait?" she said, grinning wickedly. "I know my man."

Michelle had brought a for-once/for-real spring day with her. The Mole's junkyard lanai was drenched with sun, transforming the random shards of metal and glass that surrounded the area into a glistening necklace.

"You look gorgeous, Mom," Terry told her, adroitly cuing his father, who *still* couldn't come up with the required compliment in time. Michelle generously settled for the blush that suffused the Mole's pasty skin.

The kid opened a laptop computer with a gigantic screen and fired it up, canting the screen so that I could see, blocking the sunlight with his shoulder.

The screen flashed too quickly for me to follow. A row of what looked like different-colored balloons popped up. Terry played the cursor over a red one and double-clicked. A photo snapped open, as clear as a movie-screen image.

A man in a dark overcoat, caught mid-stride moving down a sidewalk, a bulky briefcase in his right hand. A businessman, returning from a hard day?

"What's this?" I asked Terry.

"Hold up," he said, fingering the touchpad.

Another picture. The same man, just turning in to the front walkway of a house.

Click. Close-up of the house.

I'd seen it before.

In Briarwood.

"Got it?" Terry asked.

"Yeah."

"Okay . . ." He clicked again.

Close-up of a man carrying a briefcase. Three-quarter profile.

Charlie Jones.

"Are you sure he wasn't just—?"

Before I could say "visiting," Terry had clicked

again. This time, the man was standing on the front step, talking to someone whose back was to the camera. Click, click, click; each one a tighter close-up.

Charlie Jones.

"I never thought those camera phones could get anything like that," I said, impressed.

"They can't," Terry said, proudly. "But when Dad makes one . . ."

"You see?" Michelle said, preening.

"What's on the rest?" I asked Terry, indicating the unopened balloons on the screen.

"More of the same," he said. "He usually comes home from . . . well, from whatever he does, around two, three in the afternoon."

"When does he leave?"

"We didn't have infrared," the Mole said, answering my question. "You said you only needed—"

"Ah, this is perfect, brother."

The underground man blushed again.

*I*n New York, a new restaurant opens every seven minutes. Then Darwin takes over, and most disappear within a few months. But they keep coming, like a stampede off a rooftop.

Loyal was all pumped up about trying this Italian joint she'd heard about. It was on Ninth, in the Forties. Way too far to walk, especially in the high heels I've never seen her without. It was raining, so getting a cab was a crapshoot, and I didn't feel lucky.

"Is this *your* car?" she asked, looking around the

interior of the Plymouth like a girl who expected to find a baby-grand piano hidden in a tarpaper shack.

"One of them," I said. Then I gave her the whole restoration-hobby routine.

"It's nice," she pronounced. "Nice and big."

New York parking lots charge more per hour than some hookers, and they both end up doing the same thing to you. Loyal had a red vinyl raincoat and a little matching umbrella. It didn't really cover the both of us, but she insisted, molding herself against me as we walked the two blocks to the restaurant.

An olive-skinned woman in a black cocktail dress who'd spent way too much time on her hair tapped an open ledger book with a silver pen and looked at me expectantly. I was about to tell her we didn't have a reservation—it was only a few minutes past seven, and I could see a dozen empty tables in one glance—when Loyal said, "Lewis," as she squeezed my left arm with both hands.

A hatcheck girl took Loyal's raincoat, handed me the ticket and a half-wink.

"Bitch," Loyal said under her breath.

"She was just working me for a tip when we pick up the coat later."

"There's all kinds of tips," she said, grimly.

A guy in black pants, white shirt, and a black vest showed us to a table for four.

"Will you be joined by—?"

"Just us," I said. That's the way guys doing time spell "justice," but I didn't share that gem with him.

The waiter looked like he'd been betrayed, but manfully went on to recite a list of specials. Endlessly.

When he was done, Loyal gestured at me to go ahead, she was making up her mind.

I ordered shells and sauce, although they called it something else. Loyal had one of the specials, and a glass of red . . . although they called it something else.

"To drink?" the waiter said to me.

"Water, please."

"Perrier? Or—?"

"Just plain water."

"You want tap water?" he said, as if asking me to confirm I was too miserly to be at large.

"Unless you've got something cheaper," I said, smiling.

As soon as he was gone, Loyal leaned forward.

"You scared him, Lew."

"Me?"

"You scared him," she repeated. "And you scared me, too, a little bit."

"I didn't say—"

"You have an ugly smile," she said, very seriously. "Is that why you never use it?"

"That's a nice thing to say, with all the money I've invested in these teeth."

"You know what I mean," she said, hazel eyes steady on mine. "That was an ugly smile. And your voice was ugly, too."

"I guess that goes with being an actress. You pick up all these subtle little things that someone like me would never—"

"Be like that," she said, closing the subject.

My plate of shells was all-the-way tepid. The pasta was mushy, the sauce had no bite. Even the basil leaf was extra-limp. But maybe I was prejudiced.

"It's not that good?" Loyal said.

"I didn't come here for the food."

"You think I like food too much?" she said, archly.

"I like to watch you eat," I said, truthfully. Loyal didn't put away much food, ever, but when she enjoyed something, she let you know.

"You know why I love going out to eat so much?"

"Because you hate to cook?"

"I hate to cook for *myself,*" she corrected. "What fun is that? But I'm really a damn fine cook. Not fancy stuff," she said, hastily, "just regular food. Bacon and eggs, roast beef and potatoes, things like that. And I bake, too. Not cakes, pies. That's really my specialty."

"Do you scratch-bake?"

"I *do,*" she said, smiling widely. "Oh, I might cheat a little on the filling, but I never went near one of those crusts you can buy in a store."

"Sounds good."

"What kind of pie do you like, Lew? I'd love to bake one for you."

"Chocolate."

"*Chocolate?* What kind of a pie is that? Oh, you mean like chocolate-*cream* pie?"

"French-silk chocolate pie," I said, on sure culinary ground for once.

"Okay," she said, nodding gravely, as if confirming a suspicion.

Do you ever wonder about people working in places like this?" she asked, over her espresso cup.

"Restaurants?"

"Not in front, where you can see them. In the back. Doing the dirty work."

"You mean like illegals, working off the books?"

"Yes. I read in the paper this morning where they arrested a man in Queens for bringing in *dozens* of people from—I forget the exact country, but it was in South America, maybe?—and they had to work doing all kinds of terrible things for almost no money. They were all living in his basement, like pigs in a pen. It was disgusting. Like they were slaves."

"They were," I told her. "It's called debt bondage. They take out a loan to be smuggled here, then they have to work it off. That's all they do, work. Believe me, they pay 'rent' for that basement pen you're talking about. By the time they send a little money home—which is what they came here for in the first place—there's almost nothing left."

"How come the people who do them that way don't go to jail?"

"Sometimes they do, but not often. It's big business, supplying bodies for labor. There are contractors who'll find illegals for whatever you want done: picking crops, loading trucks, cleaning toilets. Guaranteed not to gripe about working conditions, complain about the pay, or join a union. They open their mouths, and they get shipped back across the border."

"But . . ."

"Anytime there's a big profit margin, you'll get people who want to play, Loyal. Going to jail, that's a business risk. And, in that business, not much of one."

"But they don't tell them, right?"

"I don't understand."

"The . . . workers. They don't *tell* them what's really going to happen once they get here, do they? I mean, they promise them all kinds of wonderful things, to get them to make the trip."

"Yeah, they do. How'd you know?"

"Because that happened to a girlfriend of mine," she said. "It almost happened to me, too."

*I*n the short time we were inside, the weather had changed again. It was warmer after dark than it had been all day, and the air smelled fresh after the rain.

"I could never do that," she said, as we stepped onto the sidewalk.

"What?"

"Not tip a waiter. I can't believe you did that."

"You think it was wrong?"

"Well," she said, taking my arm, "I don't think I'd go *that* far. But they all work for tips, don't they?"

"Yeah. And I gave him one that'll pay off a lot better than the few bucks I stiffed him out of."

"What do you mean, sugar?"

"He thinks tips are a percentage play, understand?"

"No, I don't!" she said, deliberately bumping me with her hip. She was looking up at me from under those impossibly long lashes, biting her lower lip.

"Don't use . . . language with me, Lew," she said, pleadingly. "I'm smart, but I don't talk the same way you do."

I drew in a shallow breath, thinking how right she was.

"Whoever schooled that waiter told him people always tip some set amount—in this town, most folks just double the tax and call it right. So he figures, if he embarrasses people into spending more money just to prove they're not cheap—"

"Oh! Like he tried to do with you?"

"Yeah. If he does that, the check for the meal will be bigger. And so will his tip. But that's not going to work all the time. And when it backfires, you get nothing. So if you do the math—"

"He comes out with less," she said, nodding in understanding.

"Right. Some people come to restaurants to be bullied by the waiters, true enough. But not *that* restaurant."

I paid the parking tab. Added a fin on top, since the car jockey had listened to my "Keep it ready, okay? Two hours." My Plymouth was right next to his booth, aimed out at the street.

I held the door open. Loyal sat behind the wheel for a second, then wiggled her way over to the passenger side.

"Have you ever been in one of those restaurants?" she asked, as I aimed the car at the West Side Highway. "Where people like to be bullied by the waiters?"

"I have."

"Did *you* like it?"

"I wasn't the one who had the reservations. I was the guest."

"So?" she said, not to be deterred.

"I never like it, little girl. I don't like it, period. Not when someone tries it on me, not when they try it on other people, either."

"I hate bullies, too," she said. "I always did."

Images flashed in my mind. Quicksilver fire, candle-points of pain in inky blackness. I closed them off.

"The last time I was in a big old car like this, I was in school," she said. "A boy I went out with, he was going to be a stock-car racer."

"Was his name Junior?"

"Don't be so smart," she said, reaching over to punch me on the upper arm. "His name was Holden. All the girls knew his trick."

"His trick?"

"I don't know what you call it in New York, but where I come from, if a boy had a special way he'd use to get a girl . . . to do stuff, we'd call it his trick."

"And Holden's was his car?"

"Not the car itself, the way he drove it. He'd take a girl out on the back roads and drive like the devil was in his rearview mirror. My girlfriend Rhonda told me he got her so scared she wet her pants."

"Maybe that was what—"

"Oh, just stop!" she said, punching me again. Harder. "I know what you mean, but that isn't what she was saying. She meant . . . you know."

"So you went out with him to show Rhonda he couldn't make *you* do that?"

"Well, maybe not *that*, exactly. But you're right, it was sort of that way."

"So what happened?"

"It was pretty much like Rhonda told it. Holden was a maniac, all right. A few times, I was just sure we were going to wreck. But it wasn't scary at all. I kind of liked it."

"You think Holden was disappointed?" I said, turning onto the highway, heading north.

"Oh, I *know* he was," she said, grinning.

*A*s we passed the Ninety-sixth Street turnoff, Loyal asked, "Where are we going, Lew?"

"It turned out to be a beautiful night. I thought you might want to take a little ride."

"I sure would. But where can you really 'ride' in this city?"

"Just be patient," I said.

"Watch me," she retorted, sticking out her tongue.

I paid the extortion to get onto the Henry Hudson, and finally got to let the Plymouth run a little on the Saw Mill River Parkway.

"Hmmm," Loyal said, as we shot past a big BMW sedan. "This thing feels like it's not even trying."

"Wait," I promised.

Another tollbooth allowed us to get to Yonkers. From there, it wasn't far to a narrow road that ran as jagged as a mid-attack EKG. The Plymouth had been there before, when I'd had to leave the area in a hurry—the big car acted like it remembered.

"Whooo-ee!" Loyal whooped, as I whipped around an S-curve in low gear and floored it just as I got the nose aimed right. The Roadrunner's xenon lights ripped blue-white holes in the blackness ahead. She flipped open her seat belt and slid over so she was jammed up against me, her left hand on my thigh to hold her in place.

I came off the back road into an underpass, hooked the entrance ramp, and charged onto the highway again, looking for an opening. It was there, and I had the Plymouth past the century mark in a finger-snap. We slipped off at the next exit, found the side road again, and went back to corner-carving. For a finale, I powered her through a full-sideways slide, making more noise than I needed to about it.

"Over there!" Loyal said, pointing to a side road as if we were being chased.

I nosed the Plymouth along cautiously. I knew she was a tiger on pavement—even wet pavement—with that Viper IRS under her, but I didn't want to try my luck on dirt. I spun the wheel hard left as I braked, then backed into a small clearing barely big enough to let us in.

"Oh, that was fine!" Loyal said, a little breathless. "I can see why you're putting money in this one, Lew"— patting the dashboard. "She's got a nice big butt under that shabby old skirt, doesn't she?"

"Surprised a lot of people with it, too," I agreed.

Loyal took a pack of cigarettes out of her little red purse.

"I'm a secret smoker," she said. "When I was in school, nice girls didn't smoke. But when I came to

New York, it seemed like the girls who knew what was going on, they *all* did. So I picked it up. Then, all of a sudden, it was, like, if you smoked, you were some kind of a degenerate. So I stopped. Only not really. And sometimes I just want one, you know?"

"I do," I said, taking the pack from her. I tapped out a pair of smokes, lit them both, handed her one.

*I*t's beautiful here," she said, later. "Even though you can't see the sky because of all those branches, you know the stars are out. It's that kind of night."

"It's beautiful here, all right. But it would be even if it was the middle of a rainstorm."

She moved against me. Just a tiny bit, more like a twitch than a snuggle.

"You know something else good girls didn't do?"

"Drink?"

"Yes. That and have sex in cars. Well, not have sex, even. Just be seen in a boy's car in certain spots outside of town. I did that once. Because I didn't know any better, I let this boy talk me into taking a ride, and we ended up parked in one of those places. He never did anything more than kiss me, but by the time Monday came around, it was like I was the Whore of Babylon."

"Your brother must not have cared for that."

"Oh my goodness, he did *not*. Speed went up to the boy that had been telling the story and asked him to fight. Well, the boy wasn't going to fight Speed, and Speed couldn't just up and start beating him. But Speed was so smart. He said something to the boy that made him *have* to fight."

"What was that?"

"Well . . ." She looked down at her lap. "He told the boy, 'I know you didn't do what you've been telling everybody you did. Because you can't bust a girl's cherry with your nose.' "

"I guess that would do it," I said, admiringly.

"Uh-huh. I was only fourteen then. It was right after that when Speed had that talk with me."

"He was a fine brother."

"He still is," she said. "And he'll always be."

You think I'm silly, don't you?" Loyal said. It was a little after midnight. I was lying on her bed, a pillow propped under my head. She was standing with her back to me, candlelight playing over her lush curves, holding a cigarette in her right hand.

"Because you only smoke in your house when you can open a window?"

"This is my whole stake," she said. "I can't do anything that might mess it up."

"I understand."

"No, you don't," she said, as she dropped her cigarette into a glass of water. She left the window open as she padded into the bathroom in her bare feet. I heard the toilet flush. Then the hiss of the lemon-scented aerosol can she kept on a little shelf next to the sink.

She brought the spray can back with her, gave the bedroom a liberal blast before she closed the window. She returned the can to its resting place and crawled back onto the bed. She stopped when she got as far as my knees, posing on all fours as if she couldn't make up her mind.

"I want to tell you something, okay?"

"Sure."

"Don't you want to know what?"

"When you tell me, I'll know."

She didn't move for a few seconds. Then she crawled the rest of the way toward me, gave me a soft kiss on the mouth, and curled herself into me, her cheek against my chest.

"Remember what I told you, about needing a place to stay for a couple of years?"

"Uh-huh."

"That was a lie," she said. "A little lie. But it's part of a lot of other ones."

I didn't say anything. My hand on her back didn't so much as flex.

She went quiet. I matched my breathing to hers, waiting.

"You know what I want?" she whispered.

"No."

"I know you're mad, Lew. I don't blame you. But I still want to do it."

"Do what?"

"Tell you the truth," she said.

I don't own this place," she said, as if confessing to a mortal sin. "I mean, I *do,* but I don't own it all."

It took her a solid minute to figure out that I wasn't going to be asking questions: I was the audience at a one-woman show.

"What I mean is, there's a mortgage on it. A big one. And it seems like every year the maintenance goes up, too. When I bought it, I used everything I had saved up just to make the down payment. And I had to get . . . someone . . . to lie for me about my income, too. The board here is very strict."

I moved my knuckle along her spine, just enough to tell her I was listening.

"For a long time, that worked out okay. I didn't have a job, not a real one, but I never missed a payment. It's all one payment here, every month. Your mortgage and your maintenance—the taxes are in there, too.

"But I haven't worked in . . . in a long time, Lew. If I sold this apartment tomorrow, I'd walk away with maybe two hundred, two hundred and fifty. And that's only because prices have gone up so much. So I have to gamble. I know the bubble's supposed to break, but that's what everyone said a couple of years ago, and the elevator still keeps climbing. I have to keep riding it, and jump off just before the cable snaps. That's what I meant about waiting another two or three years. But if I take out one of those home-equity loans to cover the maintenance, I'm never going to come out with the cash I need."

Time for me to participate. "So the plan is, you find another place to live, rent this one out, make enough to cover the mortgage and maintenance, build some more equity, and hope the co-op market keeps climbing?"

"That's right," she said, sounding as if she was ashamed of herself for such a devious scheme. "I could only rent to someone who the board approved, but that wouldn't be hard—other owners in the building have done it."

"Why couldn't you just do that, and use the money you get from renting this place to rent a smaller apartment? If you rented this one furnished, you could get a pile of money. If you're willing to live outside the city, it wouldn't cost all that much. Then, when you go back to work . . ."

"I'm not going back to work, Lew. Not ever again. The last job I was going to apply for changed all that."

"What was the last job?" I asked, shifting my weight slightly.

"You were," Loyal said, reaching down to cup me in her soft, warm little hand.

*I*t's all in there," she said, an hour later.

We were sitting at a café-style table that barely justified an ad that would someday read "eat-in kitchen." Loyal in a pink silk kimono, me in a white terry-cloth bathrobe that she'd given me when I got out of bed—a brand-new one, still in the original wrapper. She thrust an accordion file folder at me, as if I had demanded it, then folded her arms over her chest.

"What am I going to be looking at?"

"Everything. My bank account, my checking account, my mutual fund, my tax returns, the papers for the co-op . . ."

"I don't need to see any of this, Loyal."

"Don't you want to know if I'm telling the truth?"

"I always want to know if you're telling the truth."

"I haven't been."

"Like you said, the whole business about needing a place to stay, it wasn't exactly the lie of the century."

"You know what's not in there, Lew?"

"What?"

"How I earned my money. What I do for a living."

"That's not my business."

"No? Then how come you're so careful about condoms? Most men hate them."

"I don't want children," I said. A truth, with a lie at its heart—my vasectomy had taken that possibility off the table a long time ago.

She gave me a searcher's look.

"So if I told you I had my tubes tied . . . ?"

"I—"

"It wouldn't change anything," she said, cutting me off. "You don't know who I've been with, for one. And, for two, I could be lying. Plenty of girls who sleep with married men deliberately get pregnant, don't they? Maybe they want to force the man's hand. Or maybe it's just about collecting a fat child-support check every month. It could even be for blackmail."

"I suppose," I said, as if none of that had ever occurred to me.

"It doesn't matter," she said gravely. "I never had my tubes tied." She waited for a reaction. When none came, she went on, "And I never would," clasping her hands prayerfully. "I couldn't even have an abortion."

"You're Catholic?"

"No, no, no. I'm a . . . Well, I don't know *what* I am. Not that way, I mean. I was church-raised, but I haven't gone since I was last home. To say goodbye to my daddy. But that . . . other thing, it's got nothing to do with church. I wouldn't fault a woman for protecting herself, no matter what she had to do. I couldn't do it because . . ."

"Because . . . ?"

"Never mind," she said, moving her hands to her hips.

I nodded, accepting her judgment.

"That's it?" she said sharply.

"What are you—?"

"You just let me get away with that? What's wrong with you, Lew?"

"I don't under—"

"When a woman says, 'Never mind,' you're supposed to ask her again. At least once."

"Why?"

"To show you're *interested,* silly. Of course, if you're not . . ."

I wasn't *that* slow. "Sure I am, honey. I was just respecting your—"

She leaned forward, generous breasts threatening to spill out of the pink kimono. "That's my secret dream," she said, librarian-serious. "A baby of my own. When I was growing up, I never thought much about things like that. I never thought about a big church wedding, or having kids. I don't know when it got into me. Since I've been up here, I know. Someday, I'd love to have a little girl. I'd be a good mother. A real good one. And I could teach her things, too."

"It's a good dream, Loyal."

"It is," she said, closing her eyes for second. "I used to babysit all the time when I was in school. But it wasn't until I got out in the world that I understood what that takes. Not to have a baby—anyone could do that—to be a mother. I kept telling myself I wasn't ready. And the years kept on rolling, like a river that won't be dammed. You know?"

"Yeah."

"Remember, when we were having dinner, I told you about something that almost happened to me?"

"Your girlfriend? The one who went somewhere on a promise, and it turned out to be a trick?"

"A trick," she said, bitterly. "That's it, exactly."

S he wasn't my girlfriend, not like you'd say 'girlfriend' where I come from. Just another girl I knew, from the business."

It was like a game of chicken—the loser would be the first person to say "prostitute" out loud. It wasn't going to be me.

"I didn't come to New York to be in movies," Loyal said. "Nobody in their right mind does. I wanted to be on the stage. Not Shakespeare or Mamet, more like musical comedy. I can sing and dance, too. Not good enough to be the lead, and I'm way too short to be a Rockette, but I thought I could get chorus work."

"That didn't work out?"

She made a harsh sound in her throat, like a strangled laugh. "No. I did all the usual stuff girls like me do: went to a thousand auditions, waited on a thousand tables. I got little, little *tiny* parts. In off-off Broadway.

Plays that ran a weekend, and didn't cover my cab fare home.

"The first 'agent' I got didn't want to get me jobs; he wanted to get me. But I was expecting that, and all it cost me was time. I didn't get discouraged; I didn't think I was going to set the town on fire or anything. But I was hustling like a crazy woman just to put together the cash for head shots and audition tapes.

"That's when I started working as a B-girl. I told myself it was just like an acting job, sitting with men, listening to them go on and on. I threw down so many watered drinks, I spent half my time in the bathroom, I swear.

"After a couple of years, I'd had my fill. I'd been up here long enough so I could go home and tell folks I'd given it my best shot. I even had a couple of clippings I could show people, but . . ."

I stayed in my silence, waiting.

"Could you go in the living room?" she said.

I got up without a word. Walked over to the armchair, guided by the light spilling from the kitchen.

Time passed.

I heard sounds I couldn't identify, coming from the bedroom area but deeper, as if there was another room behind it.

Loyal stalked into the living room like a woman on business. "Here," she said, handing me a leather folder. The cover was soft, as if filled with foam. She walked behind me, turned on the lamp. My lap filled with frosted light.

"Go ahead," she said, still standing behind me.

It was a photo album. The first shot was black and

white, an eight-by-ten glossy. Loyal, in a straight chair, facing the camera head-on. She was wearing a short black skirt and a white blouse, black pumps on her feet, blonde hair pulled back into a bun. Each of her ankles was lashed to a leg of the chair. Her hands were behind her back. A white cloth was tied around her mouth, parting her lips.

"Keep going," she said from behind me. "I did."

The photographs were in some kind of sequence, telling Loyal's story. They went from ropes to duct tape, from cloth to ball gags, from fully dressed to partially, then not. The last one had Loyal on her knees, facing a wall, naked. You couldn't see her face. Her wrists were handcuffed behind her back, her ankles were bound together, and a single chain linked the two.

When I was finished, I closed the book.

Loyal turned off the light behind me.

"Say something," she said.

"You're a good actress."

"What does that mean, Lew? What are you trying to say?"

"Just that. In the earlier pictures, when they came in close on your face, you looked like a damsel in distress."

"What does that mean?" she said again, her voice tightening down to braided wire.

"You looked terrified," I said. "Like the villain had tied you up, and your only hope was that Dudley Do-Right was going to ride in and rescue you."

"That wasn't acting," she said, putting her hands on my shoulders.

*T*hey really do it," she said, standing by the window in the living room, this time facing me. "Tie you up, I mean. The first time I . . . modeled, I thought it was all fake. Like it would be Velcro or something. But it wasn't."

"So you were afraid of . . . what, exactly?"

"I don't know," she said, blowing a stream of smoke out the opened window. "Being . . . helpless, I guess. Not in control. They loved that. I had the 'look.' So I had all the work I wanted."

"Why did you stop, then?"

"Did you ever look into a fireplace when it's working? Well, that's what it was like. If you start a fire, you either feed it, or you watch it go out. Do you have any idea of what I'm telling you, Lew?"

I flashed on a not-so-young-anymore girl I'd met in Los Angeles years ago. I'd been out there looking for a photographer who took crime-in-progress pictures for money. He knew I was looking, and he'd gone to ground. I'd gotten the girl's name from someone who told me that she might have an address for him. And that she'd be stupid enough to give it up, if I worked her right.

That girl hadn't been stupid. Just sad. All done, and she knew it.

When you're fresh stuff out here, they may not treat you like a little princess, but they don't . . . torture you, you know? But every video you shoot takes a little of the bloom off you. One year, you're getting a thousand bucks for naughty schoolgirl—and I was never the lead, okay?—the next, they expect you to take some rough stuff for less money, and do it more often. And if you do that? Another year and you're down to double anals and gang bangs. After that, it gets really disgusting.

"A real good idea," I said to Loyal.

She took my tone for truth, shifted her own to one less challenging. "It's like with my apartment," she said. "I knew I had to get off the elevator before it started going down."

"They asked you to—"

"I wasn't looking at myself. Just sleepwalking through it. But I was sliding. It started with girl-girl. Not sex—they never even asked me to do that—but there'd be another girl in the pictures. Like she was the one who tied me up. Maybe I wasn't raised on the fast track, but I could feel the heat when I got close enough to the fire."

"You're not the first actress to do that kind of modeling, early in her career."

"If that was all I'd done, I could see what I want to see when I look in the mirror."

"I don't see that when I look, either," I said. "I don't know anybody who does, all the time." That wasn't the truth. I'd done time with glistening psychopaths whose self-worship was the sum total of their existence. But that was Burke, not the man she knew.

"Yes," she said absently. She gutted her cigarette. I waited while she did her full-disposal routine in the bathroom.

"All the time I was . . . modeling, I had been trying

out for parts. But I was getting used up there, too. Like I was disappearing. And the less of me there was, the less I felt I could go home."

"So you stayed. . . ."

"Until now. Yes. But I didn't just quit modeling, I quit trying to work, too."

"How could you do that and—?"

"—still afford a place like this? You know the answer to that, Lew. I'm a toy. A pet. A rich man's life-size doll. I've had four of them since I left off working. You were going to be the fifth. That day we met? I wasn't shopping for cars."

I don't know why I told you all that," she said, as the green numbers on her alarm clock blinked 4:09. "I know how it makes me look. You know, I used to be able to lead boys around by the *nose*. All I had to do was take a deep breath, wiggle a little, and talk baby talk. I never had to . . . do what I told you to pay the rent, or keep food on the table.

"I wasn't addicted to drugs, I wasn't . . . I didn't have any excuse, not really. I was just ashamed to go home. Not because of anything I did, but because I wouldn't have anything to show for it. Can you understand that, Lew?"

"Yeah. Yeah, I can. And when you go now, after you sell your apartment, you'll have been a hardworking actress who saved her money."

"I sure will. I'll be able to fix up the house so it's one of the nicest ones around. Have a swell car. Maybe even . . ."

"Meet a guy?"

"I . . . don't know about that," she said, letting me in on a conversation she must have had with herself a hundred times. "Here's what I do know: I can't go back home just to be getting a job in some store. I need to come back with enough money to live right, so people know I made something of myself while I was away, be proud of me for it. It wouldn't take a fortune for me to be somebody back home. I just don't want to be a fraud."

I touched the vertebrae at the base of her neck. She made a little moaning sound that didn't have a trace of fake in it.

"It looks like you're staying the night, for once," she said, reaching for me.

L oyal slept with her face buried so deep in the pillow I couldn't see how she got a breath, but her rib cage moved rhythmically as I punched in a number on my cell. I stepped into the living room and waited for the call to be answered.

"Gardens."

"It's me, Mama. Can you find the Prof, ask him to meet me, anytime this afternoon?"

"Twelve hours?" Mama said, making sure.

"Perfect."

"Max, too?"

"No, I won't need—"

"Yes," she said, hanging up.

Y ou don't take coffee even in the morning?" Loyal asked me. We were back at her kitchen table. She was bustling around, wearing a pair of baggy gray shorts and matching jersey top. I was just sitting still, stealing glances at my watch. Almost ten in the morning.

"Well, you have to have something in your stomach to start the day," she said, firmly. "At least let me make you some toast."

"That would be great."

"And have some juice, too. I've got . . ." She bent at the waist to look in the refrigerator.

"You keep juice on the bottom shelf?"

"Oh, you!" she said, turning over her shoulder to smile at me. "You know all a girl's tricks, don't you?"

"Not even close," I said, as much truth as I'd ever told in three words.

"Well, you sure know what a girl likes."

I chuckled. Said, "Even I know *that* trick."

"Hmmpf!" she said, turning around, hands on hips, face glowing with mock annoyance.

"Come here for a minute, girl."

She took that as a request to sit on my lap.

"What?" she said, innocently.

"Remember last night? You were telling me about how you almost got into real trouble. A girlfriend of yours went somewhere. . . ."

"Oh! That's right, I was. I forgot. You really want to know about that?"

"Yeah, I do."

She squirmed around in my lap. Not playing, getting

comfortable. "I never thought I was better than anyone else," she said, her tone telling me it was very important to her that I believe her. "I met a lot of girls like me. Not just when I was . . . modeling. When I worked in bars, too. And went on casting calls, of course. I was kind of in the middle of them. Not one of those dreamy-eyed ones who believe they're going to be 'discovered' someday, and not one of those who believe you have to put out for producers if you ever want to get a part, either.

"You know how they say there's lines you shouldn't ever cross? Well, I found out that those lines move. Right in front of your eyes. Even if they don't move for you, they move for your *judgments*. Do you see what I'm saying, Lew?"

"What you might have once thought was . . . wrong, or whatever, you learned that there might be good reasons for it."

"Yes! I may be very old-fashioned. I guess I'm even country in my heart. But, to me, there's always going to be a difference between a woman who sells herself for money to buy a fur coat, and one who does it to keep a roof over her kids' heads."

"And before you came to this city, you would have thought the same of both, that's what you're saying?"

"That *is* what I'm saying. It's easy to point the Bible at folks like you're aiming a gun, but it's just a book, isn't it? Everybody who reads it comes away with whatever they bring to it. So it wasn't going to be me casting that first stone."

"Right," I said, squeezing her waist slightly to underline my approval.

She took a deep breath. Let it out slowly. Then she

stood up, went to the sink, and drew herself a glass of tap water.

"The job was what they called being an 'entertainment hostess.' Like a B-girl, but very, very high-class. It was a six-week contract, working for this club. They paid for everything: plane fare, your hotel room, meals, the works. And you came back with thirty thousand dollars. In cash, no taxes."

"Where was this, Tokyo?"

She gave me a long, measured look. "Yes, that's right. How did you know?"

"Just a guess."

"Uh-huh. Then I bet you could guess the rest of the story, too."

"I might. When your girlfriend got there, they took her passport away. And her visa. That was to make sure she fulfilled her contract, they told her. And they told her she'd misinterpreted what they meant by 'entertainment,' too."

"I'm not sure about that last part," Loyal said. "I mean, about them fooling her. Lace—that's what she called herself—she was . . . I'm not going to call names, but I think she might have known what she was going to have to do. What she didn't know was that she wouldn't have any choices. It wasn't one man. Or even one man a night. By the time they allowed her to leave, it wasn't even one man at a *time*. When they let her go, they took most of the money away from her, too."

"She told you this when she came back?"

"Yes. I told her she should report it. To the UN or something, I don't know. I mean, Japan, that's not someplace where they don't have laws. It's a very civilized country. And we do all kinds of business with them, don't we?"

"All kinds," I agreed.

"Lace said she was mad, but she wasn't crazy. 'They've got different rules for whores,' is what she told me. It made me sick."

"I don't think you were lucky, girl."

"What do you mean?" she said, frowning.

"It wasn't luck that kept you from going over there. You were either too smart or too scared."

"Scared."

"When it comes to an offer like that, one's as good as the other."

She came back over to me, threw one leg over mine, and sat down on my lap again, this time facing me.

"I told you a lot of truth, these last few hours."

"I know."

"Yes. I think you do. I think you *do* know it was the truth." She bounced slightly, as if she were making up her mind what to do next.

"What?" I said.

"How about you tell me some truth, Lew?"

"What truth would you like, girl?"

She leaned in so close I lost focus on everything but her eyes. "Tell me why you pretend you're married," she said, very softly.

I don't like it," the Prof said. "You never get too brave around another man's cave, because . . . ?"

"That's the quickest ticket to an early grave." I finished the rule, to show I hadn't forgotten the first time he'd taught it to me, eons ago.

"You want to trap a weasel, you don't look for his den," the little man rolled on, unmoved. "What you do is, you set a trap in a chicken coop. You don't need to know where a man lives . . . ?"

"To know where he's going to visit," I said. "I know, Prof. But we've got no way to put the watch on Charlie, not in that neighborhood."

"My main man Mole—"

"He got us the pictures, sure. But that was because he knows people who live around there. They weren't watching for Charlie special; they just snapped off a shot when they ran across him."

"What'd they take the pictures with?" he asked. From the way he turned toward Clarence, I knew the old man wanted to make sure his audience was in place before he hit me with a jab.

"One of those camera phones," I said, playing along.

"Camera *phone,* you said, Schoolboy?"

"I get it, Prof. But it's not that simple. Who do they call? They don't know us. And the Mole doesn't *want* them to know us. But let's say he could get them to just ring a number when Charlie was in the street. Where are we going to be sitting in ambush? There's no hotel close by. No poolrooms or gin joints we could hang out in. Not even a lousy OTB. And we could never rent a house in that neighborhood. So?"

"If my father—" Clarence started to say.

"Nah," the Prof cut him off. "I never said Burke was wrong, just that I didn't like it. We're done, son."

Max tapped the face of his watch, shook his head in disapproval.

"You, too?" I gestured. "We only get one chance, right?" I said to them all, holding up one finger. "And, from what Mole's people told him, the window only opens at certain hours," I went on, my hands saying the words to Max. "So there's only one way I can see to make our move."

The next morning, I woke up thinking about Loyal. That hadn't happened to me before. I guess I stopped thinking of her as a party girl the minute she told me she was always afraid of ending up as one.

The newspaper had a make-you-retch story. Cop arrested for rape and sodomy. Too many counts to list, over too many years, because the victims were his daughters. The Queens DA put out the red carpet for the poor guy. They let him surrender himself at the courthouse, arraigned him in seconds, and cut him loose on his own recognizance, no bail. The paper said the DA wouldn't identify the cop, because they wanted to "protect the alleged victims." Nice.

At your age, this is supposed to be an *annual* examination," my doctor said. He's very tall for a Chinese man, good-looking enough to be a movie star, and a magazine survey I read last year said he was one of the top urologists in New York. With all that, his office is still down on Canal Street, his prices haven't changed, and his receptionist still blinks when I tell her I'm a patient, not a salesman. Or a cop.

"Sorry," I said, lamely.

"The outcome for prostate cancer is directly related to early detection," he said, for at least the fifth time since I'd been coming there.

"I know," I mumbled, holding up my hands in surrender.

"The lab is right around the corner, on Mott Street," he said, unyielding. "This time, you *call* for the results, all right? The PSA test isn't a perfect indicator, but it's the best lab screen we have now. Last time"—he glanced down at my folder—"you got the test, but you never called for the results."

"Sorry," I said again. "What were they?"

"Three point seven," he said. "That's not a cause for concern, but anything over four is something we would want to follow closely."

"Sure."

"We would call *you,* but the number on your file never seems to be up-to-date."

"I move around a lot."

"Yes. Well, we don't," he said, sternly. "We're right here. And our number hasn't changed."

*T*he blood lab on Mott Street had the decor of the waiting room at a Greyhound terminal. I was the only non-Asian in the place. The Oriental flower at the receptionist's desk took the paper I handed her, pointed at a row of plastic chairs, said, "Few minutes, okay?"

I settled in for the duration, but it turned out the girl was telling the truth. My phlebotomist was a burly Hispanic, with stress-pattern baldness. He wrapped a piece of rubber tubing around my arm faster than a junkie who hadn't fixed in days, tapped the crook of my elbow to bring up a vein, slid the needle home.

"How many of these you do a day?" I asked him.

"Many, many," he said, sliding out the needle and slipping a cotton ball over the entry wound in one motion.

As I left, I saw a sex worker waiting to be tested, a young-bodied, older-faced woman in jeans and a too-small stretch top. If she got the same blood-taker I'd had, she'd learn the real meaning of "quickie."

*B*y the time I climbed off the F train at the Van Wyck/Briarwood stop, spring had arrived, a light rain misting the streets. I walked over to the small branch library just off Queens Boulevard, spotted the Prof sitting on the steps enjoying a leisurely smoke, and strolled on past. I boxed the corner, crossed the boulevard, and set off to find the middleman.

I wore a brown leather jacket that I had picked out of a Goodwill bin, leaving a brand-new nylon one in its place. I hadn't been looking for a bargain; I wanted something I might have to leave at the scene. Something with enough random DNA on it to confuse the hounds. A white jersey cable-knit, dark-green corduroy pants, scuffed brown work boots. In the pockets of the jacket, a pair of deerskin gloves and an orange wool watch cap.

No gun, no knife, no brass knuckles. I was coming in peace.

Charlie's street was quiet, but it was time-of-day quiet, not the *peligroso* silence that falls in some neighborhoods whenever a stranger walks through. The kids were home from school—playing on their computers, not in the street. Working parents weren't back yet; retirees were watching whichever one of the endless parade of "court" shows was on at the time.

It wasn't the kind of neighborhood where you'd find basketball hoops nailed to telephone poles, or dogs running wild, but it still throbbed with the muted rhythms of life behind the well-maintained façades.

Charlie's house was a stone-and-stucco job that looked vaguely British to me. Maybe it was the ivy that trellis-climbed on one side, or the small windows broken into even smaller rectangles by the copper-colored panes.

I went up to the front door like I was expected, pushed the little white button nestled inside a silver filigree, and stepped back slightly, hands clasped in front.

"Hello?" the woman said. She was medium height, with thick raven hair pulled back into a single plait, wearing a plain blue dress that was too good a match for her eyes to be off-the-rack. Her smile was open and friendly, showing perfect teeth. I figured her for somewhere in her thirties; would have laid good odds she'd been a swimsuit model or a pageant contestant earlier on.

Was Charlie playing the Benny Siegel role so heavy he got himself a gorgeous Sabra to flesh out the skeleton? I wondered, but I just bowed slightly, said, "Good afternoon, young lady. My name is Kolchan. Meyer Kolchan. I was hoping I could have a quick word with Benjamin. . . ."

"Yes, sure," she said, smiling again, some kind of Slavic accent in her voice. Not an Israeli, then. "Ben?" she called out, sweetly. "Mr. Kolchan is here to see you. Can you—?"

Charlie Jones stepped past her, grinning. "Go fix supper, woman!" he said, mock-commanding, giving her a swat on the bottom as she turned away, giggling.

"What can I—?" he started to say. Then he saw my face.

No," he said, very softly.

"It isn't what you think," I said, not moving from my spot, radiating calm out to him. "I just needed to ask you a question, and I didn't know where else to reach you."

He looked over my shoulder, expecting . . . I don't know what.

"One question," I said. "Then I'll—"

"Pick a place," he said, his voice so tight it vibrated like a tuning fork. "Pick a time. I'll be there. Set it up any way you want. Please! Just don't—"

"You know the plaza next to Penn Station, on the Eighth Avenue side?"

"Yes."

"Say, eleven tomorrow morning?"

"Yes. Yes, I'll be there, okay?"

"Don't ruin a good thing by being cute, Benny."

He looked at me the way a steer in the killing funnel looks at the rifleman waiting at the end: a stare of dull, helpless hatred. I turned my back on him and started for the subway.

I was about twenty minutes into my meandering half-hour walk when a dark-blue commercial van with tinted windows pulled over to the curb ahead of me. The back doors opened and two men jumped out. I didn't have to see the tracksuits to know who they were.

The smaller one was a mongoose. He circled behind me, looking for the back of my neck. The big one plowed straight ahead, a charging bull. I glanced over my shoulder. The mongoose was holding what looked like an oversized plastic automatic—*Taser!* screamed in my head. The bull had his hands spread wide, like we were going to do Greco-Roman. I spun to my right to give them a visual of me running, planted my right foot, torqued hard, and rushed the big one.

I registered a broad face and a flattened nose just before we closed. As he wrapped thick arms around me, my steel-toed boot shattered his right ankle. He grunted in pain and locked on, trying to take me to the ground with him. I drove my inside forearm against his chest, jammed my right hand under his chin, and *snapped* my wrist as I forked my two front fingers past his nose into his eyes. He shrieked, grabbed at his face, and let go.

I spun to face the mongoose. He danced, looking for

the exposed flesh his weapon needed to work. I X-ed my jacketed forearms over my face and ran at him. He stepped back, surprised, and I caught him with a side kick to the thigh. I rolled with the kick and took off running.

I dashed across two lawns, looking for a back yard. Heard shouting behind me, but no shots. Cold comfort—I hadn't heard shots when they'd snuffed out Daniel Parks, either.

I ran through some back yards and pulled myself over a wooden fence, hoping there was no dog on the other side and cursing Daylight Saving Time.

I made it to the street, scanned the area. Looked clear, but I figured by then the locals were lighting up the 911 switchboard. I turned a corner, pulled off the leather jacket, and dropped it on the ground. I put on the gloves and the orange watch cap, then walked down the sidewalk until I hit the apex of a triangle— Clarence in his Rover at one point, the subway back to Manhattan at the other.

I couldn't see the blue van, but I couldn't be sure it hadn't seen me, so I chose the subway.

I looked over my shoulder as I swiped my Metrocard. Nothing. Down on the platform, I spotted a battered payphone, but the Manhattan-bound train was pulling in. No time.

Two stops later, I got out at Continental Avenue, slipping into the heavy foot-traffic that's always there at that hour. I crossed over to the cab stand, told the driver I wanted the Delta terminal at La Guardia.

At La Guardia, I dropped the gloves in a garbage

can, used an alcohol wipe to clean the congealed eye-ball fluid off my right forefinger in the men's room, and left the watch cap in a stall.

Plenty of working payphones there. I rang Clarence's cell.

"I'm out," I said.

"Saw you drop down, mahn."

I waited my turn on the airport cab line, then rode a Crown Vic with bad shocks to Broadway and Seventy-fifth, just north of what guys my age still call Needle Park. If the cabbie wondered about my lack of luggage, he kept it to himself. Or maybe he intuited that I wasn't fluent in Senegalese.

I walked over to the 1/9 line, and used my Metro-card one more time.

When violence erupts at me, the same thing al-ways happens. A tiny white dot lasers in my brain, bathing the world in a blue-edged light. I watch myself move through that blue-edged light, like a man underwater, everything so very *slow*.

Later, I can play it back, like a stored VCR tape.

Over and over again.

What I can never do is erase it.

Max tapped his temple, raised his eyebrows in a question.

"No," I told him, shaking my head. "I didn't think." The Mongol nodded approval. The foundation to all his teaching is replacement of instinct. That viperstrike he'd taught me is really an escape move; it can't be thrown from a distance. You have to give your enemy a grip on you to make it work, and that goes against every instinct . . . especially mine.

I'd been a boxer in prison—one of the Prof's endless schemes. It didn't require me to actually win any fights to pay benefits. As a fighter, I was what they used to call "pretty." Slick and smooth. Very fast hands. I didn't have one-shot KO power, but I threw cutter's punches, and I was a good finisher.

I always had plenty of backers, because, even with all my speed, I was never a runner—I stayed in the kitchen and traded. There was never a lot of money on me to win—they don't pay too much attention to weight classes Inside, and I was usually matched against bigger guys—but I was an ace at going the distance, even against the hardest bangers.

"Fighting's the same as friendship, Schoolboy," the Prof told me. "The best ones always try to give a little more than they take."

When I got out the first time, it took Max about ten minutes to show me I was never going to make a living with gloves on my fists. At first, we sparred a lot. Me trying to hit him, him watching me try. Once he had me dialed in, he worked with what he had. No more boxing, no more rules.

> *Surprise is speed*
> *Speed is power*
> *Thinking is slow*
> *Slow is weak*

I'd been ready for the two men who'd jumped out of the van. Been ready for a long time.

"It was a snatch," I said out loud, gesturing to include Max. "If they'd wanted to shoot me, I was an easy target."

"Didn't even need all that noise and nonsense," the Prof agreed. "They could have done you just the same way they did that boy who was gonna hire you."

"Yeah," I said, slowly. In our world, we know that there's no such thing as the "precision beatings" you see gangsters order in the movies. Violence isn't surgery: You send a couple of men out to break a guy's legs, the guy struggles, the bat slips, and, just like that, the beating's a homicide.

There's a thousand ways that can happen. You can't order a pre-beating medical report on a target, like those degenerate doctors who worked in Southern prison farms used to do, telling the torture-loving guards whether it was safe to keep whipping. One punch can do the trick. All it takes is a heart condition you didn't know about. Or an eggshell skull.

"It was a capture, not a kill," I said. "They wanted to talk to me, all right."

"I was in position the whole time," Clarence said. "There was nothing like a blue van by the subway."

"You said you saw me go down there?"

"Oh yes, mahn. As soon as I spotted the orange cap, I knew something had gone wrong. But you were moving nice, and I didn't see anyone interested in you."

"I had your back all the way to the hack, Schoolboy," the Prof said.

"You were in the subway?"

"The Invisible Man," the Prof chuckled. That's what he calls himself when he's dressed as a foot soldier in the Vagrancy Corps. The ankle-length coat he always wore was big enough for three of him, and they only have metal detectors in the subways on special occasions.

"They came *awfully* quick," Michelle said, grim-faced.

"It don't take a lot of time to drop a dime," the Prof told her.

"Could they have followed you, mahn?"

"How?" I asked Clarence. "From where? Starting when?"

"That clue is true," the Prof agreed. "Only way that works is if Burke was spotted same time they took out that rich guy, and followed him, right? Come on! That was so, they already passed up a hundred better shots than the one they took."

"They don't have anything," I said, checking my voice to make certain I wasn't graveyard-whistling. "That night, they never saw where I came from, or where I went. And all Charlie's got for me is a phone number."

"He's got something else," the Prof said.

"What?"

"He knows where you're going to be tomorrow morning, son. Time and place leaves him holding an ace."

"You think he'll show, then?"

"*Got* to, honeyboy. He knows where you'll be one time, sure. But we, we know where he *lives*."

*T*he flower boxes outside Penn Station were pure New York: thick concrete tubs surrounding death-brown evergreens, with spikes all along the border to prevent panhandlers from finding a seat between engagements.

I crossed Thirty-third Street to the plaza, where they get a different class of visitor, and sitting is encouraged. I took the place up on its invitation, looked around casually. After dark, this place would be a skateboarder's paradise. The broad expanse of flat surfaces would magnet the graffiti taggers, too. In another hour or so, the place would be crowded with office workers eating pushcart lunches, eyeing one another like it was a singles bar. But now it was all business.

A scrawny Caucasian in a white mesh jacket with a neck tattoo I couldn't read at the distance was performing an elaborate set of hand gestures. It looked like he wasn't having any luck persuading his audience, a big-headed black man in a hugely oversized basketball jersey, red and white, with number 23 on the back.

A flushed-faced man in some kind of green maintenance uniform stared openly at a reddish-brown man sporting an American flag do-rag, trying to make up his mind.

A black pigeon with a perfect circle of white on its head patrolled the grounds, treasure-hunting. A flock of tiny brown birds with pale undersides surrounded me, asking me to slip them something before the pigeon mob caught wise. I crumpled a piece of bagel in my fist, flicked the crumbs behind me. The little birds hit like a flight of locusts.

I didn't have to glance at my watch to know I was early. The group of Chinese teenagers catty-corner from me had been there since at least midnight. Or maybe they were handling it in shifts. I couldn't even tell how many of them there were, the way they kept drifting together, then pulling apart to float around the perimeter. They were all wearing shiny fingertip black leather jackets over goldenrod silk shirts buttoned to the throat, their obsidian hair greased into high pompadours.

The gang kids all worked for Bobby Sun, but Max had some sort of treaty with his crew, the Blood Shadows. They left the restaurant—and my personal parking space in the alley behind it—alone, and Max left them alone. But there was more to it than a nonaggression pact. Some of those empty-eyed killer children worshiped Max in a way they couldn't have explained and didn't understand . . . but trusted with all of their life-taking lives.

Anyone who moved on me in that plaza would be Swiss cheese.

Clarence posed against the entrance, resplendent in a bottle-green jacket with wide lapels and exaggerated shoulder pads, a white felt hat shielding his eyes. Charlie had never met Clarence, but he knew the Prof, who was being invisible somewhere close by. Max stood right in the center of the plaza, arms crossed. He looked as if he had sprouted from the cement, still as a statue except for his eyes, which were swiveling like a pair of tank turrets.

Clarence left his post, started a slow strut around the plaza, hands in his pockets. He looked like a peacock, hoping to audition some new hens. But he was really a coursing hound, and the under-clothes bulges he was looking for weren't female curves.

I watched as a dark-blue BMW coupe slowly drove by. It had been circling the block since before I arrived, passing by irregularly, depending on traffic. If I hadn't been looking for it, I never would have noticed. Michelle.

Nobody could miss the mammoth old Buick four-door, though. Originally painted egg-yolk yellow, years of never seeing a garage had faded the rolling hulk to fish-belly white, with a rust-red roof. The Blood Shadows' war wagon, far out of its territory, orbiting like the mother ship, ready to take everyone home when it got the signal.

Still no men in tracksuits. No blue van.

And there was Charlie Jones, walking toward me, making sure I saw him coming.

Here," I said, as he sat down next to me, "put this on."

"What for?" he asked, voice quavering as he looked down at the red baseball cap with a white bill I was holding in my lap.

"It's to make you easy to pick out, Charlie."

"Pick out? For who?"

"Who do you think I got your address from, Charlie?" I wanted him to hear his own name coming out of my mouth. Over and over again.

"I don't . . ."

"Yeah, you do," I told him. "You're a very smart guy, Charlie. You've been fishing in the whisper-stream for so long, you know what to keep and what to throw back."

"So you *didn't* die," he said. Like he'd just won a big bet but the bookie wouldn't pay off.

"We don't die, Charlie. None of us. We just come back looking different. You won't know my brother if you ever see him again, either."

"Your . . . ?"

"Put the cap on, Charlie," I said. "You wouldn't want Wesley to hit some citizen by mistake, would you?"

*I*t took him a while to put the cap on his head—his hands were shaking so badly, he dropped it the first time he tried.

"How long have you known?" he finally asked.

"Years and years," I assured him.

"So why now? What did I—?"

"That last job you had for me . . ."

"Yeah?"

"The guy who was going to hire me stepped out to get something from his car. He got gunned down on the way. It was in the papers."

Charlie shrugged, saying it all.

"What I don't know, Charlie," I continued, "is whether the shooters want to clean house. My house."

"I don't do names," he said, a little strength coming into his voice. "You know that, Burke." Saying *my* name, reminding me how far back we went, how long his own reputation stretched.

"The dead guy, his name was Daniel Parks."

Charlie just shrugged again.

"He was looking for someone. Someone he wanted me to find. Maybe the shooters were looking for that person, too."

"All I had for that guy was the number I gave you to call," he said. "That's all I ever have."

"That does sound like you, Charlie. It even sounds like the truth. There's only one problem, okay? I'm on my way back from your house yesterday and this van pulls up. Out pops some guys dressed like the ones who killed the guy you sent to me. And they try and snatch me, right there on the street. I can't quite see that as a coincidence. Maybe you can help me out here?"

He went stone-still for a second. Then a tremor shot through his body like a current. His face looked as if a vampire was clamped to his jugular.

"Galya," he said, barely audible. He slumped forward, face in his hands. The red baseball cap slid off his head and fell to the cold concrete.

I f Charlie's sudden move had been a signal, nobody was tuned in. Sometimes you can feel violence coming, like a rolling shock wave ahead of the actual impact. The penitentiary gets like that when a race war's running. When you're trapped in a tiny stone city, when your color *makes* you a combatant, it changes the air you breathe. Most of the time, you never get a warning—you go from ignorance to autopsy in a fractured second.

That's the way Wesley liked it. He wasn't programmed for fear, but he knew how it worked. Sometimes he used it—to spook the herd so he could spot the one he wanted. But mostly he liked it better the other way.

"They're easier when they're sleeping," he had whispered to me one night, after one of the dorm bosses told us if we didn't get money from home we'd have to pay him some other way.

Detectives were all over the place when we got up in the morning. Word was that the dorm boss's skull had been caved in, right next to one of his eyes. By the time they discovered the body, the murder kit had vanished: the D-cell batteries returned to the flashlight of the night-shift guard, the gym sock they had been carried in shredded and flushed down a toilet.

That joint had been lousy with rats. Some informed for favors, some just because they liked to do it. But, even then, nobody ever told on Wesley.

The Blood Shadows looked bored. That didn't mean anything—they'd look bored in the middle of a shootout. Clarence was on his second circuit. I couldn't see Max. Hadn't seen him move away, either.

Charlie hadn't brought friends.

Or he didn't have any.

I looked over at him, still slumped. Realized that I'd never seen Charlie Jones in daytime, never mind day*light*. He looked defeated. Drained. And old—he looked really old.

"Better tell me," I said.

Can I smoke?" he asked me, like I was a cop in an interrogation cell.

"Come on, Charlie," I said, trying to get him to unclench. But even a hit of liquid Valium wouldn't have gotten the job done, not once I'd brought Wesley back to life.

Charlie looked down at his shaking hands, as if to add them to the list of people who had betrayed him. "*Treyf,*" he mumbled to himself.

"*What's* not kosher?" I said. "I've been straight with you from the—"

"Not you," he said, sorrow drilling a deep hole in his delicate voice.

Max materialized to Charlie's left, just as a shadow blotted out the sun to his right. I didn't have to look to know a couple of the leather-jacketed kids were forming their half of the bracket. Suddenly Charlie and I had as much privacy as if we were in a hotel room.

"The guys who jumped me, they were either watching your house or . . ."

"Somebody made a phone call," he finished for me.

"Yeah."

"Galya."

I gave him thirty seconds, then said, "Galya. What's that?"

"My wife," he said, like a man watching his oncologist hold up three fingers.

"The girl who came to the door?"

"Yes."

I waited, patient as the stone I was sitting on. When it finally came, it flowed like pus from a lanced wound.

"Her name is Galina," he said. "This June, we'll have been married fifteen years. She was only nineteen when I found her. Nineteen. I was old enough to be her father, but she said that was what she was looking for. She wanted a man, not a boy. A man to take care of her.

"It was through one of those services. A legit marriage bureau, I mean. They screen you, just like they were the girl's parents. And it's not some green-card racket, either—I went over there, to Russia, *twice* before she . . . before she said she'd come back here with me to live."

I gave him a no-judgments look, waiting for the rest.

"My Galya wasn't one of those 'bought brides,' " the night dweller said, angry at someone who wasn't there. "That's just . . . slavery. Those people sell those girls like they're fucking cars. *Used* cars, you understand what I'm telling you?"

"Sure."

"I was . . . lonely, okay? Thirty-seven years old, but I felt like I was a hundred. This life . . ."

I let the silence throb between us, waiting.

"To you, I'm . . . Never mind," he finally said, holding up his hand like I'd been about to interrupt him. "I know what I am in your eyes. But where I live, I'm not Charlie Jones, the matchmaker. I'm Benny Siegel, the businessman. I'm respected. Part of the community. I've had my house there since I got out of the army. Cost me every dime I had saved up just to make the down, but it was worth it."

He went silent. I gave him a few seconds, to see if he'd pick it up. When he didn't, I said, "The army, huh? Were you in—?"

"Yeah, I was there," he cut me off. "Even got myself a couple of medals for it. Wouldn't have thought it, would you?"

"I wouldn't know how to tell," I answered him, truthfully.

"That's where I learned to do what I do," he said. "Down in those fucking tunnels."

No wonder he's more comfortable in the dark, I thought, but kept it to myself.

"You weren't there yourself, were you?" he said, turning his face to me. "No, that's right. Word is, you were some kind of mercenary. In Africa, right?"

"This isn't about me, Charlie."

"No," he said, forlornly. "I guess it's not. All right, you want to know, I'll tell you. Over there, once you got off the line, the whole country was nothing but a giant fucking trading post, like a flea market on steroids. Some people wanted things; other people had things. People wanted things *done;* there were people who wanted to *do* those things. Everything got moved: dope, ordnance, medical supplies. Even whole jeeps. I fell into it by accident. A guy asked me, did I know someone who could do something. It doesn't matter what. Not now. But I did. Know someone, I mean. A sniper.

"That's where it started. The middle, it's like a deep trench. You fall into it, then you find out it's not just deep, it's long. Endless. One day, you look up, and you can't see the sky anymore. That's when you know you're back in the tunnels. Tunnels so long that you couldn't walk to the sunlight in your whole life."

Charlie looked down at his hands, as if seeing the unlit cigarette for the first time. He put it to his lips, used a throwaway butane lighter to get it going. I noticed his hands were steady now. Lancing an abscess will do that sometimes.

"When I came home, I just picked up where I'd left off," he said. "I had a lot of names and numbers. For a long time, I just worked with people I knew. I'm not sure when it happened, but word got out I was down there, and people looked me up. Like it was my address. Word got around. People who needed things done would look for me. Ask around. And I knew people, too, by then. People I could match them up with. People who knew I could be trusted."

"Trusted," I said. Just the word.

"Trusted," Charlie repeated, a touch of pride slipping into his voice. "You know how the tunnels work?"

"No," I said. I didn't know which tunnels he was talking about—Vietnam or New York—but I let him run.

"You have to have something to believe in," the ferret said. "And it has to be something you can *do*. Not religion. Rules. You have to do things right. By the book. No matter what comes up, there's a plan for it. You'll be all right as long as you stick to the rules. The guys who went down and didn't come back, it's always because they forgot the rules."

"And you never did."

"I never did," he repeated, like taking an oath. "One tunnel's the same as another. Maybe one's lined with punji sticks, one's got those little gas bombs. Another one, there's a VC pop shooter, sitting there for days without moving, just waiting for the fly to stumble into the web. It doesn't matter what's down there. You can't control that. But you can control how *you* act."

"Follow the rules."

"That's right. And I have. I always have."

"You've got a good rep," I acknowledged.

" 'Good'?" he said, snapping away his cigarette. "Fuck you, 'good.' I'm not good; I'm gold."

There! His ferret's pride finally bursting through the crust of fear, the opening I'd been probing for.

"Easy to say when you're not looking at a ride Upstate," I said. And I *could* say it—everyone in our world knows that when Burke goes down he goes down alone. My diploma was from my last felony jolt, *magna con laude*.

"I've been jugged three times," Charlie said, like a tennis player returning an easy lob. "Twice as a material witness, once for some okey-doke they made up to put me in the pressure cooker. I just sat there until they cut me loose."

"So they couldn't bluff you. That's not the same as—"

" 'Bluff'?" the ferret said. "The last one, they had a body, and they had the shooter. He was a pro. A contract man."

He glanced up, as if calling my attention to something we both knew was there. The corner of his mouth twitched. Not a tic, telling me something in a language we shared.

But telling me what? That the contract man had been Wesley. Making an offering out of his honesty?

He couldn't be bragging about keeping quiet, because nobody in our world would give Wesley up. Not out of loyalty—Wesley was alone. Not out of obedience to some twit screenwriter's idea of "the code." No, out of a fear so deep and elemental that it transcended logic and reason. Everybody knew: If you said the iceman's name aloud to the Law, you were dead.

Or was the little ferret gambling? The whisper-stream had all kinds of rumors running about me and Wesley. Maybe Charlie thought I already knew about the job he was talking about, showing me he could have put me on the spot when he'd had the chance.

"Nobody could make a connection to the dead woman," he went on, not missing a beat. "They knew it had to be her husband who paid to get it done, but they didn't have a link. Oh, the shooter rolled on him," he said, contemptuously, "but the husband was ready for that. Alibi in place, lawyers spread out thick as chopped liver on a bagel. The cops needed me to make the bridge."

"So the shooter gave you up, too?" I asked, knowing it couldn't be Wesley he was talking about now.

"Tried to." Charlie shrugged. "First they offered me a free pass. Tell what I knew and walk away. Not a misdemeanor slap, not even probation. Immunity, straight up. I just looked dumb," he said, showing me the same blank face he must have shown them. "Then they tried to scare me. A skinny little guy like me, a skinny little *white* guy, everyone knew what was going to happen if I had to go Upstate, they said."

"But after the tunnels . . ."

"Yeah," he said, unwilling to dignify the attempt to frighten him with another word.

"So what happened?"

"To me? Nothing. My lawyer told them, if they brought me into the case, I was going to testify the shooter was lying—about ever meeting with me—and since the DA needed the shooter to be telling the truth about the hit, they couldn't risk letting the jury see him lie about any *part* of it. So they tried it on murder-and-motive."

"Yeah?"

"Yeah. The husband would have beat it, too. Only the DA had another card. His girlfriend. She testified she had been pressuring him to get a divorce so they could get married, but his wife had all the money, so he was trapped. He told her they'd be married by Christmas. The wife got smoked in September. When he hadn't married her by April, she went to the Law."

"Happy ending."

"That's what I want here, too," the tunnel-runner said. "A happy ending. Tell me what I have to do to get one, Burke. All I need is the rules."

You want to go back to being Benny Siegel?"

"I *am* Benny Siegel. That's what it says on my birth certificate. On my 214, too. I'm like a farmer, okay? It's not any one year's crops I care about so much, it's the *land.*"

"I get it."

"No, you don't."

"Jews weren't allowed to own land," I said, softly, remembering the Mole's lessons. "That's why they wandered."

"And did the work nobody else wanted to do . . ." Nodding for me to fill in the blank.

". . . but everyone needed done."

"Yes," he said, solemnly.

In the silence, he took out another cigarette. His hands were as steady as a dead man's pulse.

"Were the guys who jumped you Russians?" he asked.

"I don't know. We didn't have a conversation."

"My wife . . ."

"What?"

"I love her. Tell me how she survives this, and it's done."

"Meaning it was her who called in the troops?"

"I don't know that. But it's all that's left."

"Does she work with you, Charlie?"

"Galya? She doesn't even know—"

"Yeah, she does," I cut off his self-delusion at the root. "If you didn't sic those guys in the van on me— and I don't think you did, okay?—then it was her. What's she doing, calling the same crew that executed the man who was trying to hire me, Charlie? The same guy *you* sent to me?"

"I never told her a—"

"This is your *wife*, Charlie. She's not just in your house; she's in your business. And she's in deep. At least this piece of it."

"I—"

"She's in your business," I said again. "And if you

want to protect her like you say, you better get in hers."

"Just tell me," he said, defeated.

"I want to talk to the people who want to talk to me. I want someone to tell them they don't need to be trying to snatch me off the street to do that."

"But, you do that, they'll know who you are," he said, his ferret's brain back to professionalism. "And now they *don't* know—or they would have come for you already."

"You let me worry about that. I don't like things hanging over me."

"Me, either," he said, pointedly.

"Then it's time for you to have a talk with your wife."

He just nodded—a man who knew the rules.

*I*t took only another few minutes for me to run the whole deal down. Charlie didn't argue. In fact, he made himself my partner in the enterprise, suggesting a couple of ways we could get what we needed done a little better.

"Call the number I gave you," he said.

"When?"

"Anytime after midnight."

"You'll have it by then?"

"One way or the other," he said, grimly.

He lit another smoke.

"It took a lot of guts for you to walk in here," I said, making a gesture to encompass the whole wired-up plaza. "To come in all alone."

"I always work alone," the middleman said. "And this"—imitating the gesture I'd just made—"this is just another tunnel."

Charlie Jones, a tunnel rat," the Prof said, musingly. "Who would've thought there was any glory in *his* story?"

"Everybody's got a story. That's not the same thing as an excuse."

"You didn't buy his lie, Schoolboy?"

"I . . . I guess I did, Prof. Even the timing works. The woman who came to the door first—his wife, now we know—she went right back into the house, left me outside talking to Charlie. That's when she has to have made the call."

"That's why he asked you if the snatch team was Russians?"

"Has to be."

"Which means he knows more than he gave up," Michelle put in. "Which is what we'd expect."

"Yeah. But it wasn't Charlie," I said, more sure of myself after a few hours of thinking it through. "If he wanted to set me up, all he had to do was ring the number he has for me, make a meet, like he had a job—"

"Like he did before," Clarence said.

"Right. And if he just panicked, seeing me at his door, and called in muscle, why would they have tried to grab me? If they're the same crew that hit Daniel Parks, they're not shy about shooting."

"So you're going to talk to them because you think that's what *they* want?"

"No, honey," I said to Michelle. "I'm going to talk to them because the guy they hit is a money man. *Was* a money man, anyway. We've been trying to figure out if there's something for us in all this. If anyone knows, they do."

"Or your girl," the Prof said.

"Yeah. Or her. But, so far, we can't find Beryl. And we *can* find the Russians."

"Uh-huh," the Prof grunted. Not convinced, and making sure I knew it.

Any way you want to do it." Charlie's voice, on the phone. "It's not you they want, it's information."

"And if I don't have it, they're going to take my word for it?"

"They don't *expect* you to have it. They know it's a real long shot."

"*Any* way I want to do it?"

"Yes."

Two-fifteen the next morning. The man in the blue-and-white warm-up suit had been standing on the corner of a Chinatown back street for almost half an hour, as still as a sniper. He never once glanced at his watch.

When the oil-belching black Chevy Caprice—Central Casting for gypsy cab—pulled up, he got into the back seat.

From that moment, his life was at risk. Not because the hands of Max the Silent could find a kill-spot like a heat-seeking missile, but because those hands were on the steering wheel. Max drives like he walks, expecting everything in his path to step aside. He still hasn't figured out that cars are like guns—they make some morons braver than they should be.

We box-tailed the Chevy all the way out to Hunts Point. If the man in the warm-up suit had brought friends, we couldn't see any sign of them. I'd already told Charlie what would happen to whoever they sent if we found a transmitter on him. Or a cell phone. Or a weapon.

Wesley rode with me. My brother, still protecting me from the other side. Charlie couldn't be sure Wesley was really gone, but I was sure he wouldn't want to bet his life on it.

A riderless bicycle sailed past on the sidewalk. I looked over and saw a clot of kids way short of puberty. They were gathered around a few more bikes, one of them holding his hand high. I knew what would be in it—a piece of fluorescent chalk. The kids were ghost riding. You take a bike—I mean *take;* the game is played with stolen property—get it going as fast as you dare, then bail out. The trick is to jump off while keeping the bike pointed straight ahead. The bike that goes the farthest before it crashes is the winner; the chalk is for marking the spot.

After all, every educational system needs report cards—otherwise, some child might be left behind.

The Chevy stopped on the prairie. It looked like a black polar bear, alone on a dirty ice floe.

I walked over as Max opened the back door for the guy inside, who stepped out lightly and moved in my

direction. I held out my hand for him to stop. He stood
still as Max searched him. The Mongol nodded an
"okay." I gestured for the man to follow me. We walked
over to the gutted-out shell of what had once been a
car. I leaned against the charred front fender, opened
my hands in a "go ahead" gesture.

"You were never going to be hurt," he said, without
preamble.

"I couldn't know that."

"Oleg only has one eye now." Looking at my bad
one, as if we were sharing something he didn't need to
explain.

I didn't say anything.

"We don't want to fight," he said. Not pleading—
stating a fact. He was a burly man, a little shorter than
me, and a lot thicker. I could see a gold chain, more like
a rope, at his neck, and a diamond on his right hand
that threw enough fire to give a pyromaniac an orgasm. His watch cost more than some cars. And that
warm-up suit wasn't the kind you buy where they sell
sneakers.

"Me, either," I said, waiting.

"Okay, then." He put his hands together like we'd
just sealed a deal. "We did not know who you were, or
where to find you. We still do not. But we had to talk
with you, so we . . . did what we did. You know how
such things are."

I didn't say anything.

"We would have preferred to do what I am going to
do now," he said, watching my face as he spoke the
words. When I didn't react, he went on: "Pay you for
your time. For your time and your trouble."

"What's the going rate for being tortured?"

"You think we were going to—?"

"You weren't looking to hire me," I said, keeping my voice edgeless. "So you must think I know something. Something you want to know. If I told you that you were wrong, that I didn't know anything, what were you going to do? Thank me for my time and cut me loose? Or use that Taser on me?"

"We would never have—"

"I like this way better," I cut him off.

He grunted something I took for understanding. "My name is Yitzhak," he said. "But I don't have to know your name to know you are a professional. So! A man hired you to do something. All we want to know is what he hired you to do."

"Which man?"

"The man who can't pay you anymore."

"What's it worth to you to know?"

"That depends on what you tell us."

"I don't think so."

"Bravo. What is it worth to *you,* then?"

"I'm not sure," I said, making it a question he had to answer, if he wanted us to keep talking.

"This man, he stole from us. Money. A great deal of money. Wherever that money is, it's not in a wall safe. Or a suitcase."

"Why didn't you just ask him?"

"You mean, instead of . . . ? All right, I will tell you. Maybe, if you understand us, you will believe us, too."

I lit a cigarette, a signal to my backup that I was okay. For now.

"This man was in trouble," he said. "He thought

this trouble was a burden he could transfer. Do you understand?"

"He was a cooperating witness?"

"He was, if our information is correct, *negotiating* to be exactly that. But the deal had yet to be struck."

"So you needed to move before—"

"No. Not for that. This man was a thief, and he stole from many. We are businessmen, and money is important. But in *our* business, there is something much more important than money. It is not just that this man stole from us; it was *known* that he did it. Do you understand what I am saying to you?"

Understand it? I thought to myself. *I was raised on it.*

Inside, if a sneak thief takes your stuff, it's nothing personal—it's just part of living there, like rain falling in Seattle. But if the thief shows off what he took, it's like he raped you. If you don't square that up, you don't get to keep *anything* that's yours.

You've got a pack of Kools in your cell. A fresh, new pack. You go to take a shower, come back, and find it's gone. That happens. And that night, you see a guy on the tier smoking a Kool, holding a whole pack in his other hand. Still nothing—the commissary sells them to anyone with money on the books. But then the guy says, "Thanks for the smokes, punk." And now, now you *have* to hurt him. You don't do that, you're going to be meat on some freak's plate.

But all I said to Yitzhak was, "If other people thought it was safe to steal from you . . ."

"Americans see with wide eyes," he said, sounding more like a Talmudic scholar than a businessman who regarded hunter-killer teams as a line item on a budget. "You say 'Russian' to an American, and he thinks he knows all there is to know. But there are Odessa Beach Russians—you know the people I mean—and there are ... others.

"We have been on this earth for thousands of years. But, every place we go, we have to establish our own identity. In American minds, a Jew is always motivated by money. Money comes first. That is a perception we have to change, if we are to be allowed to conduct our own business. You understand this?"

"If you don't build a rep for always getting even, it makes people think you're weak."

"Correct!" he said, pleased with the pupil. "The stereotype is that we are clever people, but not strong people. In our business, it is more valuable for our enemies to believe we are crazy than that we are clever."

"Which is why this guy who stole from you couldn't just disappear. You needed his head on a stake."

His shrug was eloquent.

"But the money ... ?"

"We made our own inquiries. Before we ... acted. This was a sophisticated thief. There was some system in place—it is too complicated for me to understand; that is not my role—but the money was vacuumed right out of his accounts, and then it just disappeared. The thief himself would not know where it ended up."

"Then what good would it do him?"

"He had a confederate. Maybe more than one. Someone he trusted."

"And you think *I* know who that is?" I said, snapping my unsmoked cigarette into the darkness.

"No," he said, smiling. "If you knew where that much money was, you would be long gone. Far away."

"So what did you want to snatch me for?"

"We know you met the thief. We had to learn whether you were . . ."

"His 'confederate'? Get real."

"Yes, we understand that. We understand that *now*. The information we had was . . . sketchy. A man such as that one, he would have no friends."

I understood what the Russian was telling me. "Friends," as in those who would avenge his death.

"So what was I supposed to tell you?"

"We still want the money," the man said. "We thought maybe you could help us find it."

"You think this guy told me?"

"No," he said, brushing off my sarcasm. "We don't think this man knew *we* knew he was a thief. But he knew we would find out eventually."

"That explains it," I said.

"What?" he asked, too eagerly.

"Why in the world a white man would want to go to Africa."

"Please," he said, tilting his chin at me for encouragement.

"I did some . . . work over there. Years ago. But I keep up my contacts. It's a good thing to have people in a country that doesn't have an extradition treaty."

"Where?"

"Nigeria."

"Nigeria?" His voice reeked suspicion. "Free-lancers haven't worked there since—"

"Nineteen seventy," I finished for him. "But it's still the most corrupt country on the planet."

"You have not been to Russia recently," he said, as if his nationalistic pride had been insulted.

"I haven't been to Russia at all. But I know how to get things done in Nigeria."

"And that's what this man wanted?"

"He didn't know specifics. All he'd heard was that I could get someone set up in an African country where a lot of cash would guarantee a lot of safety. I think, from the little bit he said, that he thought it was South Africa, but he wasn't particular."

"So what happened?"

"You know better than me," I said. "I told him I needed twenty-five thousand just to start the process. I thought we'd have to make another meet, but he said he had it with him. Not on him, in his car. He went out to get it . . . and he never came back."

"Did he leave anything with you?"

"Yeah. The tab for the drinks we'd ordered."

He said something under his breath. Sounded like Russian.

"Did he come to you directly?" Asking me a question he already knew the answer to.

"No." The truth.

"Will you tell me the name of the person who introduced you?" Testing me; they already knew it had been Charlie, thanks to his wife.

"No."

"A man must choose his own path," he said, very deliberately. "Must it be your choice to stand in mine?"

"I'm no different from you," I answered. "If I gave you a name, my own name would be hurt. And that would put me out of business."

"For fifty thousand dollars? Cash?"

"No."

He made a guttural sound I took for approval. "You are a businessman, fair enough. Let us say the name of the person who introduced you to the thief means nothing to us, yes? But, should you happen to run across information—say, from *another* source—that might be of value, you understand that you would be compensated?"

"Sure."

"What do you think is fair?"

"For . . . ?"

"For your time and trouble, as I said."

"For my *past* time and trouble?"

"If you like."

"I like the number you mentioned."

"What we did was wrong, but we had no other way," he said. "That is worth something, I agree. But not fifty thousand. That was an offer for information. This you declined. So, for the time and trouble, let us say . . . ten?"

When I nodded, he unzipped his warm-up suit. "If you want to earn ten times this, all you have to do is call me."

"Call you with what?"

"With the name of anyone else who wants to go to Nigeria."

Are we okay now?" The voice of Charlie Jones on the phone. Soft, with just the faintest trace of a tremor.

"You're still into me," I told him. "Into me deep."

"Could I square it with—?"

"This isn't about money," I told him. Meaning it wasn't about money *now*.

"What, then?" he said, his voice already sagging under the weight of what he felt coming.

"I have to talk to her."

"Not my—?"

"Yeah. You can be there, too. But there's questions I have to ask."

"Just tell me and I'll—"

"You know I can't do that," I said.

His end of the line went on semi-mute; the only sounds were his shallow breathing and the cellular hum. Then . . .

"When will this be over?"

"When I know I'm safe, that's when you'll know you are, too."

That brought me more silence. I waited. Then . . .

"It can't be here. At the house, I mean."

"Of course not," I said, as if we had agreed on everything up to then. "Let me treat you to dinner. Wherever you'd like."

"Not in Manhattan."

"Wherever *you'd* like. Fair enough?"

*O*h God! How could you *know*?" Loyal squealed, staring into the box she had unwrapped so daintily that the floor was carpeted in shredded paper. "This is *just* like the dolly I had when I was a little girl. She was too big to be a baby, but that's what I called her. 'Baby.' "

"I'm glad you like it," I said.

" 'Her,' " she corrected me.

"Baby."

"Yes," she mock-pouted, cuddling the oversized porcelain doll Michelle had promised me would be worth the fat chunk of my money she'd spent on it.

"What happened to your . . . to the original one?" I asked her.

"I gave her away," Loyal said. Her eyes were damp, but her chest was puffy with pride. "When I was only . . . about twelve, I think, I saw this story in the paper. It was about this little girl, a real little girl, much younger than me. She lived in another part of town. There was a big fire, and her whole house got burned up. Her momma went right into the flames to save her, and she died doing it.

"The little girl—Selma was her name—she was in the hospital. In the paper, it said she was going to live with her mother's family. I asked my father, what about her daddy, why wasn't he going to take her home? My father told me Selma didn't have a daddy. I was young, but I wasn't dumb. I knew enough to ask Speed, and he explained it to me.

"The next day, I made him drive me over to the hospital. They wouldn't let me see the girl—she was burned up too bad to have visitors, they said—but they let me leave Baby there for her.

"When I told my father, I thought he might be mad enough to . . . Well, I thought he'd be mad for sure, because that doll had cost a pretty penny, and I knew it. But he put me on his lap and gave me a kiss and told me I was a fine girl.

"I never forgot that. Because, just the week before, when I tried to sit on his lap, he said I was getting too old for that kind of thing."

"Do you ever think about her? That little girl, Selma?"

"I do," she said. "And when I do, I think about her with my Baby, and I feel good inside myself. I could never explain it. It was like, when I heard that child's story, my heart just went out to her. Went out to her and never came back."

If you need to get to D.C., Amtrak's a lot better than a plane. No baggage scanning, no real ID check, and door-to-door quicker, too.

A business-class ticket on the Acela Express gave me access to the "quiet car"—the one place on the train where cell phones were banned. I had figured it would be packed—the cars I walked through to reach it sounded like they were full of magpies on angel dust— but it was just about empty.

I cracked open my newspaper. A human—the paper

called her a "mother"—in Florida had been prostituting her little girl for years. Twenty bucks a trick. Extras were extra. Her older daughter, almost twelve, had finally resisted the beatings. So the mother just sold her outright. A used car plus five hundred in cash, and some lucky vermin got to make his slimy dreams come true.

I wished I had a bullet for every one of them. Not a simple death-dealer, a magic bullet—the kind that would take one life and give back another.

In my world, you get even because you're nothing if you don't, but it's never enough. It can't be. You can't *really* get even. You can make someone who hurt you dead, but whatever they took from you is never coming back.

The ride was less than three hours, right on time. Even more on time was the canary-yellow Corvette convertible waiting at the curb outside, a truly spectacular redhead behind the wheel.

"Toni?" I said, as I walked up to her.

"Who else?" she answered, grinning.

Some women get annoyed if you stare at their breasts. This gorgeous Titan didn't care where I looked, so long as it wasn't at her Adam's apple.

"So you're Michelle's big brother," she said, appraisingly. "Somehow, I thought you'd be . . ."

"Better looking?"

"No!" she giggled, patting my thigh.

"More sophisticated? Smarter? Taller?"

"Stop it! I just meant . . . Well, you know Michelle. She's so . . . refined. You look a little rough around the edges, if you don't mind me saying so."

"You're not the first. And most don't say it so euphemistically."

"*That's* what I was looking for! Michelle said you were a real intellectual."

"Is that right?" I said, reaching into the breast pocket of my Harris-tweed jacket and slipping on a pair of plain-glass spectacles.

"Oh, those are perfect! You're some kind of investigator, aren't you?"

"I guess I am."

"Well, anyone who works with that husband of hers must be smart. That Norm, he's a genuine genius, she says."

"She's not lying," I promised, finally learning the name Michelle assigns the Mole for social occasions that require bragging. "He's way past being a genius. Their son's going to win a Nobel Prize someday."

"Terry? That's if Hollywood doesn't grab him first. That is a *gorgeous* young man!"

"That's outside my area of expertise."

"What exactly are we doing, you and me?" she said, making it clear she was just curious—the answer would have no effect on her participation.

"We're going to look at a house. You already have the address."

"A house you're thinking of buying?"

"No. There's a woman living there; it's her I'm interested in," thinking, *Michelle said she was one of us.* "Interested in professionally."

"Oh?"

"Michelle told you what I do for a living?"

"Well, of course. Like I said. You're some kind of investigator, aren't you?"

"An investigator who doesn't know one end of this part of the country from another."

"Toni the Chauffeur, at your service," she said, saluting.

"I appreciate it, Toni. Very much. But this isn't about finding a house as much as it is finding a way inside it, do you follow me?"

"In broad daylight?" she said, sliding the 'Vette through an intersection on the caution light.

"We're not talking about a burglary here. I want to talk to the person who's inside—who I *hope* is inside. Not because she's the one I'm looking for; because she can . . . maybe . . . lead me in the right direction."

"And you don't think she'll be, what's the word you guys use, 'cooperative'?"

"I can't even guess," I said, truthfully.

"So where do I come in?" Toni asked.

"I'm not sure yet," I told her. "I was hoping you might have some ideas."

This neighborhood is first-tier," Toni said, her sheer-stockinged legs flashing in the sun as she changed gears. "Not absolutely top of the heap—the plots are too small for that. But these are all seven-figure houses."

"There's slums in New York where you could say the same thing."

"Oh, I *know*. Michelle showed me around the last time I was up. I couldn't *believe* it."

I looked down at the map spread open in my lap. "What's a 'crescent'?" I asked.

"If you mean when they use it for an address, it's just a fancy name for 'street.' Probably shorter than most, maybe a cul-de-sac. How far . . . ?"

"Next left."

"How fast do you want to go by?"

"Like we're just passing through. On our way to somewhere."

"What number?" she asked, turning in.

"Twenty-nine."

"Be on your side."

The house was two stories with an attached garage. Dark green, with white shutters around the windows.

"Nothing special," Toni said. "Four bedrooms, three baths, probably. But they spent seriously on the landscaping."

"I hadn't noticed," I said. We were at the end of the block, and Toni turned the Corvette onto a slightly wider street.

"Those back trees are old growth," she said. "The way the plantings were arranged beneath them, it's almost like outdoor bonsai, with the flower beds and those hedges and all."

"A privacy thing?"

"Could be. You think whoever you're looking for could be staying there?"

"You should consider a change of careers," I told her.

"You mean I'm right?" she said, flashing another smile.

"On the money."

"Let's get coffee," she said.

*T*his is her?" Toni asked, holding the blown-up photo of Beryl Preston. The redhead's long nails were beautifully manicured, heavy bracelets concealing wide wrists.

"Yep."

"How long ago was this taken?" A woman's question. A suspicious woman.

"I don't know exactly. But she'd be in her early thirties now, so it looks recent, don't you think?"

"Maybe," she said, grudgingly.

"I was going to just walk up and see who answers the door. But . . ."

"What?"

"Well, you're about the age of the girl I'm looking for. A bit younger, sure, but close enough."

"Yes?" she said, widening her improbably greenish eyes.

"If you were to just ring the bell, and say you were looking for Beryl, who knows? Her mother—that's the woman who lives there—might just call her downstairs or something. Hell, it might be Beryl herself who answers the door. She's got no reason to think anyone would be looking for her here."

"But she *does* know people are looking for her?"

"Oh yeah."

"This isn't a—?"

"What did Michelle tell you?" I said, letting my voice harden.

"I know," she said, working her lips like she was making a decision.

I sipped my hot chocolate, feeling the minutes slow-click against the clock in my mind.

"Let's talk outside," she said.

I was a runaway," Toni said. "I didn't know what I was, but I knew what I wasn't. Do you understand what I'm—?"

"Yeah," I said. And I did.

"I . . . My family had money. They sent me to . . . professionals. That didn't work: I was still a girl inside, no matter what they called it. I was . . . I was sad, but I wasn't suicidal. Until they sent me to the healer."

I made an encouraging sound in my throat.

"It was a . . . They called it a Christian retreat, but it was a prison."

"Because you couldn't leave?"

"Because they had bars on the windows," Toni said, fingering the tiny gold cross that caught a shaft of sunlight as it twinkled against her white sweater, standing between her prominent breasts like a warning. "Because there was no privacy. No privacy ever. Not even in the bathroom. Because they were afraid you might . . . do something to yourself.

"What I had . . . what I had inside me, they said that was being possessed. Satan had my soul. But if I worked hard enough, if I prayed hard enough, if I did everything they told me to, I could drive it all out.

"Only I didn't *want* it out. I wanted to be . . . I wanted to be myself. Me."

I nodded my head.

"At first, I kept that to myself. When I finally said it out loud, that's when the beatings started."

She shifted position, opening her stance like a boxer loading up to throw the equalizer. Her voice dropped into a metallic baritone.

"They called it 'correction.' The rod, right out of the Bible they made me read after each time. My parents never knew. Part of the program was that they couldn't have any contact with me for the first six months. 'Total immersion in the Lord,' is what they called it.

"I was only fifteen. And sheltered, too—my parents had taken me out of school years before that. Because of my . . . problem. So I didn't know much about the world. But it didn't take me long to understand. They taught me a lot in that place. And the first thing I learned was, those beatings, they *liked* doing that. It was exciting for them. Got them all . . . you know."

"I do know," I said, reaching for her hand. She let me take it, but didn't return the squeeze I gave.

"We were at the zoo. To see the baby pandas. It was like a field trip. Only for students who had been good. Obedient, they meant. I knew how to be 'good' by then. That's when I ran.

"I knew I couldn't go to my grandmother's—she would have just called my parents. And I didn't have any other place to go. I kept seeing New York in my mind. The biggest city in the world. Magic was there, I was sure of it.

"Michelle found me on my second night. I was looking for a place to sleep. These two men were . . . taunting me. It was at this old empty building, right next to a pier, all the way downtown. But they had been there first, they said, so it was their home. And I had to pay rent.

"I would have done it. Whatever 'it' was, it would have been better than going back. And then Michelle just *burst* in. She's so small—I was bigger than her even then, and the men were *much* bigger. But they were scared of her. She was so *fierce*. And she had a razor. . . .

"I stayed with her for a few weeks. She worked nights, but we talked when she came home. Every day. I told her everything.

"One day, she told me she had to go away for a while. She promised she'd be back, and made *me* promise I wouldn't go out while she was gone.

"I don't know how she did it, but when she came back, she told me it was time for me to go home. I was so scared, but I believed her. And when I got home, it was like I had different parents. They *apologized* to me. My mother was crying, and my father was . . . well, I don't know what to call it, but he was very, very determined.

"That's when I started to become Toni. The doctor they sent me to was so good and kind. I couldn't have the surgery until I was of age, but he explained I had to live as a girl for at least two years first anyway, just to be sure."

"Your parents turned out to be really something."

"They did," she said, relaxing her shoulders, her hand soft and damp in mine. "They were Christians, but *real* Christians, like Jimmy Carter, not fundamentalist freaks. That . . . place they sent me to, it was out of ignorance. When my father found out what they really did in there, he . . . I don't know exactly what he did. But I know there was a big lawsuit, and the place ended up closed."

"That's quite a story."

"Oh, it's a *long* story, I know," she said. "But I told it to you for a reason."

"Did you, Toni?"

"Yes. I wanted you to understand what I'm going to say now."

I waited.

"Michelle said, anything I did for you, it would be the same as doing it for her. Do you understand?"

"I do."

"And I'd do anything for Michelle," the big redhead told me. "That's N. E. Thing. Understand now?"

*T*oni dropped me off at a bowling alley. Luckily, they also had a few pool tables. I wasn't even finished with the first rack before a pudgy kid in a short-sleeved shirt big enough to be a dust cover for a refrigerator wobbled over and asked me if I wanted to play some nine-ball.

The hustler was patient. I was up fifty bucks—the worm on the hook he was baiting—when Toni walked in. She sashayed her way over to me, snapping necks as she went, mane of red hair bouncing.

"How much have you managed to lose so far?" she said, hands on her hips, but smiling to show she was being the indulgent girlfriend, not a harpy.

"Hey! I'm up about fifty, right?" I said, turning to the fat kid for confirmation.

"That's right," the kid said, gravely, nodding his head to reluctantly acknowledge my clear superiority with the cue.

"Well, we are *late,*" Toni announced.

"Just one more game?"

"*One* more," she said, warningly. Then she perched herself on a high stool, crossed her long legs, and cupped her chin in one hand.

"Double or nothing?" I said to the fat kid.

"Oh, hell, it's the last game, let's make it for a hundred."

"Your break," I said, winking at Toni.

The pudgy kid's shot hit the rack like a cannonball going through crepe paper. The balls ran for cover— three of them so terrified they ducked down into the pockets. The cue ball was centered, a little short of the head spot. He cut in the one-ball, came three rails for perfect shape on the two, tapped it into the side, pirouetted like a bullfighter, and comboed the four-nine without drawing a breath.

"In between tournaments?" I asked him, as I paid up.

"You recognized me?" he said, caught between surprise and pride.

"Sure," I lied.

"You're pretty good yourself. Want to go one more time?"

"You see that girl over there?"

"I sure do, bro."

"That's all the luck I'm ever going to find in this place, son."

S he was the third house I visited," Toni said. "I'm a broker—for real; that's what I do—Michelle must have told you. I told the woman I have a client who's much more interested in the right neighborhood than in any individual house. He and his wife have three school-age children, and he's done his research. I didn't get where I am today by waiting for the right MLS to pop up—I go out in the field and scout around. Occasionally, you run across someone who wasn't thinking of selling . . . until they hear the kind of money my client's willing to put on the table."

"*Very* nice," I said, giving her a con man's respect for a superior opening shtick.

"It's actually true," she said, smiling. "If someone were to make a phone call to my office, it would get verified, too."

"Even better."

"She was last on my list," Toni said. "Fortunately, the first house I tried, no one was at home. And the second one, it was only the maid. But if anyone had been watching . . ."

"Beautiful."

"The woman who answered the door isn't your girl. Too old. Not that she doesn't keep herself up—she was all toned-and-tucked, believe me—but she hasn't seen thirty for a good long time. Has to be the mother."

"Did you get the sense anyone else was there?"

"Well, there was at least one more," Toni said. "The baby. More like a toddler . . . ? I don't know; I'm not good with guessing ages when they're that small. Young enough for the mother to be carrying her around in one arm, anyway."

"Did she act like—I'm not sure how to put this—did she act like the baby was *her* baby? Or a kid she was watching for someone else?"

"Oh, it was her baby. She had that . . . protective way of standing you see in mothers."

"Some mothers."

"Some mothers," Toni agreed. "But there was more. . . . She was, like . . . I don't know how to say it. . . . Maybe the way she talked, like the baby was in on the conversation. She didn't *treat* her like a baby. Didn't just make noises at her, she called her by her name. Elysse. That was her baby, Burke. I'd bet a month's commissions on it."

"She let you come in?"

"Not exactly. She didn't tell me to get lost, but—this is all part of the way she was standing; I can't quite explain it—she wasn't going to give any ground. She acted like she had all the time in the world. Even took my business card. But she wasn't offering me a cup of coffee. Not even when I said my client was a seven-figure buyer, all cash."

"That's great, Toni. You did a perfect job."

"Thanks. I would have felt better if she'd let me in, but I didn't want to push it." She glanced at the dashboard, said, "If you're not going back to see her today, we can still make your train."

"Let's get that train," I told her.

"When you spend your life going in and out of houses, you get a feel for them," she said. "That place was big, but it was empty, too. I got the distinct impression that she lives there by herself. Her and the baby, I mean."

"Well, it was long odds."

"She might have a cat. Everyone says cats are so curious, but some of them couldn't be bothered to get up just because someone's at the door."

"But a dog . . ."

"That's right," she said, "a dog is different. My Samson—he's a Jack Russell terrier—if you let a *mosquito* in the door, he'd have to go and see for himself."

"Jack Russells are all lunatics."

"That's true!" she said, laughing. "But there was no dog in that woman's house at all. I could just tell."

I didn't say anything, watching the scenery change as we got back inside the D.C. limits.

"Maybe she doesn't think she needs a dog," Toni said, as she pulled up to the station. "Just inside the front door, there's a blue box on the wall. Some of my clients have the same one. It's a central-station system. If that alarm goes off, it doesn't ring some clown who's supposed to dial 911 *for* you; it rings right inside the cop shop."

*T*he next morning, the newscaster said Amtrak was taking the Acela out of service for a few months. Something about the brakes not being trustworthy.

Another man might have taken that for an omen.

*T*he restaurant was Japanese, not far from the old
tennis stadium in Forest Hills. The hostess had a
treacherously demure smile, too much rouge, and
glossy black agate eyes. She showed me over to a corner booth shielded from the rest of the place by rice-
paper screens.

Charlie saw me coming, stood up, shook hands like
we were business friends.

"Hello," the dark-haired woman next to him said.
Polite smile, wary eyes.

"John, I'd like you to meet my wife," he said.
"Galina, this is John Smith."

She reached up and extended her hand. It wasn't so
much cold as neutral. Inanimate.

I sat down across from them, noting that Charlie had
set it up so that I was facing the entrance, my back to
the wall.

"Do you know my husband a long time?" Galina
asked, as the waiter placed bowls of miso soup in front
of us.

"More years than I care to remember," I told her,
smiling to show I wasn't being hostile, just regretting
my age.

All the way through the meal, we talked about everything except what I'd come for. A New York conversation, ranging from superficial to fraudulent. Taxes, real
estate, crime.

"Dessert?" the waiter asked.

"Let us think about that," Charlie told him, handing
over some folded bills.

"He won't come back until I call him," he said to me.

That was my cue. Turning to face Galina, I said, "When I came by your house the other day, you told your husband I was there, then you went back inside. While you were there, you made a phone call."

Her face was a mask of polite interest.

"Your husband promised you would explain that to me," I went on. "I'm sure he told you how important . . . how very important this is."

"Yes."

"Then, please . . ."

She looked over at Charlie. He nodded.

"I am Ashkenazi," she said. "You know what this is?"

"Jews born in Eastern Europe?"

A quick flash of surprise registered in her dark eyes, opening them to a new depth. "It is more complicated than that, but yes. I was born in Russia. My family, too. And their family. My ancestors *fought* the Nazis. In the Red Army. Many died. Those who lived, maybe they thought things would be different for them when the war was over. But it was not.

"To be a Jew in Russia was always dangerous. And so it is today. More than ever, maybe. The skinhead gangs, they say they are targeting immigrants, but their alliances are with their brothers in Poland. In Croatia, too. The fascists are there in strength.

"The way we survive is the way we have always survived—we do not look to the government for protection; we look to each other."

My eyes never left her face. A faint flush rose in her cheeks.

"You do not believe me?"

"About what you just said? Sure I do. But I guess I don't understand what all that has to do with the phone call you made."

"Because you are not a threat, so why should we need protection from you?"

"You *don't* need protection from me. I didn't even know you existed until a few days ago. You made that phone call because you *already* knew whoever you called wanted to talk to me."

"So?" she said, raising her chin as if I was the butler, defying the mistress of the manor.

"That's it?" I said to Charlie.

"No," he said quickly. "Just have a little patience, all right?"

I sat back, waiting. He looked at his wife.

"The people I called are my family," Galina said. "They ask; I do. This is always."

I didn't move. She looked at her husband.

"Yes, I knew they wanted to talk with you," she finally said. "They are . . . crazy people. But they are my people. By blood. So if they want something from me . . ."

"They want a lot more than phone calls from you, Mrs. Siegel," I said.

"What do you mean?"

"Remember I said I didn't even know you existed until recently? Well, your people knew *I* existed before that. They knew I went to a meeting. A meeting with a client. Nobody knew about that meeting but me and the client. Your people might have been following the client. Maybe that's how they spotted me."

Her dark eyes never left my one good one.

"But I don't think so," I went on. "I think they knew my client had a meeting. I think they were listening in on his calls. And there's only one way they get his number to do that."

"We already talked it over," Charlie said. "Galina was just doing—"

"Please don't say 'what she had to do,' " I said, chopping off whatever speech he was going to make. So long as Charlie Jones stayed a lizard, he could survive in the desert world of middlemen. But if he tried to go warm-blooded, the climate would kill him.

I squared up so I was right on Galina. "You understand what's at stake?" I said.

"Yes," she answered. She put her left hand to her mouth, kissed her wedding ring. Her way of telling me the man next to her wasn't some long-term meal ticket; he was her heart. Charlie had been right—this one was no "bought bride."

"I want to walk away from all this," I said, just barely above a whisper. "That's what you want, too. Your husband and I, we're never going to do business again. You go back to your life; I go back to mine. If you ever see me again, feel free to call whoever you want. Understand?"

"Yes." Ice-cold, now, and at home with it.

"Showing up at a man's house without being invited, I understand how that could be seen as an act of aggression," I said, rolling my shoulders slightly to include both of them in what I was saying. "But you understand . . . you understand *now* . . . I didn't come for that reason, don't you? You understand I had no choice."

"Yes," they replied, as one.

I shifted my total focus to the woman.

"I will never need to do that again," I said. "I know how to reach your family now. I met with—"

"—Yitzhak, yes. He is my cousin."

"And I know how to reach him," I repeated. "But that would be my choice, not his. If I see him again, if I see *anyone* connected with you, even by accident, everything changes. I have people, too. Ask your husband."

"I understand," she said. "And it is fair."

T hat's not what we sell in our store, and you know it," Pepper said, her voice a hard, tight ball of Freon.

"It's information. And you deal in—"

"It's information we can't get."

"Yeah, you—"

"*We* can't get it," Pepper said, as clear as spring water, and as cold. "Only *she* could do that. And you were already told—"

"I'm not coming sideways, Pepper. There's only one thing I want," I lied.

"Yes, one thing: You want her to take a risk. Worse, you want her to ask someone *else* to take a risk. More than one, actually. What you want, it's complicated."

"I know."

"We came all the way down here," she said, looking around at the restaurant, "because you said you had something very important. Too important to say on the phone."

"And it was, right?"

"Important? I don't have any idea. Important to you, maybe."

"It's . . . Look, Pepper, here it is. I told you what I want. What I want to *buy,* remember? I'm not asking to meet with Wolfe. I *got* that message, all right? I just want your crew to do what you do. Not for me, for—"

"Money."

"Not for that, either. This is something . . . this is something you'd want to do."

"Yes?" Skeptical-suspicious.

"I can't tell you any more than I already have," I said, knowing I'd already blown it. But I'd had to try.

Pepper exchanged a look with Mick. I couldn't see a muscle move in his face, but she nodded like she'd just finished reading a long letter. Mick got up from the booth and walked out the front door. Max waited a few heartbeats, then moved out in the same direction.

Pepper stepped out of the booth, took out her cell phone, and deliberately turned her back to me as she walked off.

In a minute, she was back. "You have the best food in the whole city," she sang out, as Mama passed by on her way to the kitchen.

Mama held one finger to her lips, but she was smiling.

One of the payphones rang.

Mama came back over to my booth.

"Police girl," she said.

I thought we had an understanding." Wolfe's voice, through the receiver.

"We do," I said. "But this, what I need, you're the only one who can get it for me."

"Even if that was true, why should I?"

"I'm back to . . . what I was when you met me."

"When I met you, you were a lot of things."

"You know what I mean."

She was quiet for a few seconds. Then: "Yes, I know what you mean. What I don't know is whether you mean it."

"I swear I do."

"On what?"

I stayed silent, waiting.

"What does a man like you swear on, Burke?"

I'd never said it before. Not out loud. And, probably, if I'd thought about it, I wouldn't have said it then. I was just reaching for one true thing, and . . .

"I swear on my love," I told the woman who had always known.

W on't you have another slice, sugar?"

"Slice?" I said, looking at the gaping empty wedge in the French-silk chocolate pie sitting on the kitchen table. "That was a *slab,* girl. Three normal pieces, easy."

"Didn't you like it?"

"It was the best pie I ever had," I told her, holding

up my palm in a "the truth, the whole truth" gesture.
"I'm just not used to eating so much."

"Oh, I can see that. You're way too skinny, Lew.
You're not one of those men who think skinny means
high-class, are you?"

"Come here, brat."

*M*en are so lucky," she said, an hour later. "Fash-
ions don't change for you. A big deal is when ties
get narrower, or lapels get wider—stuff like that. For us,
you can go from being just right to all wrong in a month."

"I don't see what that mat—"

"Do you like these jeans on me?" she said, turning
her back and looking over her left shoulder.

"Who wouldn't?"

"Uh-huh. Except nobody hardly even *makes* jeans
like this anymore."

"They're just regular—"

"They are *not*. These are old-fashioned. See how
high the waist is? The new ones, they ride so low on
your hips they almost make your butt disappear."

"There's no chance—"

"Don't you even *say* it!" she said, her voice caught
between threat and giggle. "The *point* is, I'm not built
for the new ones. Everything they make now is for
those girls with Paris Hilton bodies."

I made a sound of disgust.

"What? You don't think she's cute?"

"I think she looks like a really effeminate man. And
when she opens that lizard-slit of a mouth, she makes

Anna Nicole sound like Madame Curie. I wouldn't just kick her out of bed; I'd burn the sheets."

"Oh, you're so *mean*."

"You asked me."

She came over to where I was sitting, turned, and dropped into my lap. "How about we go for another ride in that car of yours, big boy?" she giggled. "I'm all dressed for it."

*P*eople around here don't do this," Loyal said, her shoulder just brushing mine. "Go for drives, I mean. They get in their cars to be going someplace, not just to be going."

"We're going someplace," I said.

"Where, Lew?"

"I don't mean tonight. I just meant, you and me, we're going someplace, aren't we?"

"You're the driver," she purred.

*W*here do you get all that music of yours?"

"The CDs? A friend of mine mixes them for me."

" 'Mix' is the truth," Loyal said. "I never heard such a . . . collection of different songs before."

"You like any of them?" I asked her. Between the Midtown Tunnel and the Suffolk County line, the Plymouth's speakers had gushed out a real medley: Little Walter's "Blue and Lonesome," Jack Scott moaning "What in the World's Come Over You?," Dale and Grace begging you to "Stop and Think It Over," even a rare cut of Glenda Dean Rockits, "Make Life Real," sounding like Kathy Young backed by Santo and Johnny.

"That 'Talk of the School' one was so sad. Kids can be so mean, especially in high school."

"You know who that was, singing?"

"No. But I'm sure I never heard him before."

"But you did, girl. That was Sonny James."

"*The* Sonny James?"

"Yep."

"But he's country, not—"

"Not doo-wop? Roy Orbison had a doo-wop group himself once."

"For real?"

"Sure. Roy Orbison and the Roses."

"My goodness."

She drifted into a sweet, connected silence. We were encapsulated, the Plymouth sliding smoothly through the night.

"I *loved* that girl singer," she finally said. "You know the one?"

"Sounded like a young Patsy Cline?"

"Yes! Can we play hers again?"

I hit the "back" button until I found the cut. A driving, insistent bass line, the plaintive haze of a steel guitar hovering over the top. A nightingale's voice cut through the steel like an acetylene torch:

> *You say that was your cousin*
> *But I know what I saw*
> *And if that girl was your cousin*
> *You both was breaking the law*

"Oh, I know I should just hate that," Loyal said, chuckling, "but that Kasey Lansdale is just too good! That child's going to be *big* someday."

"Why should you hate it? The song, I mean."

"Well, it's another of those stupid stereotypes, isn't it? You know, rednecks and incest. Tobacco Road stuff. We're supposed to be all kinds of bad, Southerners. To hear some of the people around here talk, we're all Bible-thumping, ignorant racists with no teeth, living in shacks. Well, you know what, sugar? That's just another kind of prejudice."

"It is."

"You're not going to argue with me?" she said, lightly scraping her fingernails over the top of my thigh. "Or are you just making sure I'm going to be nice to you later?"

"I can't speak for the South. I haven't spent enough time there to say. But anyone who thinks there's no racism in New York hasn't lived here long."

"I *know,*" she said, vehemently.

"And anyone who thinks one part of the country— one part of the *world*—has got a patent on incest is in a coma."

"There's good and bad people everywhere," Loyal said, a schoolgirl, reciting a hard-learned lesson.

I'm a lifelong gambler, but I never go all-in unless we're playing with my deck. Hedging bets is more my style.

When I left Loyal's apartment building, I drove downtown. I like the subway better, but this time of the year it's a hermetically sealed disease-incubator, a particle accelerator for germs. Winter flu's bad enough, but springtime flu can drop you quicker than a Jeff Sims overhand right.

Chicago is a city of neighborhoods. New York is a city of streets. Five blocks away from where I stopped, ruptured-synapse zombies trembled in doorways, down to nothing but the prayer that the next rock they bought with blood-bank money would be a sweet crackling in their glass pipes, not a tiny chunk of dry-wall pretender. But I was standing in that sparkling piece of Manhattan where they shoot those perky and precious romantic comedies. The block was lined with wonderful little shops and reeked of *ambiance*. The princes who lived there kept their organically grown marijuana in rosewood humidors.

I used my cell phone instead of ringing the bell. Stayed on the line until I was buzzed in. Took the tiny little elevator cage to the top floor.

The man who let me in was built like a jockey, all muscle and bone. He had a shaved and waxed skull, a ruby in his ear so heavy it had elongated the lobe, and a red soul patch under his lower lip, the same color as his tank top. His eyelids sagged, dark half-moons stood out against the bleached whiteness of his cheeks. He looked as weary as a platitude in a mortician's mouth.

"So?" he said, exhaustedly stepping aside to let me in.

I walked over and took a seat at one end of a long, narrow slab of butcher block. He followed me lan-guidly, sat down at the other end.

I slid a copy of the CD Clarence had made over to

him like I was dealing a card. It was an edited version of the one Daniel Parks had handed over.

"I'd like to find that woman," I said.

"That's nice," he said. Like any good psychopath, he lived in the Now, and whatever ethics he had were long past their sell-by date. He knew that the only way the meek were going to inherit the earth was if the last predator to go left it to them in his will.

"I'd consider it a big favor," I told him.

"Redeemable for . . . ?"

"The last job I did for you . . ."

"You were paid for that, as I recall."

"I was paid to do one thing," I reminded him. "The job turned out to be more than you said it was going to be."

"I never promised—"

"You told me someone had something that belonged to you, and you'd pay me to get it back."

He raised what would have been his eyebrows, if he hadn't shaven them off.

"It wasn't yours," I said, placidly.

"Well, that's a matter of some dispute."

"The dispute turned into a bullet wound."

"So you're here for more—"

"I told you what I'm here for," I said. "Be a good listener; that's how people stay friends."

"I'm not alone here," he said. "You don't think I would have just let you come over if I was, do you?"

"You don't think, if I wanted to do something to you, I'd call first, do *you*?"

He folded his arms across his chest, eyes involuntarily darting over my left shoulder. "Point-blank, I didn't know Hector was going to go psycho on you, Burke. Polygraph that."

"Oh, I believe you. I just figured you'd feel bad about how it turned out. And you'd want to make it up to me."

"And if I don't?"

I looked over at the wall of glass to my right. "You know how people talk about a 'window of opportunity'?" I said. "You know why leaving it open a little's always better than keeping it shut?"

"I'll bite."

"Because that way the glass never has to get broken."

He touched his temples, tuning into whatever frequency guided his ship.

"I can't promise anything," he said.

When I got up the next morning, the whole right side of my head throbbed. A quick glance at the mirror showed me my right ear was inflamed. I get that from grinding it against the pillow all night. Only happens when I dream so deep and dark that it's a blessing not to remember any of it.

I stepped out of the flophouse into the red-and-gold blaze of a chemical sunset. That's this city for you, a toxic-waste garden, full of beautiful artificial flowers.

The pit bulls let me reclaim my Plymouth, even though all I had was a couple of gyros I bought from a

vendor on the walk over. It wasn't about the quality of
the bribe for them; they just wanted to be shown some
respect.

The orca female sat and watched me for an extra
minute. I tossed her a cube of steak I had saved from
Mama's. She snapped it out of the air without a sound.
We both looked at the other two pits. Neither of them
had seen a thing. Our secret.

*T*he windowless, slab-sided building in Sunnyside
had a fresh display of swastikas, spray-painted
by some glue-sniffing member of the master race. I
thought how nice it would be to introduce him to my
new pal, Yitzhak. Or dip him in a vat of meat gravy and
throw him over the fence that surrounded my car.

The bouncer looked like a recycling project from
wherever they dump disbarred bikers: greasy hair
pulled back into a Shetland ponytail, jailhouse tattoos
across the knuckles of both hands, bad teeth, wrap-
around shades. If he had a name, I didn't remember it.

The first time I'd been there, he had followed me
out into the parking lot.

"Hey!"

"What?" I had said, turning to face him.

"You a cop?"

"Sure."

"You don't want to fuck with me," he growled, moving in.

"That's right, I don't."

"We don't like motherfuckers coming in here asking
questions."

"I'm not a fighter," I said, edging backward.

"I heard that one before," he taunted. "You're not a fighter, you're a—"

"—shooter," I finished for him, showing him the .357.

"Hey!" he half yelled, spreading his arms wide. "I was just—"

"No, you weren't," I told him, cutting off the "just doing my job" speech he was going to launch into. "Go back inside, call your boss on the phone. You handle it right, he'll think you're being smart, just checking out this guy who was acting suspicious. Instead of shaking down the customers, that is."

"You don't know my boss."

"Tell Jiffy, Burke said hello," I told him.

The next time I visited, the bouncer had pointedly ignored me. He did the same tonight.

"Hello, Dolly," I said to the waitress who came over to my table. It wasn't a line; that's her name.

"Hey!" she said, giving me a smile as genuine as Ted Bundy's remorse.

"Sit down with me for a little bit."

"You know I can't do that, baby. Only the dancers . . ."

I spread five twenties on the tabletop. "So you'll share," I said.

Dolly had been a dancer once. A drop-down after she started sagging too much to work escort. She'd kept sagging all the way down to table hostess in a Grade C strip joint. I didn't want to think about what was next for her. Neither did she. Cocaine helps her with that.

"Nope," is all she'd said when I showed her Beryl's picture. It had been a long shot, but that's what you do when you're killing time.

"Show it around," I told her. "I've got a grand for an address."

"These girls," she said, glancing at the stage, where a scrawny brunette with ridiculously huge breasts was humping a pole, next to a cellulite blonde who was fingering herself and moaning from boredom, "they're all on drugs. They'll tell you anything you want to hear."

"An address," I said again. "Not a story."

"I got to get back to work," Dolly said.

*E*ven in springtime, the basement apartment was cold. Not A/C cold, but the clammy cold of damp, moldy rot. The man who lived there was dressed for his role: He wore enough layers of clothing to pass for the Michelin Man. Had the right skin color for it, too. Fingerless gloves on his hands—hands he warmed over the glow of the money he had stashed somewhere in the place.

I knew about the money, but I didn't know how much it really was, never mind where he had it hidden. It would take a team of greenback-trained bloodhounds years to dig through the fetid swamp of that basement to find it.

If it was even there.

A long time ago, a no-neck mutant named Harold who lived in the same building figured out that the man in the basement must be hoarding something. After all, he never went out. Never. Lived on take-out food passed through a slot cut into the steel door to his den, the same way they do it in supermax prisons. He hadn't needed the landlord's permission to put in that door—he owned the building.

The mutant didn't know that; he wasn't the research type. His idea of a complex extortion scheme was to pound on the man's door and scream, "Give me money, motherfucker!" When that didn't work out for him, he remembered a technique he'd heard about in prison. So the next time he came back, he had a plastic squeeze bottle full of gasoline with him. Told the man inside that he was going to roast him alive unless he got paid.

I was the one who got paid instead. I used some of the money to buy my partner Hercules a nice suit. Had to go to a tailor for it—department stores don't make suits to fit guys who spend most of their time Inside hoisting iron.

"What?" the mutant yelled in response to my knock.

"Open the door, Harold," I said. "Mr. G. sent us."

"Who the fuck is Mr. G.?"

"Harold . . ." I said, my voice clearly losing patience.

He flung open the door like a Bluto cartoon. "What the fuck are—?"

The sight of Hercules calmed him right down. I guess he remembered more about prison than just the burnouts.

We had a nice talk. I explained that the man who

lived in the basement was the crazy old uncle of a very important individual. Harold the Mutant never asked who "Mr. G." was; maybe he thought he knew. In fact, he seemed to be getting smarter by the minute. When I told him if he ever went near the basement again he was going off the roof without a parachute, his comprehension was perfect.

*H*ow many steps?" the man in the basement asked me, through the slot in the door.

"Eleven," I said.

"You're sure?"

"Positive. I counted them," I told him, connecting us.

The door swung open soundlessly. That always surprised me—I expected it to squeak like the ones in horror movies—but I guess he kept it lubricated, somehow.

I didn't offer to shake hands; I knew he didn't like that.

He didn't offer me a seat, just looked at me with the beyond-disappointment eyes of an orphan staring into a shopwindow at Christmastime. I don't know how he ended up where he is now. But I know he knows money.

"Is it hard to set up an account in Nauru?" I asked him, without preamble.

I waited for him to count the syllables in my question. I knew it had to be an even number, or he wouldn't respond. He doesn't care how the dictionary breaks up a word, only how it comes out of someone's mouth.

"No," he said, playing out his ritual: questions are even, answers are odd.

"Why do people do it?"

"Secrecy."

"Like a Swiss bank account?"

"Liechtenstein."

"Like that?"

"No."

"What's the difference?" I asked, knowing he'd hear "difference" as two syllables.

"Government."

"You need big money to do it?"

"Yes."

"Do they *make* money doing it?"

"Yes."

"So it's like a big laundry job?"

"Yes."

"For criminals, then?"

"Yes."

"And everybody knows?"

"Yes."

"Do you have any contacts there?"

"No."

"Thank you."

He made some noise. I wasn't sure what the word was, but I knew it was a single syllable.

I tried other places. Other people. Other possibilities. Even a "journalist" who spent his slimy life pawing through garbage looking for morsels to peddle to the sleaze-sheets. He promised he'd sniff around. I believed him—that's just what dung beetles do.

I wasn't holding good cards, but I wasn't down to drawing dead, either. Not yet. Beryl's picture was circulating all over the city. Favors were being called in, pressure was being put on.

You can't really do surveillance on houses as isolated as her father's, or in neighborhoods as ritzy as her mother's. Not unless you have a government-sized budget and government-level immunity for felonies. I know how to get in touch with some sanctioned black-bag boys, and I know what it takes to turn their crank, too. But telling your business to people like that will guarantee you go on a list. The bone-and-pistol package Morales had planted had gotten me off a bunch of those, and I didn't want to start new ones.

With the kind of money that Daniel Parks had made disappear, Beryl could have disappeared, too. She could be anywhere. But it didn't feel like that to me. And I'd found her once. . . .

S ay where and when."

"You know where I used to work? There's a parking lot, the public one. The upper deck is outdoors."

"Got it."

"I'm there now."

"Give me an hour."

I thumbed off the cell phone, slipped it into the pocket of my jacket.

"That's her, isn't it?" Loyal said.

" 'Her'?"

"Yes, 'her.' Not that fake 'wife' of yours, the one woman you really love."

"This is just business," I said.

"Sure," she said, soft and somber, like in church. "When you're done with your 'business,' you come right on back here, sugar, and I'll fix whatever she broke. That's the kind of woman *I* am."

*T*he Chrysler was standing by itself in the farthest corner of the lot. I parked at the other end, backing into the open space. At midnight, the lot was empty. The courthouse was closed, visiting hours were over at the jail, City Hall was shut down.

The Chrysler's passenger door opened and Wolfe got out. Instead of moving toward me, she opened the back door, and a thick black shape flowed onto the ground.

Great! I thought. *Just what I need, another one of my big fans.*

Wolfe snapped on the Rottweiler's chain and stepped over to where I was parked. Her shiny lime-green raincoat was tightly belted at the waist, blazing in the night.

I got out of the Plymouth. Slowly.

Not slow enough. The Rottweiler let out a threatening growl.

"Bruiser!" Wolfe said. "Enough."

"Hey, Bruiser," I greeted him.

He said something like "Go fuck yourself!" in Rottweiler. The barrel-chested beast had decided to hate me the first time he saw me. And once he locked his bonecrusher jaws around a feeling, he never dropped the bite.

"Your dog's a real party animal," I said to Wolfe.

"Bruiser? He's a sweetheart," she said, patting the monster's huge head. "You're the only one he doesn't like."

Wolfe walked over to the edge of the lot, leaned her elbows on the railing, and looked down at the dark. I stayed where I was.

"Down!" she told the Rottweiler.

He did it in slow motion, his "give me a reason" eyes pinning me all the way.

I moved over to the railing, my hands already coming up with a flared match for Wolfe's cigarette.

"Thanks," she said.

"I'm the one who needs to be thanking you. You found—?"

"Maybe not much," she said. "Maybe enough."

"How did you—?"

"That little tombstone was a perfect surface for prints." I didn't bother telling her that that was why I'd pocketed an item from the shelf full of artifacts bestowed on little Beryl by professional revolutionaries grateful to her parents for their financial support. It was a lead-cast miniature of a clenched fist rising from the engraved tombstone of Fred Hampton. "You're lucky nobody had polished it."

"Just how lucky did I get?"

"There were three different partials that could be lifted. One of them matched to a Beryl Eunice Preston, DOB nine, nine, seventy-two. That's her, right?"

"Right," I said, not surprised to see Wolfe's hands holding nothing but her cigarette—I'd seen her cross-examine expert witnesses for hours without ever glancing at her notes.

"She was in the system," Wolfe said. "Arrested eleven, twenty, ninety-seven. Attempt murder, CCW, whole string of stuff."

"All one event?"

"Yes," she said, exhaling so that smoke ran out of her nose. "This was in Manhattan. She was working for one of the escort services, claimed the john had demanded she do something she didn't want to do, then got violent with her when she refused."

"A self-defense case?"

"It might have been, if it had ever gone to trial," Wolfe said. "The escort service said they'd never heard of her, big surprise, but she posted bail and walked. Then the complaining witness stopped complaining. When the detectives leaned on him, he said the whole thing had been a mistake. He was showing her the knife—said he was some kind of collector, and this was a fancy one he'd just bought—and he slipped and fell on it. The hotel never should have called the cops."

"Anyone buy that?"

"Why would they?" Wolfe said. "But what were they going to do, threaten to tell his wife he was using his credit card to have some fun? Bluff the girl into taking an assault plea? This is real life, not a TV show. They dropped it like it was on fire."

"Nothing since? For Beryl, I mean?"

"As far as the system's concerned, she could have joined a convent."

"You pulled an address?"

"Sure," she said. And gave me the condo in Battery Park.

When I didn't say anything, she said, "You had that one, didn't you?"

"Yeah," I admitted, not trying to keep the disappointment out of my voice.

"The arraignment judge played it like it was a stand-up assault with a deadly weapon," Wolfe said, grinding out her cigarette with one precision stab of her spike heel. "Set bail at a quarter-mil. Your girl, she didn't use a bondsman."

"She put up that much in *cash*."

"No," Wolfe said. "A friend put up his house."

"Must have been some house."

"Oh, it was." Her white teeth flashed in the night. "Want the address?"

S he had that hideout in place for a *long* time," Michelle said. "Even before she met that Daniel Parks guy, you think?"

"Yeah. That *is* what I think. She bought the property in '94."

"She would have been . . . twenty-two years old then," Clarence said, looking up from his laptop.

"Pretty young to be that smart," Michelle said. "She must have had a crystal ball, too, buying a house in that neighborhood back then. I'll bet it's worth five times what she paid for it."

"It wasn't leveraged, either," I told them, tapping a stack of paper in front of me. "She put a hundred down, leaving her with a twenty-one-hundred-dollar-a-month nut for everything—mortgage, taxes, insurance, the whole thing. It's a two-family, and she was getting eight fifty for the first floor, seven hundred for the second. The C of O for the building says it's strictly a two-family, but I'll bet the basement's another apartment, off the books."

"You sure it's our girl?" the Prof said.

I looked around the table, ticking the points off on my fingers: "One, the name on the ownership papers is 'Jennifer Jackson.' That's a motel-register name. Two, whoever owned that property put up the whole thing, deed and all, to make bail for Beryl when she was arrested. Three, we know she knows how to change her name, and how to move money around, too. And, four, she's the kind of operator who never builds a house without a couple of back doors."

"Park Slope's gone way upscale, but it's no gated community," Michelle said, looking over at the Mole.

I love these," Loyal said, fitting the blue leather bustier over her breasts. "But you can't get into them without help."

"At your service," I said, slowly pulling the laces tight.

"That's what you think I am, don't you?"

"Huh?"

"You know what I mean, Lew. I've been so honest with you. Now it's coming around to hurt me."

"I don't—"

"You know what? I thought you loved me. I don't

mean I was your *great* love. Not that special, once-in-a-lifetime-if-you-get-real-lucky love. But a whole lot more than . . . than just *liking* me, I guess. I guess I just told you too much truth, didn't I?"

"No, you didn't. You told me just enough. And you *showed* me a lot more."

"But I'm not the one you—"

"You *are* the one," I said. "Not like you think, but . . . Look, Loyal, to me you're a princess. A little princess. And I've got a plan for this to have a happy ending."

"But not a *marriage* plan, right?"

"Better."

"What could be—?"

"Just wait," I said. "Wait a little bit. You wanted to know what I do for a living, remember?"

"Yes. But I don't—"

"I'm a gambler, little girl. And I've got something going now. The dice are already tumbling. If I can throw the hard eight, you're going to have your happy ending. That's all I can tell you now. Is that enough?"

Loyal paused in the act of pulling on one of her stockings. "A coral snake is one of the most beautiful things you could ever see. But one bite and you're all done. Then there's milk snakes. They're just as pretty, but they're harmless. You know how to tell them apart?"

"Red and black, he's a good jack. Red and yella, kill the fella."

"Oh!" she said. She raised her chin, looked down at where I was sitting. "You've spent some time in the South, haven't you? I wondered about that, ever since

I told you about people saying I looked like Jeannie, remember? And you said I do favor her. That's not the
way people around here talk."

"I've traveled a little bit."

"Gambling?"

"That's right."

"And you're going to win me a happy ending?"

"I'm trying."

"That would be the sweetest thing a man could give
a woman, a happy ending."

"I—"

"I'm a girl who gives as good as she gets," Loyal
said, turning away from me and bending over the
couch. "And you don't have to wait for yours."

*T*hat's her?" Clarence asked, pointing at his laptop
screen.

"Go through them one more time," I said.

He trailed his finger over the touchpad, and a new
set of thumbnails popped into life. He clicked on them,
one by one, and each new image burst into full-screen
life.

A woman in a beige parka, so densely quilted that it
was impossible to tell if she was a stick or a sumo,
walked down a tree-lined street, carrying a large green
tote bag with a yellow logo.

The same woman inside a market, the tote draped
over the handlebars of a shopping cart. She had pixie-
short light blonde hair, bright-red lipstick.

"I can zoom in on that one," Clarence said.

"Go."

The woman had china-blue eyes, a beauty mark at the corner of one of them. It looked like one of those tattooed tears gang kids put on their faces, one for each jolt Inside.

"That's her," I said.

"Are you sure, mahn? She looks nothing like the girl on that—"

"Her stuff is tough," the Prof interrupted his son, "but it ain't *close* to enough. That's the same girl Schoolboy and me snatched."

"You have not seen her for—what?—twenty years?" Clarence said. Not challenging, fascinated.

"She's still got the look," the Prof said.

"She does not look afraid to me," Clarence said, respectful but doubting.

"She never did," the Prof answered. "Ain't that right, Schoolboy?"

On the move." Terry's voice, over my cell. "Walking."

"Probably a Starbucks run," I said, glancing at my watch. "Gives us twenty minutes, tops."

"I can double that for you," Michelle said. "Drop me off at the next corner."

I glanced over my shoulder at the Prof. He patted the outside pocket of his ankle-length canvas duster. "I already been in once," he said. "I left it so's I can pop that box like I had me the key."

"Eight-fifteen," Clarence said. "The tenants have all gone to work."

"You take the wheel," I told him.

I heard the sound of a key working the lock. Pointed my finger at Max to warn him.

She walked into the living room, one hand holding a paper cup. A sixteen-ounce double skinny mocha latte, if she hadn't changed her usual order.

"Hello, Beryl," I said, from the darkness of the couch.

She was fast, but Max was ready for the move, wrapping her up as she bolted back toward the front door. He held one finger against the buccinator muscle in her right cheek, nerve-blocking the pressure point so she couldn't scream.

He lifted her off the ground with his left hand, letting her feel the price of resistance. She got the message and sagged, allowing him to deposit her next to me on the couch.

"Nobody's going to hurt you, Beryl," I said. "Just the opposite. We know people are looking for you; we're here to fix that."

"Who are—?"

"You know who we are, child," the Prof said, as he stepped forward. "We're the ones who got you back from that pimp when you were just a kid. Remember?"

"You're . . ." She paused, looking at Max. "You were there," she said to the Prof. "And him, too"—nodding at Max. "But who are—?"

"It's me, Beryl," I said. "I had some work done on my face, but—"

"It *is* you! I would never have known your face, but that voice, it's . . . it's the same."

"You have your father's gift."

"My . . . what?"

"Your father's gift," I said again. "He's real good with voices, too."

"My *father* sent you?"

"You mean, like he did before?"

"That wasn't him," she said, as if the words were poison in her mouth.

"I know," I told her. "I didn't know then, but I do now."

"You think so?" she said, curling her lip. She shrugged out of her coat, crossed her legs, telling us she wasn't going anywhere.

"Let's see," I said. "You were involved with a man named Daniel Parks. A money manager. He siphoned off money from a hedge fund he was running. A lot of money. He probably knew a lot more about high finance than he did about the people who put their money into his fund. So maybe he figured the most he was risking was a civil suit. Or even a fraud prosecution he could lawyer his way out of. How am I doing so far?"

"You're talking," she said, opening a silver box on the coffee table. She took out a prerolled joint, lit up, and pulled a heavy hit of Maryjane into her lungs.

"We don't know exactly how much Parks stole. Probably take years to figure that out. But we know you ended up with a pile of it. He thought you were his secret bank. But the first time he started talking about making a withdrawal, you disappeared on him. You must have been planning it for a long time. It's easy when they trust you, huh?"

"He was in love," Beryl said, her drawl suggesting, "If God didn't want them sheared . . ."

"Men aren't your favorite humans, huh?"

"Good guess, Sherlock. If it weren't for my mother, I'd be as queer as Ellen and Rosie combined."

"Got it," I said, trying to get her train back on the track I wanted. "You figured it for a low-risk play too, and *you* were right. So Parks gets arrested, so what? So he decides to name names, big deal. Far as *you* were concerned, he was just a generous lover."

"Some men are," she said, smiling ugly and dragging deep on her joint. She didn't even bother to hold the smoke down—plenty more where that had come from.

"Then he gets himself gunned down, right on the street. Now you know the people he ripped off aren't going to the Better Business Bureau. And they're going to be looking for their money."

"And so are you," she said, her voice so thick with contempt I could barely make out the words. "Just like you were the last time."

I could feel the Prof vibrating in the corner, a step away from erupting. I held up my hand to silence him.

"Don't put it on anyone but me, Beryl," I said. "The whole thing was mine. Everyone else just backed my play. I thought I was doing the right thing."

"You know what they say about the road to Hell."

"Yeah."

"Well, you don't even get *that* much slack. I *know* you got paid to bring me back."

"I did you wrong. I didn't know it then. I know it now. That's why I'm here."

"What, to make it up to me?" she asked scornfully.

"I can't do that. Because it can't be done. Nobody could do it for me; nobody can do it for you."

She gave me a sharp, appraising look, but she didn't say anything.

"Here's what I can do," I told her. "I can get you safe. Not just off the hook—safe forever."

She gave me a serpent's grin, certain she was back on her home ground now. "Sure. All I have to do is give back the—"

"Not a dime," I cut her off. "You walk away free and clear. You won't have to hide in this basement. You can go right back to being Peta Bellingham, if you want."

"Just like that, huh?"

"There's more," I said. "To sweeten the deal, I'll even throw in some justice."

S he might still run, son," the Prof said on the drive back, signing with his fingers so that Max could follow along.

"No," I said, shaking my head. "She knows we found her once, we can find her again. Probably thinks we have her watched twenty-four/seven," I went on, turning my hands into binoculars, then cupping my right ear in a listening gesture. "The deal I offered her is the only way out."

I turned slowly in my seat, capturing each of them with my eyes until I had them all with me.

"There's something else, too," I told them. "She *wants* to do it."

Isn't this a little flashy for a lawyer?" I asked Michelle. She was busy adjusting the lapels of my tuxedo-black suit, threaded with a faint metallic-blue windowpane pattern. Under the jacket, my shirt was royal purple with vertical stripes of pale lemon. French cuffs, with Canadian Maple Leaf gold coins for links. My tie was a Dalíesque riot of color that you couldn't look at for long without vertigo. The shoes were black mirrors, softer than most gloves.

"Not for the kind of lawyer *you're* supposed to be, sweetheart," she said, confidently. "And this is the pièce de résistance." She meant the black leather Tumi attaché case, gusseted to expand to carry a laptop and whatever other tools a bar-certified extortionist might need.

The initials on the case were "ROM." Roman Oscar Mestinvah wouldn't come up on a Martindale-Hubbell search, but he *was* registered with OCA—the New York State Office of Court Administration. Admitted to practice in 1981, and a member in good standing. Roman was an elite lawyer, with a very narrow practice—Gypsies only. I don't know his real name—no Gypsy ever has only one—but the one he'd used since law school gave him those inside-joke initials.

If anyone speaking English called his office, his girl

would know it was for me, and message me at Mama's—
my rental of his name included a few extra services.

"No diamond watch?" I said, sarcastically.

Michelle gave me one of her patented looks. "You'll
be driving a Porsche, not a Bentley," she replied, as if
that explained the Breitling chronograph she had
handed me.

"I guess I'm ready," I told her.

She stepped very close to me, stood on her toes, and
kissed my cheek. "I'm proud of you, baby," she whispered. "This is the real Burke now. My big brother.
Coming home."

Y ou want to go over it again?" I asked, as I plucked
the EZ Pass transmitter from the inside windshield of Beryl's metallic-silver Porsche and stowed it
in the glove compartment before we hit the Holland
Tunnel. She was wearing a navy-blue pinched-waist
jacket over a beige pleated skirt, sheer stockings, and
simple navy pumps. A successful woman, on her way
to work.

"I've got it," she said. "Don't worry; I've been doing
this kind of thing all my life."

"Even before I—?"

"Years before," she said, flatly.

"Why didn't you say anything?"

"To you? What for? You were just another hired
man. And it wasn't me paying your salary."

"I would never have brought you back," I said,
hearing the defensiveness in my voice. "That happened before. More than once."

"Sure."

"It's the truth," I said. Hearing *You know it is* in my mind. Realizing it was Wolfe I was talking to.

"Even if I believed you, which I don't, where were you going to take me? You think I hadn't *tried* telling before then? *Way* before then? You know what that got me? More hired men, doing more things to me. Before they sent me back, that is. I'll give you that much: You just drove the merchandise home like you were paid to do, didn't even make me blow you first."

I shook off the image, said, "But you weren't really running away."

"What's that supposed to mean?" Turning to give me a quick, hard stare.

"That pimp, the one you were with, he hadn't kidnapped you. I've seen enough of those to know."

"Because I didn't throw my arms around you for rescuing me from the big bad man?"

"Because you weren't scared," I said. "You weren't stoned. And you weren't hurt."

"You're smarter than you look," she said, smiling sardonically. "At least, you're smarter *now*. That's right. You think some half-wit nigger could have tricked *me*? I was playing him, not the other way around. But I didn't know the game then. Not the whole game. I never figured he'd try to actually *sell* me."

"What's with 'nigger,' Beryl?"

"You don't like the word?"

"It sounds nasty in your mouth, and—"

"Ah. When you spoke to my dear daddy, he told you we were all such wonderful liberals, yes?"

"He did say they were—"

"Fakes," she said, spitting the word out of her mouth like a piece of bad meat. "Both of them, complete frauds. Every word they ever spoke was a lie. The big 'radicals,' fighting oppression. That whole house was a nonstop masquerade ball. Everybody had their own mask. Especially me."

"Your father was—"

"Weak," she dismissed him with a single word. "A pathetic, cringing weakling. Funding the revolution from the safety of his living room."

"And your mother?"

"Oh, she was never weak," Beryl hissed. "She was even harder than the steel she used on me."

*W*e gassed up on the Jersey Pike. While Beryl used the restroom, I thumbed my cell phone into life.

"Anything?" I said.

"Nothing," Michelle answered. "You know I would have called you if—"

"Yeah."

"Relax, baby. We've got a Plan B, remember?"

*B*eryl accelerated back onto the turnpike, her fingers relaxed on the wheel. As she settled into the middle lane, I said, "You're sure you—?"

"If you say fucking 'reparations' to me one more time, I'm going to throw up all over that cheesy suit of yours."

We stopped at a diner off the Baltimore-Washington Parkway. Beryl wanted the restroom again. And a cigarette. She was a heavy smoker, but she wouldn't light up in her car.

"You don't smoke anymore?" she'd asked me, the first time we'd stopped.

"No."

"Doesn't go with the new face?"

"You're smart enough to be anything you want," I told her. The truth.

"Oh, Daddy!" she mock-squealed, clasping her hands behind her back and stepping close to me. "That's so sweet. You just want your Berry to be the very bestest little girl she can be, don't you?"

I looked away.

"Now I made you mad," she said, reaching down and pulling the hem of her skirt high over her thighs. "You think I should be punished?"

"Give it a rest, Beryl."

"Why? You're not much of a conversationalist, but it's been a while, and I could always use the practice."

I looked away.

"Makes you mad, that I'm such a little whore?"

"That's your business," I said.

"Exactly," she retorted, sticking out her tongue in a deliberately cold parody of a sassy brat.

Did you ever tell him?"

"Who? My father?"

"Yeah. You said you *tried* to tell people, but you never said you actually did it."

"He knew," she said, with a sociopath's unshakable certainty.

"Just like that? You said your mother had a special—"

"Just because he was a coward doesn't mean he was a stupid one."

"But you couldn't be—"

"Yes, I could," she snapped. "I *could* be sure. I'm sure he would have just closed his eyes, no matter what I showed him. You know why?"

"No."

"Because my mother had the *power,*" she said, licking her lips as if the very word was caressing her under her skirt. "If you have power, you can do anything you want, go anywhere you want, get away with anything. It's all yours. Everything. And you know what makes power? Money. If you have enough money—"

"It's not that simple."

"You're right; it's not," she snapped. "If you'd let me finish what I was going to say, you would have heard this: If you have enough money, *and* the spine to use it, every door opens. The whole world is nothing but a market. And humans are just another commodity."

"In some places—"

"In *every* place! You think it's not a market just because the buyers wear masks when they shop? If you have the price, you can have whatever you want—it's *just* that simple."

"Not all prices are money," I said, thinking of Galina's cousin.

"I don't like word games. They're just another way for liars to lie. I don't care what you call it. Some say money; some say God. Some call it a button—a button you push to make people do what you want. Everybody's got one; you just have to look for it.

"And if you don't know where to look, there's tricks to make it come to the surface, where you can see it. I learned something from everyone who ever had me. And I *took* something from them, too. Like a vampire does. It all comes down to the same thing. Power. That's all that counts."

"If that's all that counts, then most people don't."

"Good boy!" she said, rewarding a dog.

Why do you want to know?" she asked me, a few more miles down the road.

"So I can learn."

"How *bad* do you want to know?"

"I don't know how to measure that."

"Did you ever fuck a girl outdoors? Like in a park, where anyone might come along and see you?"

"What diff—?"

"We're trading," she said. "You tell me, I tell you."

"And me first, right?"

"Money in front," Beryl said, giving me a whore's wink.

*T*hose so-called feminists make me retch," she said, lighting another cigarette. We were sitting at a wooden picnic bench at a rest stop. We were the only customers. "They say they're all about choice—like abortion, how they *adore* abortion—but you're only allowed the choices *they* say are okay. They whine about 'empowerment,' but you can only be empowered if you lap up every word they say, like a tame dog."

"You're talking about—?"

"You know what the great buzzword is now? The high-concept plot for the movie they all think they're starring in? 'Trafficking.' This great evil that's been set loose on the world. It's all those kind of people can talk about."

"It's not worth talking about?"

"Why? Because, if enough people talk about it, someday they'll actually *do* something about it? That was my parents' line. All that 'consciousness raising' they wrote checks for."

"What's your answer, then?"

"My answer?" she said, twisting her lips to show teeth, not smiling. "I don't even have a question. Because this 'trafficking' thing, it's all just another mask. Read the papers. Watch TV. Go to a cocktail party. Nobody cares about trafficking in children so long as you're going to use them the way they're *supposed* to be used," she said, planting the barb and twisting to make sure it hooked deep. "You know, like making them work in diamond mines, or sewing soccer balls, or plowing fields."

She turned to me full-face, her own beautiful mask crumbling against the acid of her hate.

"Every kid's nothing but property, anyway. If you want to sell your own property, who cares? The only time anyone bitches about it is when they get sold a lemon, like when some yuppies adopt one of those Russian babies with fetal alcohol syndrome.

"And the media? The only time *those* whores get excited is when they can do a story on 'sex slaves,' because that's what *sells,* okay? And you know what? Most of those girls, they're not slaves at all. They're just women who made a deal. A *choice,* okay?"

"You mean, like to be hookers?"

"You think that's *never* a choice?" she said, mockingly. "You think every stripper is a domestic-violence victim? You think every girl who acts in a porno movie is a drug addict? You think every escort was sexually abused as a child? You think Linda Lovelace didn't *like* fucking and sucking?"

"I wasn't saying—"

"That's right," she said, making a brushing-crumbs gesture. "You weren't saying *anything*. All that 'trafficking' hysteria is just so much political bullshit, a good way for thieves to get grants. A woman grows up in a country where there isn't enough food to eat. She makes a decision to come to a place where she can make more money on her back in an hour than her whole family could earn in a month—what's wrong with that? She's a whore to you, fine. But she's a hero to her family."

"What about the girls who think they're coming here to work in factories, not whorehouses?"

"Grow up!" she snapped. "You really think even

they believe that? You really think they're going to pay twenty, thirty grand for the chance to earn five bucks an hour?"

"That's not an investment," I said, my one good eye scanning her mask, looking for an opening, "that's debt bondage. They have to work off the cost of their passage. And if they open their mouths, they get deported."

"Isn't that a crying shame."

"Not enough to make *you* cry, I guess."

"Who cried for me?"

"So that means—?"

"It means *I* found my own way out," Beryl said, pure self-absorption wafting off her like thick perfume. "You think anyone cares about slavery? There's people in slavery all over the world, aren't there? You buy something made in China, it was probably out of some forced-labor camp. Are you going to pretend that makes a difference to you?

"Slavery, my sweet white ass. All anyone pays attention to is the sex part. And here's a nice irony for you: That *is* a choice, okay? These women, they come here, like you said, they know they have to work off their debt. They can be maids, take them twenty years to get caught up. Or they can gobble some cock for a few months, and end up flush.

"You think if you 'rescued' them they'd jump at the chance to be stuffed into some basement, sewing until their fingertips got paralyzed or they went blind from the lousy lighting? Fucking's not just better paid; it's easier work, too."

"Work?" I said, thinking back to how I had dis-

missed that woman in the blood lab as a "sex worker."
Not liking myself for it now.

"It *is* work," she said, as hotly composed as a high-
school debater. "The higher up the scale you go, the
better it's paid. And safer, too. You know those legal-
ized houses they have in Nevada? When's the last time
you ever heard of a girl being killed in one of them?"

"I don't think I ever did."

"Right!" she said, triumphantly. "Those serial
killers, they grab girls off the streets, not out of houses."

"So an escort service is better?"

"You know about that, too, huh? That was when I
was still learning. I worked in houses, too. But, really,
it's all the same. You only have yourself. They promise
you all the 'security' in the world, but when you're
alone in that room, it's all on you."

I didn't say anything. It wasn't a strategy—her hate
had just run me empty.

"And it's the same when you're all alone in the
world," she said. Slowly, as if concerned I'd miss something important. "You know where I learned that?"

"Yes."

"Yes, that's right, Mr. Knight in Shining Armor. In a
little room. A little girl in a little room. All alone. That's
what you brought me back to. My hero."

We stopped one more time, to switch places. The
Porsche was supposed to be the lawyer's car,
not the client's.

I hit my phone. "It's me," I said, when it was picked
up at the other end.

"She was home an hour and fifteen minutes ago," Toni said. "I dropped by with an even better offer. She wasn't any more interested than she was the last time."

"You're a doll," I told her.

She blew a kiss into the phone.

*T*he woman who came to the door was dressed in workout clothes, a sweatband around her head, towel around her shoulders.

"What can I—?" she started to say, then froze as her eyes went past me to Beryl.

"Hello, Mother. You're looking good."

"I . . ."

By then we were inside. Beryl closed the door behind us as her mother stood there, mouth half open, as if frozen in the act of speech.

"Good afternoon, Ms. Summerdale," I said. Oil in my mouth, too-bright smile on my face. "My name is Mestinvah, Roman Mestinvah. I represent your daughter—"

"Represent?" she said, voice hardening. "What do you think you have to 'represent' anyone about in *this* house?"

"Let's all sit down, Mother," Beryl said, sweetly. "This won't take long."

"It will take less than that for me to call the police," her mother said, standing with her fists clenched at her sides.

"Do it!" Beryl suddenly hissed at her. "Do it, you fucking cunt. Come on!"

Her mother sagged like she'd been body-punched.

We all sat down in the living room, like the civilized adults we were. Nobody offered coffee.

Beryl lit a cigarette.

"We don't allow smoking in—"

Beryl blew a puff of smoke in her mother's direction.

"Ms. Summerdale, I understand this all may be a bit . . . traumatic for you, seeing your daughter after all these years," I said. "We came here in the hopes we can settle things without the need to . . . well, without the need to leave this room, frankly."

"What 'things'?" she said, as Beryl flicked the ash from her cigarette into a crystal vase that held a single blood-red rose.

"Reparations," Beryl said, on cue.

"What are you—?"

"My client," I said, holding up my hand as if to stop Beryl from saying anything more, "has a number of causes of action she intends to pursue, Ms. Summerdale. You would, needless to say, be the defendant in any such litigation. And please don't tell me about the statute of limitations," I went on, as if she'd tried to interrupt. "A team of eminent treatment professionals has already provided sworn affidavits that my client had suppressed all memory of the horrors inflicted on her until very recently. We are quite confident that we could survive any motion to dismiss."

"I don't under—"

"I told them everything, *Mother*," Beryl said, vomiting the last word.

"I have no idea what you think you might have 'told'

anyone," the mother said, strength coming back into her voice. "You have a very troubled history, Beryl. Your mental state was never—"

"That's what happens to little girls who get turned into trained dogs, Mother. *Lap* dogs, remember?"

"You're being—"

"You still have your collection of baby-sized speculums, you filthy fucking bitch? You still have your model-train transformer? The one with the extra wires for bad little girls who don't learn to make Mommy happy?"

"You are insane," the woman said. Emphatically enough, but I could hear the stress fractures in her voice. "You've been insane since you were a child."

"Nobody's insane here," I said, soothingly. "Nobody's even unreasonable. You see, your husband—your ex-husband, I should say—was very forthcoming, Ms. Summerdale."

"He never knew any—" she blurted out, before she realized what she was saying, and clamped down on the words.

"He knew more than you ever imagined," I said, finishing her thought. "And it wasn't just that he had an idea; he had proof. I wonder if the people who bought your house in Westchester ever found the wires for the microphones."

She sat there, stone-still, not moving a muscle. Her face was a frozen, expressionless mask.

"Your 'crafts room,' " I said. "The one with the lock on the door, the double-pad carpet, and the acoustical tiles on the walls. The room where you were teaching Beryl private mother-daughter stuff. The room your husband was never allowed in. You thought he bought that, didn't you? Everybody needs their own space, right? And, after all, he had his den, didn't he?"

She still didn't move. Didn't react when Beryl dropped her burning cigarette butt into the vase, and immediately lit another.

"There are over twenty *boxes* of cassette tapes," I lied. "No video, but the audio makes it clear enough."

"I was in therapy for years and years," Beryl said, on cue again. "But I could never figure out what was *wrong*. If it wasn't for those tapes, I'd still be loaded up on antidepressants, walking around like a zombie. Good old Daddy. All those years, you thought you had him castrated. But he was doing just what *you* were doing, only coming at it from a different angle. You were both fucking me. Fucking your little girl. You did it for fun, and Daddy did it for money. Your money. Now it's my turn."

"What do you want?" the woman said, dead-voiced. Speaking to me as if Beryl wasn't in the room.

"My client is going to need a lot of treatment," I said, greasily. "Expensive treatment. This is much more important to her than digging up the past. What good would that do?"

The mother's mask shifted. "You think you can come into my own home and blackmail me, you grubby little shyster? I've got lawyers that would crush you like the cockroach you are."

"I'm sorry you characterize a sincere attempt to settle a viable case out of court as 'blackmail,' Ms. Summerdale," I said, reaching for my attaché case. "I did warn you this was a possibility," I said to Beryl.

"I like it better this way," she said, licking her lips. "I can't wait."

We hadn't even gotten to our feet before the mother caved.

How do I know you won't be back?" the mother said, a half-hour later.

"Because we're going to give you not only a properly executed and fully binding release of any and all claims against you for any reason, covering my client's life from birth to the present day, but a cast-iron confidentiality agreement, one that requires my client to pay you triple the amount of the settlement as liquidated damages should she disclose any of the . . . material we discussed."

"I . . ."

"And," I said, "something even better. A notarized affidavit from my client acknowledging that the . . . allegations we discussed were a complete fabrication. I have all the documents right here," I said, soothingly, fondling the black leather attaché case. "You're not settling a lawsuit; you're agreeing to pay for your daughter's desperately needed long-term treatment."

"It's a lot of money."

"Oh, please, *Mother,*" Beryl said, in a teenager's voice. "It's, like, only a fraction of what you'd be leaving me in your will anyway, isn't it? Just look at it as an accelerated inheritance."

"When do you expect to—?"

"Right this second," Beryl told her, both hands on the leash. "You've got a computer somewhere in this house. And you've got online access to your money, too. Maybe not all of it, but more than enough to cover what you're going to pay me. A few mouse-clicks, and it's all wire-transferred."

"Even if I could—"

"Oh, you can, *Mother.* Come on, let's go play."

Beryl tapped keys on her cell phone.

"It's there," she said. "Move it out, and close the account down. Now!"

"I never want to see you again," the woman said, spent.

"Oh, you won't, *Mother.* Just one more thing, and we're out of here forever."

"What?" she said, hollowed out way past empty.

"The baby," Beryl told her, a hideous smile playing over her lips. "After what you taught me, I always wanted a little girl of my own."

"You're . . ."

"You can just buy another one. And I know you will. After all, you haven't even started 'training' this one yet. But I need more than money, Mother. I need to take something from *you.*" She clasped her hands in a prayerful gesture, said, "Oh, please, please, tell me you understand," as soft-voiced as a scorpion.

Sign there . . . and there," I told Beryl.

"I still don't see why I should have to split the money with you. It was me she did those things to, not you. And if you hadn't brought me back . . ."

"We went over all that. You keep what you got from Parks; we split what we got from your mother."

"Maybe I changed my mind."

"Don't do that."

"Are you threatening me?"

"Yes."

"Haven't you already stolen enough? From me, I mean."

"You already played that card."

"I always thought my so-called father was the most pathetic man on earth," the beautiful viper said. "Thanks for showing me otherwise."

"Sign *both*," I reminded her, pointing at a line on the papers below which her name and Social Security number had been typed. An embossed notary's seal was already on the page.

"What do you want that baby for?"

"What do you care?"

"I don't," she said. I believed her.

Her silver Porsche pulled away, leaving me on the downtown sidewalk with a baby girl in my arms.

Toni's Corvette came around the corner.

I punched in a twelve-digit number. When Yitzhak answered, I said, "I have something for you."

She has all of it?" he asked me later that night, out on the prairie.

"I don't know how much 'all' is," I said, reasonably. "But she has out-front assets of something like thirty mil. On paper, it was all supposed to have come from her father's business, but all that paper's bogus . . . just a screen."

"How do you know this?"

"Daniel Parks wasn't just stealing from you," I said. "He had a whole long sucker-list. But he had to find a place to stash the money. Spend some money yourself, check out the divorce papers his wife had filed. Parks had a mistress. Her name, her real name, is Beryl Summerdale."

"Beryl Summerdale," the Russian repeated carefully, committing the name I'd given him to memory.

"That's right. And I've got something else for you, too. She's got access to her money online. Right over a modem. If you could get her to tell you the right numbers . . ."

*T*he AP wire said, "Luxury Home Firebombed!"

Beryl Summerdale's neighbors hadn't heard a thing until the house on Castle Crescent suddenly burst into flames at approximately three in the morning.

It took the local Fire Department only minutes to respond to their frantic calls, but the house was already incinerated.

The Arson Squad said a highly sophisticated series of incendiary devices had been used, but no more information could be released at this time.

The crime-scene investigators said "human bone fragments" had been located.

The lead detective on the case said that the house was known to have been owned and occupied by Ms.

Summerdale and her infant daughter. Both were presumed to have perished in the explosion.

The Special Agent in Charge of the local FBI office said that speculation about terrorists targeting the wrong house "has, to the best of our knowledge, no basis in fact at this time," although he acknowledged that the neighborhood was home to several prominent D.C. insiders.

Beryl Summerdale had no known enemies. Her ex-husband had been ruled out. The police had no suspects.

Loyal stood on the sidewalk outside her building. A white Cadillac sedan was at the curb. The trunk was full of luggage. The back seat was full of baby stuff.

"Her name is Charisse, after my mother," Loyal said. "Of all the things you did for me, she was the best. I never even knew how much I wanted—"

"It's what I wanted, too," I said. Pure truth.

"You know where I'll be, Lew."

"You'll be home."

"Home with my little girl," Loyal said. She stood close, her heart in her eyes. "Your home, too, if you ever want one," she said, very softly.

"I just might," I said, lying to her for what I knew was the last time.

EXCERPT FROM

TERMINAL

BY ANDREW VACHSS

Available in hardcover from Pantheon in Fall 2007

I got to the job site a couple hours early. The kind of work I do, you show up too late, sometimes you don't get to go home when it's over.

Gigi was already planted in his spot, his enormous body mass taking up most of a wooden bench, a half-empty pitcher of beer on a little table to his right. The behemoth had a perfect sight-line on the front door, but his tiny eyes were too deeply flesh-pouched for me to tell where he was looking. Wrapped in a faded gray jersey pulled over drawstring pants of the same material, he looked like a moored battleship.

I found a stool at the far end of the bar. The guy behind the stick had a little slice of forehead and less chin. His eyes showed signs of life—I guessed somewhere around geranium level.

I ordered a shot—nobody does brand names in a joint like this. The inbred blinked a couple of times, then brought me some brown liquid. I asked him for a glass of water. He stared at me for a minute. You could see his mind working—it wasn't a pretty sight. Finally, enough tumblers fell into place. He reached under the bar and came up with a glass the EPA wouldn't allow you to dump without a permit.

The TV set was suspended from the ceiling by cables at the opposite end of the bar from where I

was sitting. Some baseball game was on. I was too
far away to hear the sound, or even make out who
was playing, but I watched the moving images. Reminded me of being Inside. They rig the TV in the
dayroom the same way, probably for the same reason. Most guys want to be outdoors every chance
they get, but there's cons who know their soaps better than any housewife.

Usually, I drink the water, slip the whiskey into
the water glass, let the ice melt into it, and then ask
for another. If I think anyone might be watching
close, I transfer by mouth. I was raised in places
where you learn to do that with meds you don't
want, watched by "staff" who hoped you'd refuse—
restraints and hypos were more fun for them.

Eventually, the bartender takes away both
glasses, brings me a "same again," and everybody's
happy. Any regular interested in the stranger sees a
man drinking solo, dedicated to his work. In a place
like this, you sit by yourself *not* drinking, it's like a
red neon arrow pointing at you. *Down* at you.

But I watched how other guys at the bar had to
practically scream to get the inbred's attention. He
mostly just stood there, in the Zen state of just
being the mouth-breathing genetic misfire that he
was. So I nursed my drink the way a crack-addict
mother nurses her kid—if it could figure out how to
drink itself, fine.

Forty minutes later, a man in a bone-colored
leather sports coat shoulder-rolled in and sat down
in an empty booth. Late thirties, with a tanning-bed

complexion. He sported a hundred-dollar short hair-cut—gelled, not spiked. His wristwatch was crusted with diamonds; a three-strand loop of eighteen-karat draped against a black silk collarless pullover.

The battleship slowly broke loose from its mooring and started across the room. From behind me, two torpedoes cut across his wake. As the first passed by where I was sitting, I slid the length of rebar out of my sleeve, gripped the taped end, and took out his knee from behind. The other whirled at his partner's scream, but I was already swinging. His collarbone snapped under the ridged steel whip.

The guy in the bone-colored jacket never made it out of his booth.

I was one of the men who flowed around Gigi like river water around a big rock, all of us heading for the door. The sidewalk was empty, except for a squat-bodied man in a wheelchair. He had a begging cap on the ground next to him, one hand under the army blanket spread across his lap. Nobody gave him a second glance.

*T*he battleship was docked at a pier overlooking the Brooklyn Navy Yard, behind the wheel of an ancient black Caddy. He covered more than half of the front seat; the steering wheel was hidden somewhere under his upper body. A thick skullcap of wiry black hair covered his bowling ball of a head. I was standing next to him, talking through the opened window. I'd done time with Gigi—keeping something solid between you and him is always a good play.

"Didn't expect you," Gigi said. "Never saw you before."

I shrugged, wasting fewer words than he had.

"I did time with your boss. Thought he'd be sending Herk to watch my back."

I shrugged again. "Herk" was short for "Hercules," named for his hyper-muscled physique. Everyone but Gigi called him "Big Herk," but Herk's 275 pounds of prison-sculptured, Dianabol-boosted chassis made him a middleweight in Gigi's league.

The man Gigi thought was my boss was me, the Burke he knew years ago. My face had changed—bullet wounds and trainee surgeons will do that for you—but the payphone that rang in the back of Mama's restaurant still took my calls. And my voice was still the same . . . when I wanted it to be.

"He still in your crew, Herk?"

I gave him the look.

"What?" he said, insulted. "You think I'm a fucking cop? They wanted to wire *me* up, they'd have to use a motherfucking bale of the stuff."

I shook my head.

"You're a dummy? You can't talk, that it? Look, pal, I can see you're not Herk, but I sure as fuck *know* you ain't Max, either."

Gigi meant Max the Silent, a Tibetan combat dragon. Max can't speak, but that's not how he got his name.

"I'm not a dummy," I said, softly. "But I know when to dummy *up.*"

"Not everyone does," he said, a tinge of nostalgia in his guttural voice. "Things ain't the same. These days, you got to pay a man to watch your back even when you get hired just to do a simple job like pounding on that mook. But with these punk kids taking over now, fucking *bosses* they are, you never know when they're gonna watch too much TV, start thinking all *plots* and shit."

"Those two guys, you don't think they were his?"

"Mario's? The guy in the pretty white coat? Yeah, they were his all right. Even a fucking *stugotz* like him knows when he's been put on the spot, marked down for some serious pain. But he's still got to do business, got to make his rounds, show some face. It was just a matter of time. Wasn't me, it would have been someone else.

"Besides, if those guys you took out were from the . . . people who hired me, they would have been shooters. Those guys, they were just dumbass muscle."

I nodded agreement. If they'd been experienced bodyguards, one look at Gigi would have had them heading for the back exit. Probably a pair of strip-club bouncers, used to flexing their gym muscles at drunks.

"Mario could've got himself some shooters, but he'd have to go to the yoms, get someone to do that for the kind of chump-change money he's holding now. Can you imagine a nigger walking into that place? It'd be like one of them wandering onto our range, Inside."

I shook my head.

"You know what, pal? This is seriously fucked. I get paid to do some work on a guy, I got to pay a piece of that just to make sure my back don't get cold. Turns out, I wasted the money."

"You could have handled both of those guys, too?" I said, pretending mild surprise. I'd seen Gigi waddle up to whole *groups* of men Inside, then go through them like an enraged kid busting up balsa-wood model airplanes. He had all the speed of a fire hydrant, and about the same pain tolerance. Gigi wasn't any good at chasing you down, but that's the thing about prison . . . nowhere to run.

"Ask your boss," the battleship said.

I didn't say anything.

"Hey, fuck you, you don't want to talk. Here's the other half of your money. Tell Burke I still owe him a glass of *vino*. . . ."

I used to find people. Kids mostly. I was good at it—the best tracker in the city, the whisper-stream said. But I'd finally learned that bringing kids back to the people who paid me didn't always make me a hero.

And the last job I'd done had changed that for-ever. The man who used to send me tracker work would never be calling me again, either.

I scratch around now. Helping people go and stay gone, that's something I know how to do. But there's not a lot of that kind of work around. And most of it just *vibrates* with danger, like the hum in an electric fence.

The thing about doing crime for a living is that you have to *keep* doing it. And, every time you do, the odds shift . . . in the wrong direction. I'm not going Inside again. Not for all the usual reasons—although every one of those is a good one—but because I can't play that hand anymore. At my age, with my record, any sentence would come with a lifetime guarantee. So when I do violence-for-money, like covering Gigi's back, I make sure I'm nowhere near the fallout zone.

Still, in my world, being "sure" is just another way of saying you had cut down the odds. Nobody was supposed to die in the job Gigi had hired me for, but accidents happen. What I *was* sure of was that nobody was going to talk. Not because of some bullshit "code," because it was the smart play. The only play.

Nobody was even going to *call* the cops, much less talk to them. And if some passing citizen had a cell phone, good fucking luck interrogating that bartender—he wouldn't be *playing* dumb.

With all that, I still should have passed. Anytime you cover Gigi while he's working, you could end up watching a homicide.

I've got some money. That last job had turned out to be worth a lot more than I'd thought it could be. Cost me a lot more than I thought I had, too.

No reason why I couldn't go the rest of the way on that one score. I live small. I have the whole top floor of a flophouse that's been scheduled for the wrecking ball for years, but the bribery they call "paperwork" in this town had prolonged the process through two administrations already. In the meantime, I don't pay rent. Or utilities.

I don't have a phone. For outgoing, I use an ever-changing batch of cloned cells the Mole puts together for me. For messages, there's the same number the underground has been using for me for years. The same one Gigi had called.

I've even got cable, a feeder line from the ground floor of the flophouse. I see whatever I want on the screen, but I never see a bill.

Thanks to my sister Michelle, I don't pay retail for clothing. Except when she gets in one of her "You need this *now*!" moods. Then I end up paying through both nostrils and a few assorted veins.

My car is as maintenance-free as an I-beam, a '69 Roadrunner two-door post. It looks like a derelict from the outside but underneath is an all-new chassis, complete with a transplanted Viper IRS, and a bulletproof, injected Mopar wedge, hand-assembled for torque. Purrs on pump gas, never uses a drop of synthetic between changes, and wouldn't overheat in a Saharan summer.

I shoot pool, but for nickels and dimes. I play cards, but only with my family—my brother Max is into me for over a couple hundred grand, but we agreed we'd settle up when we both reach the Other Side. He's my partner in our two-man betting syndicate, too, but we've never gone more than a few hundred plus-or-minus there.

I don't drink. Even when I did smoke, I only bought Dukes— meaning straight from North Carolina, without those pesky New York tax stamps. Later on, I used one of those hundred-foot Indian reservations they have on Long Island, the ones they built to display the government's deep respect for its favorite Native American tribe: the Casino Indians.

I don't use drugs for the same reason I don't drink. Some kids who come up the way I did use stuff like that to get numb. Others, the ones like me, take hyper-vigilance as a sacred vow. No woman who ever loved me cost me money. But none of them are still with me. Some are dead; all are gone.

Max has his family. His wife, Immaculata; his daughter, Flower. The Prof, my only true father, has another child—a young gun he had picked up and lifted up, like he had done with me. I was way older than Clarence, but I'd never felt replaced; I felt added to. He calls us both "son," but, to the Prof, I'd be "Schoolboy" forever.

He and Clarence had a crib together over in East New York. Michelle had the Mole; together they had Terry. I had snatched him from a pimp in Times Square years ago, before Giuliani cleared up midtown and left the boroughs to rot. Mama had all of us, but Flower, her granddaughter, was the pick of the litter, and none of us had a moment's doubt about that.

It wasn't so much that they all had each other—I had them, too, and they me. It was that they all had something to *do*.

I walked in the glass door with the taped-over cracks, found myself facing a man in a wheelchair, sitting behind a wide wooden plank that holds a register nobody ever signs.

"Gateman," I said.

"Hey, boss. You had a call."

That meant someone had called me at Mama's and she had left word with Gateman. I wouldn't carry a cell on a job like the one I just did, and none of us would ever use an answering machine.

I nodded, then handed him an envelope.

"Thanks, boss."

"Count it."

"For what? We didn't set no exact price."

"Yeah, we did. Remember?"

"For real?"

"Count it."

"There's—fuck me!—five large here. What'd that humongoid pay?"

"Ten. Knowing Gigi, he probably got twenty-five, minimum."

"He's worth it," Gateman said, reluctantly respectful. "That monster motherfucker never misses. And he don't even know how to *spell* 'rat.'"

"True," I said, remembering a conversation I'd had with Gigi on the yard, a long time ago.

"I'm kind of like a whore," the monster said, *shocking me into silence. "I mean, we both rent our bodies, right? You know what makes me different?"*

I made an "I wouldn't even guess" gesture, afraid to say anything out loud.

"We got different values," the monster said, solemnly. "There ain't a whore in the world you can trust to keep her mouth shut. And there ain't a thing on this earth that can make me open mine."

"Nobody rats *on* him, neither," Gateman said. "You know I was at a trial of his once, over in Brooklyn?"

"Yeah?"

"Square business. It was hilarious, bro. The whole courthouse was cracking up. See, Gigi rolled up these three jamokes who got behind in their payments. Probably three separate jobs, but you know that whale-scale bastard—he does them all at the same time, save himself a few steps maybe. So, anyway, while they're in the hospital, probably flying on morphine, they all give statements, and Gigi gets taken down.

"But comes time for trial, one by one, the three witnesses get up on the stand, point over at Gigi sitting there, and *swear* that he wasn't the one who did them.

"The DA, some kid probably a week out of law school, one of those Daddy's-got-connections clowns the DA's always hiring, he's fucking *screaming* at his own witnesses: 'Are you trying to tell this jury that you were beaten by *another* four-hundred-and-fifty pound white male with a red lightning-bolt tattoo on his right forearm!? That *is* the exact description of your assailant that you gave the police, isn't it?' And the witness, *each* witness, mind you, stares him straight in the eye, says, 'That's right. All's I know, it wasn't him.'"

"Yeah. Gigi's a few hundred pounds over the ninja limit, but he can sure disappear right in front of your eyes."

Gateman high-fived that, said: "Five large, boss. Damn! So this is—"

"Half. Like we agreed."

"Ah, come on, man. I didn't think you was—"

"I said *partners,* Gate. Partners don't cut pieces, they split. Equal shares."

"You don't just *talk* it, man."

I tapped fists with one of the city's deadliest shooters, and headed up the stairs to my place.